False Memoir
Based on an Untrue Story

By Katherine Luck

:

All of it is true and none of it happened.

.

First things first

Nine days and three dead bodies later, I would wish I'd never met Jack O'Lies.

Jack O'Lies

Monday, March 19, 7:03 a.m.

From Wikipedia:

Jack O'Lies (born August 4, 1965) is a crime reporter at the *Washingtonian*, a daily newspaper in Seattle, Washington.

He was nominated for a Pulitzer Prize for investigative journalism in 1998 for his coverage of his wife's murder and the subsequent trial of her killer, the Westgate Serial Killer. He came in second to Gary Cohn and Will Englund of the *Baltimore Sun* for their series on the international shipbreaking industry, which revealed the dangers posed to workers and the environment when decommissioned ships are dismantled.

Slaughterhouse 98271

Monday, March 19, 9:22 a.m.

I'd never met Jack O'Lies, award-winning crime reporter from Seattle's venerable *Washingtonian* newspaper, but I knew so much about him. I also knew about his boss, *Washingtonian* Deputy Assistant Editor John Whiteclay. I first encountered young Mr. Whiteclay at the Society of Professional Journalists' annual awards ceremony a couple years ago, when I was but a slip of a staff writer at an obscure monthly newspaper outside Seattle and he was an investigative journalist at the *Tulalip Tribune*, which was headquartered on an Indian reservation a handful of miles north of my house.

He owned that awards ceremony, raking in five or six second-place medals and a gleaming first-place statuette. I remember he had the longest hair I'd ever seen on any man or woman: a raven-black braid that hung past his belt, tied off with what was either a thin strip of leather or a garbage bag twist-tie. He was all of 27.

I didn't talk to John Whiteclay at the time. I remember being profoundly embarrassed that I hadn't realized there was a legitimate newspaper up in casino land. Last night I finally read his first-prize-winning investigative journalism article from that awards ceremony so long ago, "Slaughterhouse 98271." It took me all of five minutes to realize why it won, why he had accumulated at least eight more first-place statuettes since I last encountered him, and why he has since ascended from lowly reporter at a weekly tribal newspaper with a circulation of maybe 2,000 to an editor gig at the *Washingtonian*, a hallowed bastion of journalism and one of the last print dailies in the country. My own journalistic ascension has been far less impressive: no statuettes and a lateral drift from staff writer to editor at the same obscure monthly newspaper outside Seattle.

When I called Jack O'Lies to set up an interview (multiple times, all sent to voicemail) and when I emailed him (multiple times, all unanswered), I never thought I'd eventually have to resort to the lowest of tactics, namely contacting his boss. But I tended to get pushy when I was ignored.

After checking my email one last time and finding no response, I decided to place a call to John Whiteclay, one newspaper editor to another. Very collegial, I figured. As I dialed, I wondered if he still had the incredibly long braid.

I was transferred, put on hold, transferred again, then put on hold again. While I hummed along to a canned version of the theme from *Titanic*, he picked up.

"John Whiteclay."

How much humming did he hear?

"Hi there. This is Katherine Luck from the *Journal*," I said.

"The *Business Journal*?"

"No. The *Journal Newspapers*."

Did he hear my attempt to hit the high trill? What sort of monster would set their on-hold music to a Celine Dion song, then abruptly pick up? And what the hell was the lyric after "my heart will go on?" It was going to bug me all day.

"The *King County Journal*?"

"Yes. No—not the one you're probably thinking of. That folded, like, ten years ago."

I just said "like." That was not a good sign. It meant he was rattling me.

"Who are you with?" he said. He sounded annoyed.

"We're a monthly newspaper. We have two editions—the *King County Journal* and the *Snohomish County Journal*. But officially or collectively or whatever, we're the *Journal Newspapers*."

I just said "whatever" to an award-winning investigative reporter who was now an influential news editor. I sounded like I was thirteen. I was thirty-three.

"I've, uh, been trying to get ahold of one of your reporters for a piece I'm working on," I said.

"Permissions can be obtained by calling extension 102—"

"No, no, I don't want to reprint anything," I said. "I want to interview him."

I heard the chatter of a keyboard through my phone. He was checking his email as we spoke. I knew he wasn't looking for a message I might have sent—no, he was multitasking, barely listening to me. I knew this because I often did it myself.

"Who were you trying to reach?" he said. He sounded uninterested.

"Jack O'Lies. He's a crime reporter, it says."

"It" was the ten-year-old byline that Google supplied three months earlier when I typed five simple words into the search bar: "husbands of serial killer victims."

On the other end of the phone, John Whiteclay stopped typing and sighed.

"Jack O'Lies," he said. "Why would you want to interview him?"

"Research. Um…that I'm doing. For a book. That I'm working on."

John Whiteclay sighed again.

"Is this some kind of backgrounding thing?"

"Yes?" I said. I had no idea what he meant.

"Okay," he said. "I'll see. What's your number?"

"425-775-2400," I said. I didn't bother to give him my extension. I only did so when I feared a potential source would mistake me for a mere blogger. Besides, I wanted him to tangle with my newspaper's on-hold music, just to even the score. Mine played Sonny and Cher tunes.

"Okay," John Whiteclay said. "Jack will get back to you."

He hung up. I hung up.

Jack did not get back to me.

It made no sense

Thursday, March 22, 9:11 a.m.

Over the past three months, with the aid of the internet and back issues of the *Washingtonian* that were squirreled away at my local library, I'd learned that Jack O'Lies was a crime reporter at the *Washingtonian* in the late 1990s. That made sense.

In 1998, he was covering the ongoing hunt for the Westgate Serial Killer. Made sense.

The same year, his wife was killed by the Westgate Serial Killer. That...that made no sense.

His wife's killer was caught. Made sense.

Jack O'Lies covered the trial of the Westgate Serial Killer, his wife's murderer, for his newspaper. That made absolutely no sense.

He was nominated for a Pulitzer Prize for his coverage of the trial. That made sense—tragic sense.

He came in second and received nothing more than a two-paragraph write-up in his own newspaper for his trouble. That made no sense—not in the slightest.

Twelve years later, he was still a crime reporter at the *Washingtonian*. I wasn't sure if that made sense or not.

After weeks of shady cyberstalking on my part, the question remained: Why did he cover the trial of his wife's killer? According to my research, he was also a witness at the trial. He went to court in the morning, he testified, then he went back to the *Washingtonian* and wrote articles about it. Day after day.

Was it a coping mechanism? A way to keep himself emotionally detached so he didn't have to deal with the pain? Or was he a cold-hearted bastard? He'd managed to stay employed as the industry bled newspaper journalists. I voted cold-hearted bastard. But I wanted to find out for sure before I started writing about him.

Four days after promising that Jack O'Lies would get back to me, his editor called. I had no idea why. He, John Whiteclay, deputy assistant editor at one of the last major metropolitan newspapers in the United States, surely had at least twenty-two better things to do at 9:11 a.m. on a Thursday. Could it have been professional courtesy that motivated him? One newspaper editor to another?

"Hi, this is John Whiteclay at the *Washingtonian*," he said, keyboard chattering in the background and not a hint of a hum in his voice.

"Hi there," I said. I tried not to sound too eager.

"Sorry, I set it up to have Jack O'Lies call you today at ten, but I had to send him to Lake Washington. Breaking news. Can I have him call you to reschedule?"

"Okay…sure," I said, though I doubted I'd ever hear from him. Among those who knew me, "Jack O'Lies" had become a slang term for a person who didn't return phone calls.

"So you'll handle this between the two of you," he said.

It was not a question. It was a managerial brush-off. I'd never had the chance to do such a thing myself, since I was my own staff, save a few dissolute freelancers who existed as disembodied entities suspended in the ether of voicemail and typo-ridden articles emailed past the deadline. I'd had it done to me plenty of times, however. I knew the drill.

"Yeah," I said. "Sure."

"Great. Bye," he said.

He hung up. I hung up. I brooded for thirty seconds. I knew I'd never hear from Jack O'Lies.

Breaking news at Lake Washington.

Lake Washington was about forty-five minutes from my newspaper office in morning rush hour traffic.

I brooded another thirty seconds, then grabbed a pen. I scrawled, stood, and put a Post-it note on my office door stating:

"Interview in Seattle. Back noon-ish."
Given my poor handwriting, it probably read:
"In stes m Settle. Be bl nons."

The AP Stylebook has no entry for "lakeside murder scene"

Thursday, March 22, 10:12 a.m.

In my experience, all newspaper journalists wanted to win a Pulitzer Prize.

Local TV reporters wanted to get hired by Fox News, CNN, "60 Minutes," or "Dateline NBC"—whichever called first.

Writers at too-hip alternative weeklies wanted to become the next James Frey or David Sedaris and craft bestselling false memoirs.

Bloggers wanted to be real (i.e., newspaper) journalists.

Staff writers turned editors at obscure monthly newspapers wanted to write a book about a serial killer.

But what did crime reporters want? I didn't know.

I found it hard to believe that a professional journalist with such an esoteric specialty still existed in this day and age, yet I was about to meet one in his natural habitat: a crime scene. A murder scene. A possible serial killer murder scene, if the live radio reports were to be believed.

The crime scene was located on the western shore of Lake Washington, where the coarse gray sand met rain-churned mud. I parked between a Washington State Patrol car and a Seattle Police Department cruiser. The King County Sheriff was on scene too, his car sandwiched between a pair of TV news vans. I'd never understood the division of labor among the various cop agencies. I wasn't that kind of journalist.

I didn't get out of my car. Outside, chaos reigned as cops and marauding ducks fought to defend their strongholds between the mucky bank, the gently lapping water, and the yellow tape emblazoned with the warning "Police Line Do Not Cross" that separated them. Through my windshield, I could see a major media convergence zone just outside the yellow tape. I covered a story here once before, under far more mundane—yet equally duck and reporter infested—circumstances, when the shoreline was submerged by a minor flood and some flunky from the mayor's office held a press conference. I ought to have felt right at home. Except for that whole "dead body found floating on the water" thing.

Stumbling over the waddling wildlife, the perpetually jeans 'n' sweatshirt clad TV cameramen (they were always men) poked their lenses into the faces of sundry cops, while the on-air talent—no one I recognized—fiddled with their handheld mics and tried to keep their hair neat. Nearby, half a dozen newspaper reporters were standing together gossiping, jeans-clad like the TV cameramen but sporting out-of-style sports jackets and clutching reporter's notebooks. Their photojournalist counterparts, decked out in full-body khaki like war correspondents, were picking their way through the ooze to shove their telephoto lenses over the yellow tape. Several radio reporters stood well apart from the mob and recorded their reportage on their iPhones, a feat that impressed me excessively the first time I witnessed it at the likewise heavily-policed Shop With a Cop charity event held at the mall last December.

Keeping a safe distance from the edge of Lake Washington, where the corpse recently washed ashore, were a clutch of hungover and under-caffeinated kids from the alternative weekly papers. Given their smeared eyeliner and excess of sequins, I was willing to bet they got pulled directly off late-night club scene coverage to report on this murder. Appearing uncomfortable and gripping homemade press passes, a few lonely souls drifted through the crowd. As soon as I saw their expensive digital cameras, I pegged them as bloggers.

If this was indeed the crime scene of a serial killer, the FBI ought to be in attendance as well, dressed in their iconic trench coats. I myself was wearing a trench coat that I bought a few years ago because I thought it looked reporterish, according to my vague memories of 1940s movies from the film noir genre. The coat once got me erroneously pegged as a private investigator while I waited for a respectable local businessman I was supposed to interview in front of his tattoo parlor. Maybe the intimidating cops and the cliquish reporters would think I was a Fed or a private eye. I was way, way outside my journalistic beat at this crime scene. In more ways than one.

I got out of the car. I needed to find Jack O'Lies. As a real-life crime reporter, he'd be able to steer me safely through this murder morass. Alone, I was likely to gain instant immortality on the 5 o'clock news when I blundered across the "Police Line Do Not Cross" tape and tripped over the corpse.

I paused next to the Channel 5 TV news van. I had no idea what Jack O'Lies looked like. I knew he was 45. Because I was white, I whitely assumed he was white. He lived in Ballard, Seattle's historic Scandinavian ghetto, so he pretty much had to be white. There were no photos of him online. There were plenty of images of his wife's killer, Robert "Bobby Dean" Clasky, the Westgate Serial Killer, however. They ranged from wild-eyed courtroom sketches to stone-cold mug shots going back fourteen years to a single school photo taken when he was a kindergartener that wrecked all wrath with his black eye, split lip, and tentative, battered smile.

The air was crisp and reeked of fish, waterfowl excrement, and cheap aftershave. I wended my way over the slippery ground toward the water's edge. Up to their thighs in Lake Washington, the crime scene investigators were slowly trudging with their eyes on the rippling water. Red and white lights atop three useless ambulances circled silently. Police radios jabbered urgently and, incongruously, the cops attached to them burst out laughing. I saw a TV cameraman aim his all-seeing lens at a kid in a state trooper uniform who couldn't be a day over 18. "Why so much police interest in an eviscerated and mutilated body? Can you confirm this is the work of a serial killer, and is all of Seattle in danger?" the heavily made-up TV reporter inquired.

I spied an idle newspaper reporter, identifiable by her jeans, sensible shoes, and decades-old but carefully pressed suit jacket. She was leaning against an ambulance, smoking and poking at her iPhone with a short-nailed thumb.

"Excuse me? You don't happen to know if Jack O'Lies from the *Washingtonian* is around here somewhere?" I said.

She pointed her cigarette at an open space beyond the yellow police tape.

"Over there with the coroner. Can't believe Muhammad actually came to the mountain for once," she said.

The cigarette indicated a black guy in his fifties who was talking with a white guy. The white guy looked to be in his forties, with graying hair hacked into a super-short crew cut. He sported a couple days' worth of beard growth that would have looked sexy on a movie star in his twenties but didn't work for a professional man over the age of thirty. The black guy was wearing a dark blue windbreaker that loudly proclaimed "King County Coroner" in a sans-serif font across the chest.

I took a deep breath and contemplated the forbidding yellow tape that separated us. I'd only seen such a thing in real life once before. Granted, it was labeled "Fire Line Do Not Cross," but close enough. It had cordoned off a crucial cross-street in the wilds of Ballard (Jack O'Lies country, before I had heard of him) when I was working on a Halloween article about bugs as a culinary option.

Yes, I ate bugs in Ballard. For journalism. But I didn't disobey the official yellow tape.

I glanced around. A gawky kid in a trench coat was wandering around beyond the yellow tape. His trench coat screamed, "I'm a reporter!" more blatantly than mine. He was carrying a fantastically expensive camera. He was clearly a blogger. I ducked under the tape and approached the coroner just as the blogger turned and made a sudden beeline for the same.

Blast these tenacious amateurs! I picked up my pace as best I could, but I was slow and unsure in the slick mud. The blogger reached the coroner before I did and pointed the camera in his face.

What happened next confused me. I was out of earshot. The blogger and the white guy—Jack O'Lies, I presumed—appeared to exchange words. Angry words. Because the blogger was attempting to horn in on Jack's interview, perhaps? In my peripheral vision, I saw a couple TV cameramen jump the yellow tape and hustle toward them.

My view was abruptly blocked by a radio reporter, a newspaper journalist, half a dozen photojournalists, uncountable bloggers, and all the cameramen and audio techs from the TV crews. Everyone suddenly coalesced into a noisy, jostling, desperate media-mob that I had only ever experienced on those rare occasions when I was covering an event graced by a celebrity. Someone was shouting, then the white guy with the graying crew cut and last week's 5 o'clock shadow shoved his way through the crowd of reporters. All lenses, boom mikes, DSLR cameras, and iPhones swiveled to point at him.

I had no idea what just happened. But according to the cigarette, that was Jack O'Lies.

The lenses and the reporters attached to them turned back to the coroner, the lake, and the blogger, who was being hauled to his feet, his trench coat covered in mud. I hesitated, then followed my retreating interviewee. I had a very fast car at my disposal. I had no doubt that I could catch him.

As I navigated the slippery ground to my loaner press car, anxious to avoid biting it in the mud like the blogger, I figured there was a fifty-fifty chance Jack O'Lies was heading back to *Washingtonian* headquarters. I didn't know exactly where the *Washingtonian* building was located, beyond the mythology of the so-called Paper Triangle formed by the Interstate 5-hugging *Seattle Times*, the comatose *Seattle Post-Intelligencer* with its waterfront view, and at the apex pointing north toward Ballard, the *Washingtonian*.

Lucky for me, I had GPS in this week's press car. It was an awesome ride—an Infiniti convertible, $80,000 manufacturer's suggested retail price. It was by far the best car I'd ever driven in my life. And it was mine for a whole week, courtesy of the automobile advertising firm that loaned me a new car every week in exchange for a review, which my newspaper's plucky sales staff leveraged into revenue by selling ad space around said review to local auto dealerships, mechanics, and oil changing outfits.

Even with GPS, I managed to get lost. Forty-five minutes later, I penetrated the Paper Triangle, pulled into the *Washingtonian*'s "staff only" parking lot, and hid the press car between a couple Fords. If it was towed, I'd be stranded but not liable for the impound costs, since it wasn't my car. The automotive advertising firm would send me nothing but base-model Mazdas and retrograde Nissans forever after, however, and my newspaper's ad revenue would suffer. I experienced a momentary twinge of doubt, shook it off, and made for the massive gray building before me.

I'd walked past the corpse of the *Seattle Post-Intelligencer* once. I'd entered the *Seattle Times* building twice. But the *Washingtonian* was a complete mystery to me. I pulled open the frosted glass front door and stepped into an echoing, marble-coated expanse of soulless 1960s architecture. The building felt bereft. It appeared to have been designed for a bustling community of hundreds that had been decimated during the past decade. It was creepy.

Just like at the *Seattle Times*, there was a front desk manned by a security guard. Unlike at the *Seattle Times*, there was a two-story waterfall behind the front desk that would have been quite impressive if it wasn't bone dry. Also unlike at the *Seattle Times*, I was treated with little caution. The *Seattle Times* had a formidable security gate. There was no security gate in sight. I informed the drowsy guard that I had an interview scheduled with Jack O'Lies. He barely looked at me in response.

"Know where he is? Third floor," he replied.

I waited, but I was not asked for ID, issued a visitor's badge, or ordered to sign in. I drifted uncertainly past the front desk to a bank of elevators. I entered the first one I encountered, pressed the button for the third floor, waited, waited, waited, and eventually ascended at an indolent pace.

On the third floor, I wandered through a lonely cubicle farm dominated by row upon row of empty desks. I was on the verge of giving myself up for lost when I ran into Deputy Assistant Editor John Whiteclay under the least desirable of circumstances: He was stepping out of the men's room. There was no doubt that it was him. He was hard to forget. The last time I saw him, he had a waist-length black braid and was wearing a Che Guevara T-shirt (red, of course) under a dun second-hand corduroy jacket with fake leather elbow patches. He had accessorized his tight jeans with a hole in one knee that definitely hadn't occurred naturally, and completed his ensemble with a turquoise and silver bracelet and a pair of beat-up cowboy boots. He was such a 27-year-old rez-cred cliché punk when he strutted up to collect his prizes at the Society of Professional Journalists' annual awards ceremony, lo those many moons ago.

But as he made his egress from the gents' powder room, I noted that his hair had been shorn to corporate shortness. He was wearing a pair of unattractive pleated-front Dockers, a department store golf shirt, and unobtrusive lace-up leather shoes. And a watch. Pushing thirty, his face was about a decade older than it was two years ago.

"Oh, hi," I said. "You're John Whiteclay, right?"

Looking surprised, cornered, and yet so very professional as the bathroom door swung shut behind him, he replied, "Yes. I'm sorry, you are…?"

"Katherine Luck from the *Journal*. We set up an interview with your staffer, Jack O'Lies, remember?"

Not surprisingly, he looked very surprised that I was here after he gave me the big heave-ho over the phone this morning. However, he hid it with supervisory speed.

"Right," he said. "Coffee? I was going to grab a cup."

"Sure, I never say no to coffee," I said, trailing him to the breakroom. "So, I went on down to Lake Washington, but I didn't manage to hook up with Jack."

Mr. Whiteclay grabbed the Mr. Coffee carafe and a probably

clean mug from the counter. His face again registered surprise before he hid it ever so judiciously.

"I thought you two were going to schedule things over the phone. Were you covering the murder for your paper?"

"Oh no, we don't do hard news. Nothing too controversial," I said.

He did not offer me a cup of coffee. He leaned against the counter and sipped.

"Okay," he said.

"I just figured it would be easier to get in touch with Jack in person, maybe," I said.

John Whiteclay said nothing. He crossed one Dockers-encased leg over the other, leaning against the counter in a way that announced that this was where we were going to wrap things up. I'd been long-form dismissed before. I knew the body language all too well. I, however, tended to become stubborn when professionally thwarted. I knew I could (and would) stay there all day if that's what it took. I was saved from making myself obnoxious by a reporter who poked his head into the breakroom.

"Oh man, Chief, you gotta see this! O'Lies punched the hell out of that idiot Seattle Crimeologist blogger."

Chief Whiteclay's face registered alarm. Still clutching his coffee mug, he followed the reporter. Since I wasn't explicitly uninvited, I trailed them to a low-walled cubicle in the middle of the newsroom. Half a dozen reporters were crammed in it, their eyes glued to a computer screen. Their Chief, John Whiteclay, shouldered his way through to stand next to the cubicle owner, who was seated in front of the computer.

"Did you see this, Chief? It's all over his blog," she said, hitting play on an uploaded video.

The glossy-gray spectacle of the Lake Washington crime scene came into focus: reporters, camera crews, cops, ducks, and all. Behind the camera, a whiny, juvenile sort of voice was saying, "It is a measure of the depravity—nay, the sheer brutality—of modern American culture that a police force immobilized by—"

Off-screen, someone said, "Jack? That really you? What're you doing here today?"

The camera swung from the slate-colored lake filled with wading cops to focus on a black guy in his fifties standing with a white guy who looked to be in his forties. The black guy was wearing a dark blue windbreaker that loudly proclaimed "King County Coroner" in a sans-serif font. The white guy had graying hair hacked into a super-short crew cut and a couple days' worth of beard growth that would have looked sexy on a movie star in his twenties but didn't work for a professional man over the age of thirty.

"Tell me about it. I feel about a hundred and forty today," the white guy said.

Within the video frame, the black guy leaned closer to the white guy. Within the cubicle, we all leaned closer to the computer speakers. The coroner said something that sounded like, "Jack. What're you doing here, really? You know what today is."

Unseen on the screen, someone let out a gleeful chortle. The shot began to wobble as the cameraman walked toward the pair.

"Jack O'Lies, *Washingtonian* crime reporter," said the unidentified voice.

Both the coroner and *Washingtonian* crime reporter Jack O'Lies turned and stared into the camera.

"What, indeed, are you doing at a serial killer crime scene today, of all days? Are you trying to finally win that Pulitzer? Today's the perfect day to give it another shot!"

The white guy, Jack O'Lies, went whiter. Then whiter still. His eyes were fixed on the camera. On all of us in the cubicle. He stepped forward.

"Jack," said the coroner. Then he exclaimed, "Jack!" as the camera made a rapid arc up to the cloudy sky.

"You don't ever speak to me, you ignorant little bastard," shouted a voice beyond the view of the heavens. There was a commotion, then some scuffling sounds as the video whipped wildly around. We viewers were treated to scraps of cop uniforms, blurry reporters, a few fancy TV cameras and boom mikes—look, that's me!—then a shot of the back of Jack O'Lies' head and jacket as he pushed his way through the crowd.

"And it's on the Channel 5 website, too," said the cubicle owner, tapping at the keyboard as her fearless leader, the stricken Chief, stared at the monitor. There was a snippet of happy talk from the Channel 5 in-studio talent, then their faces and voices abruptly went serious.

"A body was found in Lake Washington today," said the blond (female).

"The nature of the as-yet unidentified man's injuries has officials from the Seattle Police Department speculating that it may be the work of a serial killer," chimed in the blond (male). "Bill Arpaggio is live on scene. Bill?"

They cut to one of the heavily made-up TV reporters I noted earlier. He began to speak earnestly into the camera, clutching a large microphone that I suspected was purely a prop, given all the boom mikes I saw.

"Thanks, Shannon and Greg. I'm here on the shore of Lake Washington, where police have discovered a body that officials suspect may be another in a string of—"

Off-screen, there was a commotion, then some scuffling sounds. The TV camera slid smoothly left to take in Jack O'Lies shoving a gawky kid who was wearing a trench coat that screamed "I'm a reporter!" more blatantly than mine. The kid slipped in the mud and landed on his back.

"There appears to be some sort of incident here—hold on," said the unseen yet unflappable TV reporter as his cameraman zoomed in on Jack O'Lies's enraged face.

"You don't ever speak to me, you ignorant little bas— BEEP!" he said.

I wondered, was "bastard" really on the FCC's infamous profanity list? Or was Channel 5 hyper-vigilant?

Just at this moment, a man with a graying, super-short crew cut shoved his way through the crowd in the cubicle. He slammed a galley sheet covered with text in 12-point Times

New Roman font onto the keyboard. Like meerkats sensing danger on that meerkat nature show I watched once, dozens of reporters around the newsroom poked their heads up from their cubicles.

"Here," he said to Deputy Assistant Editor John Whiteclay. "And you don't ever, *ever* send me out into the field again."

I glanced at the graying crew cut, then at the copy, which was bylined "Jack O'Lies."

Gossip

Thursday, March 22, 11:53 a.m.

Trapped within the cubicle by his subordinates, 29-year-old Deputy Assistant Editor John Whiteclay, boss of veteran crime reporter Jack O'Lies for barely five months, made steady managerial eye contact, then bravely invited his disgruntled employee to discuss his grievances "in the privacy of Conference Room B." I took this to mean that the *Washingtonian*'s deputy assistant editor had naught but a cubicle to call his own. Even I had an office with a real, closeable door. I had no staff to reprimand behind it, however.

"The web designers are using B. They booked it for all day," the cubicle owner, seated in front of her computer, meekly volunteered.

"Jack, why don't we grab a cup of coffee?" John Whiteclay suggested redundantly, given the full cup he held in his hand.

I had already spent time in The Chief's coffee-having employee lounge of disrespect. Jack O'Lies appeared to be wise to the routine as well. He stared at The Chief—could a stare be slurred like speech?—in a slurred manner.

"I gotta go to the can," he announced.

Jack O'Lies stalked off.

John Whiteclay, award-winning journalist turned editor, elbowed his way out of the cubicle with mutters of, "pardon," and "excuse me, please," and followed Jack as he wended his way through the maze of cubicles towards the men's room.

Later, much later, I would learn what happened after Jack stalked angrily away with his young editor in hot pursuit. But for the time being, I remained ensconced within the cubicle of *Washingtonian* Staff Writer Bididiana Gomez, awkwardly chatting with her about meteorology (whether the weatherman on Channel 5 was hot or not).

Out of eyeshot and earshot, John Whiteclay was closing in on his retreating reporter.

"Jack? Jack. Jack!" he said ever more insistently, as Jack approached the same men's room I'd caught The Chief emerging from earlier.

Young Mr. Whiteclay told me this later. Much later.

"Jack, you and I need to have a conversation. Immediately. And probably with the legal department involved."

Jack made a derisive grunt, rolled his eyes, and shoved the men's room door open with his shoulder.

The Chief followed him. Jack repaired to a stall and slammed it shut.

"Fine," said The Chief. "You think this is the first time I've debriefed a writer in the Cone of Silence? You can't hide in there forever."

He started to drink his coffee, decided it was gross to do so in the john, set it down next to the sink, then picked it up and drank anyway. Jack began to throw up loudly within the stall.

Jack told me this later. Much later.

"Jeez! Are you okay, Jack? Jack?"

A reporter entered.

"Out!" barked The Chief.

"I gotta—"

"Use the ladies' room."

"What? Hey, who's yakking up?"

"We're having a meeting. Use the ladies' room."

"No way, Chief!"

"They won't care. I'm in there all the time when I've got to have a private conversation because I've got no damned office, and the damned web jack-holes are in Conference Room B again, and we can't use Conference Room A because of the asbestos, so use the damned ladies' room!"

The reporter retreated. Jack emerged, his face almost as white as it had been on the blogger's video. He bent over the sink next to The Chief and washed his face.

"Are you sick? I mean, with the flu or something?"

"It wasn't the crime scene," Jack said. "I'm hungover as hell. I spent an hour in traffic with no coffee. I will not take shit from a journalism school dropout blogger who thinks a three-month internship here qualifies him to write news."

"He used to work here? Jack, we've got to go talk to legal immediately."

Jack shook his hands dry, then wiped his palms over the back of his pants.

"He'll get over it."

"He'll sue us, is what he'll do! I would," said The Chief.

Jack eyed his boss, some sixteen years his junior.

"File the damned copy and leave me alone," Jack said.

He shoved the men's room door open with his shoulder and exited.

"It was shockingly good copy," The Chief told me later. "He knocked it out in just twenty minutes. It was all gold—I fact-checked it myself. His quotes were exact. I watched two hours of TV footage to be sure. He did it without a recorder. Just a notebook and a pencil. Hot damn."

Maybe I shouldn't include the deputy assistant editor's involuntary profanity (surely on the FCC's notorious list). But unlike Jack O'Lies, I was doing it with a recorder. I liked to be accurate when I transcribed an interview.

As The Chief slunk off to his cubicle to fact-check and copy-edit Jack O'Lies' 850 words on the Lake Washington murder scene, I decided to risk a shove and confront my illusive interviewee.

Hear Lies

Thursday, March 22, 12:04 p.m.

I followed the chittering danger signals of the reporters to Jack O'Lies' cubicle. It stood isolated amid dozens of empty desks along the west wall. He had removed one of the cubicle's sides, giving him an unbroken view of the cobalt blue water of Puget Sound. I wondered how often he took in the stunning vista. His head was down, his eyes on his keyboard.

"Excuse me?" I said. "Hi. Are you Jack O'Lies?"

He looked up from his keyboard. His eyes were pale blue: a shade not captured by the offensive blogger's video camera, the Channel 5 TV lens, or even my brief glance at him as he glowered at his boss.

Impulsively, I decided my best tactic in this case was to play dumb.

"I'm Katherine from the *Journal*. We had an interview scheduled for ten today. Sorry, I'm kind of late," I said.

I forced a phony giggle.

"Can we grab a cup of coffee?" I said. "My treat. This won't take more than fifteen, maybe twenty minutes."

That was what I always told my sources—fifteen, maybe twenty minutes. Occasionally it was true.

Jack O'Lies stared at me, but not in the slurred way he stared at his boss. He let out a rough sound that wasn't a laugh.

"Coffee? Is that the new corporate buzz word around here? Are you from the legal department?"

"No, I'm Katherine from the *Journal*. Your editor set up an interview between us. Remember?"

"I'm supposed to interview you *why*, exactly?"

"No, no, I'm supposed to interview you," I said.

There was a long, long, long pause. I could hear my own breathing. I held my breath.

"I've got work to do," he said.

"It'll just take a couple minutes," I said.

"Not today."

"Ten minutes, max," I said.

His gaze slipped back to his keyboard.

"I'm on deadline. Go write your blog and leave me alone," he said.

"But—"

"Not today," he said again.

He said it softly, but not kindly. Dismissively. If he'd shouted, if he'd added a bit of choice profanity, if he shoved me, I would've felt a sight less offended.

"Okay, then," I said.

I huffed back to work, some twenty miles north in light, pre-rush hour traffic. I fumed. He thought I was a blogger. I was many things that journalists didn't want to be, but I was not a blogger. I was stubborn at inappropriate times. I could be insufferable when professionally thwarted. But I was not a blogger.

As the afternoon wore thin, I sat at my desk and assembled short write-ups about recent local happenings of minor importance to fill holes in the next edition of the *Journal*, while Jack O'Lies sat at his desk and assembled obituaries to fill holes in the next edition of the *Washingtonian*. Both of us brooded. He brooded about…well, he never did tell me exactly what. But I was able to surmise later.

I brooded about my impending trip back to Seattle that evening. His fellow *Washingtonian* journalist, Bididiana Gomez, had told me plenty about his habits.

I knew he liked to drink.

I knew he was on deadline.

I knew his deadline was five p.m.

I knew he retired to the Three Coins Restaurant (where "restaurant" was a loosely applied term) every night after work and drank scotch on the rocks. More than one.

I knew that I would be joining him tonight.

"Not today," he warned me. Too bad I was obtuse. Things wouldn't have gotten so out of control if I'd listened to him.

Where we fellows drink

Thursday, March 22, 2:49 p.m.

His editor was right to say "hot damn." Hot damn was exactly right.

Jack O'Lies' article on the Lake Washington murder hit the web at 2:46 p.m. I read it. I felt depressed. I was at the same murder scene four hours earlier. Could I have written an article even half as comprehensive and insightful in less than half an hour? Could I have done it in half a day? Half a week? Half a month?

Yes, given half a month, I might have been able to. I worked at a monthly newspaper, so I was comfortable with such a deadline. But in less than half an hour...hot damn. I started to doubt whether I ought to try to interview him tonight—or ever. I was so far beneath him as a journalist. Compared to him, I was barely better than a blogger.

Then I started to think. I started to think cynically, a bad habit of mine. Had he really wrung all those stellar quotes from the coroner? Or were they manufactured, id est, made up? Had his years—decades—of experience gifted him with a reserve of stock phrases and lexical tricks that made banging out hardcore murder reportage a mere paint-by-the-numbers effort? Could I do it too, if he told me how?

Only one way to find out.

At five p.m., I jumped in the press car and drove in rush hour traffic from my newspaper's suburban headquarters south to Seattle for the second time today. Evening traffic was always worse than morning, and the trip took an hour and thirteen minutes. By the time I located a parking spot outside the Three Coins Restaurant, it was 6:24 p.m. I stepped into the leathery gloom and glanced around halfheartedly. I was sure Jack O'Lies had gone home by now. Nevertheless, I took it upon myself to dodge first into the petite soi-disant restaurant section, then into the vast bar-without-end to check.

According to the bartender in the ox-hide-bound lounge, Jack was still in situ, seated in his usual booth in the back, drinking his usual scotch on the rocks. I ordered a Diet Coke and a scotch on the rocks. I carried them into the seen-better-days murk. I didn't normally do this—stalk men to their favorite watering holes, buy them drinks, refuse to take "no" for an answer.

But I was working.

Sometimes I was simultaneously amused and appalled at the lengths to which I would go when it was for work. For fun, for friendship, for my own edification, there's no way I would have skipped dinner to drive through Seattle's monstrous freeway system and force a middle-aged widower to tell me how he came to his sorry state. I didn't cross the line—any line—in my private life. But for a story...I marveled at what I'd done.

Seated within a semi-circular banquette, Jack O'Lies was stationed behind three empty highball glasses. The tall sides of the booth were like his cubicle walls at the *Washingtonian* office, but covered with scarred sorrel leather, studded with tarnished brass buttons, and reeking of sixty years of cigarette smoke. His head was down, as if he was studying his keyboard at his desk. He didn't look up at me. As I approached, a glass in each hand, I felt like the embodiment of stranger-danger. Want some candy, little boy?

"Jack?" I said. "Hi again! Katherine from the *Journal*? Mind if I sit?"

He didn't look up. I slid into the booth uninvited and sat across from him.

"Wow," I said. "Cool place. I've never been here before. But I've heard of it. It's pretty historical, right?"

Jack still didn't look up.

"Traffic was crazy. I swear, it's worse every time I come

down to Seattle. You're drinking scotch, right? That's what the bartender said. Want this? I didn't feel like breaking the ten," I said.

I thought this sounded very sophisticated. But if he were to ask me why, exactly, I felt obliged to dispose of a ten-dollar bill rather than accept change, I would've stuttered stupidly and exposed myself as one of the world's worst liars. I had formal training in acting during my formative years. Fat lot of good it had ever done me.

"Here," I said, sliding the highball glass, filled to the brim with scotch and slowly melting ice, across the sticky tabletop.

Jack looked up. His pale blue eyes moved from the glass to my face, where they locked on my pupils. He had the stare of a basilisk. I couldn't move. I sensed the poison flowing through his eyes into mine too late to save myself.

"Um," I said, breaking eye contact nervously. "I read your article."

He said nothing. He was still staring at me. I could feel it, though my gaze was on my glass. I played with the red straw that bobbed in the soda.

"It was great. Very thorough. I was there, too. At the murder scene, or whatever. I really like your writing style."

I'd just said "whatever" to a veteran crime reporter and Pulitzer Prize nominee. His silent stare was rattling me badly.

"Here," I said, shoving the scotch closer to him. "I was hoping to talk to you for a minute or two. About a piece I'm working on. Totally off the record, obviously."

Jack O'Lies let out a sound that would have been a laugh if it hadn't sounded so painful. I winced at the harsh, throat flaying sound.

"There is no 'off the record' after deadline. You're a blogger, aren't you? The one that's been emailing and calling me over and over?"

I bristled.

"I am not a blogger. I work for the *Journal*. I'm an editor. A newspaper editor."

"BFD," he muttered, dropping his gaze to the scotch. He

grabbed it and took a sip. "Never heard of it."

"We have a circulation of over ninety-three thousand," I retorted.

"Never heard of it."

"We have two editions. The *King County Journal* and the *Snohomish County*—"

He let out a groan and looked up at me. His eyes, so light and so blue, grew drunkenly merry.

"You mean that *thing*, that neighborhood rag that used to just show up once a month in my mailbox?"

"Yes," I said.

"Oh, good God," he chuckled. "We used to wonder why the hell we got it. We never subscribed. We recycled the thing every month. Why don't we get it anymore?"

"We're advertiser supported," I replied. "We stopped mailing to undesirable lower income households."

Ah, the mean satisfaction I felt as his smirk morphed into a glare and he let the highball glass clunk too hard onto the mahogany tabletop. I raised my eyebrows innocently.

"I'm not interested in being in your paper," he said.

"This isn't for my paper," I said. "This is a writing project of my own."

He lowered his eyes, picked up his glass, and drank.

"So...how do you like The Chief? He said you'd be calling me," Jack said.

"Do you guys really call him that? Like, openly?" I said.

He stared at me. I fumbled.

"I mean, isn't that racist, or whatever?" I said.

"He's our newsroom's editor-in-chief. Why else would we call him 'The Chief?'"

Back when I was a lowly staff writer, I would have put my foot squarely in my mouth.

"He's nice," I said.

"He's an ad department tool. A tool. In all five senses of the word," Jack replied.

"Well, he's a very good writer."

"Good writers don't make good editors," he said.

So…I could be offended in one of two ways. My choice. I took a long sip from the red straw. My hands were shaking.

Jack drained the scotch.

"Thanks for the drink," he said. "Now, you'll have to excuse me."

He didn't make to rise or to grab his jacket, which was hanging on an old-fashioned brass hook just outside our private banquette. It was the big brush-off, the ol' heave-ho.

I refused to play along.

"Oh, sure, sure," I said agreeably. "I'll get out of your hair, just let me finish my drink, okay? Why don't we talk about that writing project I'm working on? It's a book. I just had a couple questions I wanted to ask you. It'll take five minutes, tops."

Jack O'Lies neither sighed nor rolled his eyes. Instead, he turned that icy blue stare on me.

"I'm planning on doing something. I'd like to be alone," he said.

"What are you planning to do?" I asked in the sweetest, fakest, most engaging voice ever to come out of Acting 101. "You can tell me. I'll keep it a secret."

Later, much later, I wished I'd kept my mouth shut.

Pictures of hell

Thursday, March 22, 7:53 p.m.

In the brown, dim lounge, alone in our womb-like corner, Jack took out his wallet. He held it a moment, then set it on the table beside the four empty highball glasses.

He inhaled deeply. He stared at the flat, coffee-colored lump on the table. He sighed shakily.

"You know what today is, right?" he said. His voice was soft and prone to cracking. "You must. Why else…why else would you hound me like this all day?"

I was at a loss, so I said nothing. I surreptitiously signaled the bartender for another round for both of us. I would be insomniac from the caffeine; Jack would be chatty from the booze. I hoped.

He reached for his wallet.

"They're in a secret pocket," he said, opening it. "Inside the money fold. There aren't many. It's easy to forget they're in here any other day of the year. I never show them to anyone. Never look at them myself…except today."

Jack slowly fingered photo paper hidden in the wallet and I suddenly felt apprehensive. Was he going to show me some kind of sex thing? Some horrifying pornography? He pulled the pictures out and laid them in a small pile on the table.

There were five pictures. They were creased and split in places from being sat on for years.

"All the other pictures were thrown away or lost after…" he hesitated. He didn't speak for a long time. "I do this every year. They're more faded every time."

All of a sudden, Wikipedia hit me between the eyes. Oh, holy crap!

I forgot.

I forgot!

I understood why the coroner was so upset to see him at the murder scene.

I understood why he shoved that blogger.

I understood why he kept telling me, "Not today."

His wife was killed twelve years ago today.

How, how, how could I have forgotten?

How tactless was I? How unprofessional? How stupid?

What must he have thought of me, following him here tonight of all nights?

"Oh Jack," I said. I reached my hand across the table toward his, then withdrew it hastily. "I'm sorry, I didn't realize. I really didn't, I swear…"

"We were so dumb," he said. "I was, what? Thirty-three? She wasn't even thirty yet. I was gonna do something special when she turned thirty. She invited my whole newsroom to an over-the-hill party when I hit the big three-oh. I was going to get her back."

The waitress set my soda and his scotch on the table. Jack grabbed his drink. I ignored mine. He drained half of his. He hadn't looked me in the eye since he took out his wallet. He stacked and smoothed the fragile pictures once, twice, a third time.

"Lucy was in preschool. Three. Not four, not quite. We were talking about having another. My wife wanted a boy. A matched set. I didn't care. I wanted another, boy or girl, healthy and who cares? You know? The thing was, we couldn't afford another kid. That was the huge issue—the worst thing in our lives. How to pay for another crib. Jesus Christ."

Jack suddenly jerked his gaze from his glass to mine. I flinched.

"Do you have any idea?" he said.

"No," I said, because I didn't understand. Not just his words, but the meaning behind them.

"I can't really remember what she looked like anymore. Not what she really looked like. She laughed like Lucy, but Lucy doesn't laugh much now. I have this picture of her in my head, but it's not real. But..." he ran his thumb over the stack of photos, tracing an invisible diagonal line, then a circle, then an X. "There are these..."

He looked at me.

"Do you want to see?"

The wedding photo

Thursday, March 22, 8:01 p.m.

"Sometimes I have this dream where I can see her. It's so damned mundane. I'm sitting at the breakfast table, harping on about the tax return. She's tying up a garbage bag and blowing her bangs off her forehead. She used to do that all the time, never cut them until they were past her nose. Then suddenly I wake up and I'm...shocked that she isn't beside me in the bed. Understand? Do you have any idea?"

"No," I said.

Jack reached for the pictures. His eyes were averted to the fake wood paneling that covered the wall of this dive bar that grandly called itself a lounge. He pulled one from the pile. It looked very old. Its corners were rounded. He stared at it, then handed it to me.

I took in the faded image of a much younger Jack O'Lies, clad in a salmon-pink tuxedo with black piping all over the sleeves and lapels, dude cowboy style. He had pushed the sleeves up, a Don Johnson wannabe. His hair was puffed out in a sort of white guy afro. His expression was smeared into a bleary grin. He looked nothing like the haggard widower seated across from me.

I inadvertently laughed.

"That's you? What year is this?" I said.

"Late eighties. Why?"

"You look like 'Miami Vice.' How old were you?"

"Twenty-three," he said.

"Wow. You got married young."

He shrugged.

I knew better than to laugh at his bride. Her wedding dress

was horrible. It was made of some kind of white and ivory checked gingham, all puffed sleeves and western flounces like a virginal square dancer. Her hair was in braids. Her veil appeared to have been secured by a bit of knotted Christmas tinsel. She carried a mixed bouquet of yellow roses and dandelions.

"Was…was it a theme wedding?" I asked.

"No. We were young. And broke."

I felt I was allowed to be judgmental, since I—not broke, but cheap because my sorry salary meant mine, too, was an undesirable lower income household—got my wedding dress for thirty-five bucks at the same thrift store from whence my reporterly trench coat was sourced. I looked a thousand times classier. Then again, maybe everyone at my wedding was secretly snickering.

"She was very beautiful," I said.

And she was.

The crayon portrait

Thursday, March 22, 8:11 p.m.

Jack shifted the wedding photo to the bottom of the stack and pulled out a scrap of fragile, holey paper. This one wasn't a photo. He gently unfolded it.

"I accidentally made a tear in it last year. Be very careful," he said.

He handed it to me.

A big red blob dominated the fragment of construction paper. It had wild green hair and broom-like arms and no legs. Its eyes were askew like a Picasso. A series of letters, unconnected and jagged, spelled out…something.

"Did your daughter make this?" I said.

He nodded.

"When?"

"In preschool. Maybe a week before the murder," he said.

I looked at the paper to hide how uncomfortable I was. I wished I'd never sat down at his table, laden with empty booze glasses and pictures from his dead past.

"What does this say?" I asked.

"'Hi, I love you, Mommy. Love, Lucy,'" Jack spelled out, tracing the text with his finger. The nail was nipped down so far it was painful to look at. He must have chewed it mercilessly, relentlessly over a period of months.

"Very sweet," I said.

"It took me three of these days, three years, to figure it out," he said. "It's the only picture Lucy drew as a little kid that I have."

"Did you throw the others out?" I asked.

Jack shrugged.

"Things turned bad after she died. Things disappeared. I have no idea why this didn't."

He signaled the waitress. He was already so drunk. He looked at me in a way that made me shrink.

"Things went very, very bad after she was murdered," he said.

The picnic photo

Thursday, March 22, 8:34 p.m.

"I've got just one photo of the two of them together," Jack said.

He brushed the remaining photos aside impatiently. A dark one, shot through with alarming slashes of red and white, flashed out from the bottom of the stack. He snapped his eyes shut and slammed his hand over it.

"Not yet," he said.

He pulled another photo out, opened his eyes, and relaxed.

"Here. One week before it happened. That's my Lucy. With my wife."

I took the proffered photo.

Lucy, the crayon portraitist, was a chubby, cheerful three-year-old caught in mid-laugh, her baby teeth shining. She was dressed in red cable-knit tights and a plaid dress. Her dishwater blond hair was pulled back in two messy ponytails. She was standing outdoors in early spring. It looked windy.

Jack's wife, ten years older and fifteen pounds heavier than in the wedding photo, was kneeling beside Lucy. One arm encircled the little girl, the other pointed at the camera. She was nearly thirty and looked it. Her face was careworn and her eyes were tired. But she was still very beautiful.

"This was a week before she died?" I said.

Jack nodded.

"We went on a picnic. We did that every weekend. Except when I had to work."

I squinted at the enormous, oddly shaped gray smokestacks that towered over the blue pond behind Lucy and Jack's wife. Black blobs dotted the water.

"Where were they?" I said. "Are those ducks?"

"Yeah. We used to drive up to the Indian reservation to feed the ducks. There was this animal farm…well, later I found out it was the front end of a slaughterhouse. But there were cows and horses, and there was this duck pond. It was open to the public. Lucy loved feeding the ducks," he said.

I studied the photo. Cold spring sunshine gleamed on the faces of the mother and daughter. Their cheeks were the same shade of pink. Behind them, the fat industrial smokestacks seemed ominously familiar to me. On the ground, between Jack's wife's feet, lay a bag of white sandwich bread that was clearly destined for the ducks.

Was this the Last Known Photo of Jack's wife? The one the TV news displayed as they detailed the fate of the latest victim of the Westgate Serial Killer? Why did all Last Known Photos have this same hazy aura of finality? I wondered if mine would. I wondered if it had already been taken and was waiting patiently in the digital camera I used for work, or my family's cheap snapshot-taker, or my husband's cell phone.

"When it was warm," Jack said. "We…my wife and Lucy and me…would sit on a ripped old quilt by the duck pond. Talking nonsense and tossing stale bread at the ducks. They knew us. They begged like puppies."

Sitting across from me tonight, he was so diminished. He wasn't the husband behind the camera anymore. I wished I knew how to help him.

"When it rained or was cold, we huddled up in the car. My wife brought these great thermoses of soup and we tuned the radio to this oldies station. We didn't actually like the music, but it reminded us of what our parents played when we were kids. The Beatles. The Rolling Stones. Janis Joplin. It was our version of church."

He killed the last of the scotch on the rocks. He was so far from sober that I felt exploitative.

"It was going to be a car picnic, the day he killed her," he said.

The Weegee photo

Thursday, March 22, 9:21 p.m.

The fourth photo found its way from Jack's hand to mine. It was a strange image: a Polaroid taken by a neighbor the day before his wife was no more. It was a real slice-of-life shot, unposed, the subjects unaware of the cameraman's presence. Jack and his wife were in their kitchen. They were sitting at their kitchen table, one on each side, facing off. I knew this posture. They were in the middle of an argument.

"Lucy let the neighbor guy into the house without us knowing," Jack said, as I peered at the photo. "I had a long talk with her that night about not letting anyone in without asking Mommy or Daddy first. For all the good it did."

In the photo, Jack of twelve years ago was slumped in his kitchen chair, his head leaning heavily in his cupped hand. The other hand was balled up in a fist that rested on his thigh. There were stress lines carved into his forehead. His shoulders were up around his ears. He looked a lot less like the dork in the wedding photo and more like the drunk, widowed, ruined man seated across from me. He was exactly the same age as me in the photo. Did I look like this?

His wife was in mid-sentence, frowning with her mouth open on a vowel, her hand splayed near her chin to help make her point. She looked even more upset than he did. Twelve years later, Jack could remember every word of their conversation, thanks to this picture. Unasked, he recounted it.

"She said, 'I hate this.'

"I said, 'What?'

"She said, 'Seeing you like this. You look terrible. You aren't eating, you aren't sleeping—'

"I said, 'How would you know?'

"She said, 'Well, unless you're sleeping somewhere I don't know about, you're only in our bed a good three hours a night. And even then, you keep thrashing around and muttering. Are you having nightmares?'

"I said, 'Can we just drop it, please?'

"She said, 'Fine.'

"And she did drop it. For about thirty seconds.

"Then she said, 'You're on a team, you know. You don't have to do it all. Can't some of the other reporters pull their weight a little?'

"I said, 'All of the other reporters are working just as hard as me! Do you have any idea how hard this is? If the cops nail this guy and the *Seattle P.I.* or the *Times*—or, God forbid, the Associated Press—are there and we aren't, do you know how many heads will roll—starting with mine?'

"She said, 'I just think you could...I don't know. I just wish you didn't have to put so much of yourself into some son of a bitch serial killer. It's such a waste.'

"I said, 'It's been months and months of work—a waste? How the hell would you know? You never read my stuff! You don't give a damn what I do for a living, do you? You just bitch about it.'"

Jack hung his head.

"I said that. She was dead eighteen hours later. I didn't know what was coming, but still...I said that. I knew she never read my articles. She never had in the ten years we were married. It hurt. She complained about how much time my job took, but she never bothered to check out the result. How many people turn out a product the whole damned world can see—with their name on it?"

I could relate. But I said nothing.

"She said, 'Honey, I just mean it's terrible that a good man has to give himself to a killer he doesn't even know, not to the family that loves him. And misses him. Jack? Do you understand?'

"And right then, the flash went off. We both jumped and

yelled, and our neighbor was all, 'Hey, thought you'd be used to the paparazzi thing, Jack! Got any beer?'"

Jack sighed. He was silent for a long time.

"I was about to say to her, 'Yes. I'm sorry, baby. I miss you and Lucy. I love you.' But I lost my chance. And I never got another."

The crime scene photo

Thursday, March 22, 9:23 p.m.

The time had come to look at the final picture: the very last photo ever taken of his wife. Jack shuddered.

"It's a horrible photo," he said. "But I want you to see it. Nobody's ever seen it but the cops and the lawyers. And me."

I wasn't sure I wanted to see it. I was pretty sure I didn't want to see it, actually.

Jack's hands were shaking. He rubbed them over his face.

"Today was so bad. I haven't been at a murder scene in years. Twelve years. My old editor never made me go after what happened. It was the same today—the smell, the chaos."

I expected him to add, "The corpse," but he didn't.

"Maybe you shouldn't show me," I said. "Maybe you shouldn't look, either. Why not put the pictures away and I'll call you a cab so you can go home to bed?"

Jack uncovered his face and gave me the basilisk gaze that I found so intimidating.

"Fall asleep, forget, and sink back into the mindless routine for another year? Right?" he inquired in a tone that sought to entrap me.

I knew better than to answer. He wanted me to argue so he could attack me, releasing his pent-up anger. After I remained silent for a full ninety seconds, he scraped his nearly nailless fingers over his scalp.

"That was what got her killed. A mindless routine. Every Sunday, we went to the same store at the same time to buy the same stale bread to feed to the ducks. She and Lucy always went in while I waited in the car. I'd been writing about the murders for months. He was escalating. That's what the police kept telling me whenever a new body surfaced. He was about to be caught, and they thought he knew it. He was getting careless. I know exactly how it happened when he took her, even though I wasn't there."

"Maybe we should call it a night," I said. "Let me take you home. I've got a very cool press car this week. You've had a lot to drink. Where do you live?"

"I'd gotten so in-tune with his methodology—the dump sites, the choice of victims, the things he liked to do to them. I should have been smarter. I was so stupid."

Jack picked up the last photo. He didn't look at it. He closed his eyes.

"We were all set to go on our Sunday picnic that morning. I'd been putting in fourteen-hour days for weeks. No time off, not even weekends. I told my editor I wasn't coming in that Sunday. We were in the kitchen getting ready to go. Lucy was begging for a doughnut to feed to the ducks. She really wanted to eat it herself. She was three—thought she was so crafty."

Jack's face smoothed out, though his eyes remained closed. The crime scene photo was in his hand, turned away from me. I did not want him to show it to me.

"My wife told me she'd seen a crib on sale at the consignment shop up the street. We weren't really broke financially. But emotionally...in our relationship, as a couple, we were almost broke. It was all my fault and we both knew it. It was my job. My ego. But we were trying."

I said, "Jack—"

And he said, "Let me tell you. Please."

So I shut up and listened.

His eyes were still closed. Their absence was more unnerving than his poisonous stare.

"So many late nights, so many weekends spent writing about this guy. One day off sounded so wonderful. One day to sit in the toasty car with my family, singing old Elvis and Beach Boys songs, squeezed close, drinking hot soup. Lucy telling me all her silly stories from preschool, and my wife whispering that if we tried real, real hard, she could buy that crib before the sale ended."

"God, Jack, are you sure you're not ready to go home?" I said. "I'll take you. Your daughter's probably worried about you."

"Then my beeper went off. And my home phone rang. And everything went wrong."

Jack bit the inside of his cheek hard, making a concavity on the left side.

"My wife picked up the land line. She lost that...that lightness. Turned all brittle. She said, 'Jack, it's work.'

"I said, 'Look, tell them it's Sunday. I'll call them back tonight.'

"She said, 'I already did. They say it's urgent.'

"She looked at me, holding the phone halfway between me and the cradle where she could hang it up. God, I thought all I wanted was to relax and spend the day with Lucy and my wife. But what I really wanted was to take that call. Because I knew, I *knew* that it was big."

Now it was his turn to go silent for a full ninety seconds.

"You took the call?" I asked.

He nodded.

"I remember the exact thought I had: What can it hurt?"

He ought to have laughed humorlessly at this. He ought to have shaken his head or slammed his fist on the tabletop. He did nothing. Nothing. He was so still that I got scared.

"Jack? Jack? I think we should go. It's a work night—"

"I told her to have fun with Lucy. I went to work. Why the hell did I do that? Why didn't I know what would happen? I knew him. I knew how he operated. Better than the cops did. I should have known..."

He opened his eyes at last. They hurt me so bad when they met mine.

"The last thing I said to her was, 'Honey...' And the last thing she said to me was, 'Jack. Just go. We'll see you at dinner. Maybe.'"

He was wounding me mortally with his eyes.

"Are you married?" he asked.

"Yes," I said.

"Any kids?"

"Yes," I said.

"Do you do stuff like that?" he asked.

I didn't answer. I was in a bar, at ten at night on a Thursday, listening to a horrific story told by a miserable man. He knew the answer.

Jack slowly reached across the impassable space between us. His hand shook as it snaked between the empty highball glasses in pursuit of mine, which were clenched together in a knot on the sticky tabletop. He knocked a glass to the carpeted floor where it bounced, rolled, and did not break. He withdrew his hand, leaving mine unsqueezed.

"Don't," he said. "Just don't."

The most gruesome image ever

Thursday, March 22, 10:18 p.m.

When Jack showed me the last photo ever taken of his wife, my heart stopped. My breath stopped. My blinking, my nervous toe-tapping, and my thoughts stopped. The entire world stopped.

It was the most gruesome image I had ever seen.

I'd seen a hospital snapshot of a woman whose face had become a comma courtesy of a shotgun blast; her forehead, eyes, and gaping throat were all she had to call her own. I'd seen a glossy, full-color image of the top half of a man's head staring up from the gritty ground of Rwanda, bisected above the nose by a machete strike. I'd seen photos of Mary Kelly, whose internal viscera were removed, breasts cut off, and face hacked to hamburger by Jack the Ripper. I'd seen crime scene photos of the Black Dahlia's severed torso, displayed in the tall grass a good foot from her severed hips and legs in an empty lot in Los Angeles.

But this...

Jack was talking. I couldn't hear him. My ears were buzzing. I'd never seen a picture like this in all my life.

"There were no witnesses," I heard him saying, as I tore my eyes away from the photo.

I let my gaze lose itself in his. His stare was so cold, so intimidating, but I didn't care—it was a sweet relief after what I'd just seen.

"No witnesses," I repeated.

"Except Lucy," he said.

"Put the picture away. Please," I said.

Jack set it face-up on the tabletop. I couldn't keep my eyes from wandering to it. I forced myself to lock my gaze into his reptilian stare. His eyes were so penetrating and so drunk. He did not blink.

"He followed a routine, just like my wife did. For the past month, he'd seen her buying bread with her little girl at the same store, at the same time, every Sunday. There was no one else with her. Apparently. He didn't know that I talked to the cops about him, that I filed stories about him on a daily basis, that I went to all the autopsies of his victims, and that I was always sitting right outside in the car."

"Why?" I said. "Why didn't you go in the store with her?"

"I was smoking," he said. "My wife wanted me to quit. Things were tense between us. I told her I had. I hadn't. Every Sunday, I watched her through the big fishbowl windows the entire time, from bakery to checkout, while I sucked down a cigarette. I tossed it before she came out. I never noticed him watching her. He never noticed me watching her. I guess that makes us even, right?"

Jack fell silent for three painfully long minutes.

"If I'd been there," he finally said. "Smoking in the car and watching her, I'd have seen him grab her. I'd have saved her. Goddamn."

Jack fumbled in his 1980s-era Members Only jacket and produced a pack of Marlboros. He set it on the table. As he hunted through his pockets for a lighter, I snatched the cigarettes and stuffed them in my purse.

"No smoking. We're in a restaurant, it's illegal," I said.

Jack drunkenly kept searching for a moment, then seemed to forget why his hand was questing within his pockets.

"I was at work," he continued. "Everyone was at work. We got a tip from the King County Sheriff's office. Then the Washington State Patrol called us. Then the Seattle cops called. Something big was about to happen. The kids who went to the press club mixers called their buddies at the *Times* and the *Seattle P.I.* They were in on it, too. The cops had him."

"What do you mean, they had him? He killed your wife," I said.

"They had him. His name, his address. They were gonna raid. They tipped off the TV stations before the papers. We found out late, but we were saddling up fast. Then the kid outta journalism school who monitored the police scanner came running in. He was so freaked out..."

Jack stopped talking for another three minutes. To keep myself from looking at the photo lying face up on the table, I counted the seconds. It was one hundred and eighty on the dot.

"I did a lot of research after he killed her. During the trial...what else could I do? I talked to everyone. He was waiting in the bakery department for her. He knew it was always deserted on Sunday—no baking till Monday, all the brunch shoppers gone by ten a.m. Mike Kraft from the *Times* got an exclusive interview with him after the trial. He gave me his notes—he couldn't publish most of the interview. Too graphic."

Jack paused. I didn't count the seconds this time.

"Lucy saw. I've never..." he hesitated. "She was three. He let her go. My wife went with him so he would let her go. That was his thing. He targeted women with small children. They always went with him after he showed them his gun and threatened to shoot their child."

Jack took the photo and held it in both hands. He didn't look at it. I didn't look at it.

"He told Mike Kraft that he waited for her. He pretended to be checking out the day-old pastries, knowing she'd stick to the bagged bread. He liked her slim arms, her good wrists. He loved her bangs hanging over her face until she blew them away."

"Okay, Jack...Jack? I really think we need to stop. Let me take you home," I said. "Please? I don't think you should tell me this story. I don't think I'm the right person."

"He got lucky that day," Jack said. "The little girl wandered away from her mother, straight to him. She stood on tiptoe so she could see the doughnuts in the glass case. He told her he'd get one for her, grabbed her hand, and told her not to say anything till he asked her mommy. Lucy told me that."

I ached. She was three years old. I could imagine.

"So, when he approached my wife with the gun, he was holding Lucy's hand. Of course she went with him. What else could she do? Lucy wandered around the store for twenty minutes before anyone realized she was lost. The cashiers told Channel 5 that she sobbed, 'Mommy left! Mommy left with a stranger!'"

Jack was so very drunk. He was slurring his consonants. His neck was wobbly, sending his head into odd orbits.

"But if I'd been out in the car...I could have taken him. Gun or no. He was five-foot-four, a hundred thirty pounds. You could have taken him. Goddamn it."

Would I have done what his wife did? I liked to think that I wouldn't have. I liked to think that I would have fought him off, or talked my way out of it, or escaped in the nick of time. A true hero in a true story. But I had no idea.

Jack O'Lies always wanted a Pulitzer Prize

The Washingtonian
Westgate Serial Killer Captured
By Jack O'Lies

March 23, 1998 — Robert "Bobby Dean" Clasky, identified by police as the Westgate Serial Killer, was arrested yesterday and charged with eight counts of murder in the first degree. He was apprehended in the immediate vicinity of his eighth victim, Jennifer Elaine O'Lies of Seattle, who had been stabbed to death in a wooded area outside Seattle city limits. Clasky was found covered with the victim's blood and in possession of a weapon that police classified as a homemade bayonet.

Law enforcement from three jurisdictions worked in collaboration for 19 months to track Clasky, who is described by the King County Sheriff's spokesman as a drifter. Clasky, who has an extensive arrest record in King County and the city of Seattle, confessed to the murder of Jennifer Elaine O'Lies upon being read his rights.

Clasky kidnapped the victim at the Ballard Stop 'n' Shop market near her home. He is believed to have forced the victim at gunpoint to drive her car to the murder site, where he raped and mutilated her with a crude weapon. Paramedics were unable to resuscitate the victim, who is estimated to have died just minutes before police arrived on scene. Her extensive wounds were inflicted while still alive, according to King County Coroner Harry Dekins.

"We had pinned him down to his last known address, but we missed him," said Seattle Police detective Allan MacIntosh. "We were just too late."

Police were able to track Clasky to the remote murder site due to assistance provided by the victim's 3-year-old daughter, who witnessed the kidnapping. The child was not harmed by Clasky.

Jennifer Elaine O'Lies, age 29, is survived by her husband, Jack O'Lies.

Too late

Thursday, March 22, 10:39 p.m.

"Less than an hour after my wife was kidnapped, Lucy told the police what our car looked like. It was bright orange. And she gave them the license plate," Jack said.

"She knew the plate number when she was three years old?" I said.

"Yeah. We bought the car right after my wife gave birth. We got a vanity plate: LUCYCAR. Lucy loved telling people about it. The cops got a bead on it right away. I rode in the KIRO Radio van. They drove crazy fast. The entire ride, I was praying that the cops got there in time. I was actually on my knees in the back, wedged in between the audio guy and a box of tuner equipment, saying Hail Marys and Our Fathers."

I wanted to say something. I felt I should. But my throat was cinched shut.

"I figured that there was…hope still out there. The cops would shoot him, just like in some cheap novel. I'd run to her and she'd wrap her arms around my neck. She'd cry and I'd cry and we would go home to Lucy and just…clutch each other, safe, all three of us. I thought we were inseparable."

I couldn't say anything. I tried, but I couldn't.

"It was dark in the woods where we found her. The sun was setting through the trees, redder than I've ever seen. Three canine units were there. The dogs were going crazy. They could smell her blood. The King County Sheriff's dog was the one that took him down. It was so chaotic. Reporters everywhere, cops shouting, dogs barking. My wife's car was abandoned by the side of the road. We jumped out of the news van and ran into the woods and…"

Jack held the photo of his wife's dead body. He stared at it, unblinking, his eyes enormous.

"The woods smelled sour. It was frigidly cold. I ran and ran, tailing the dogs. I remember thinking, I have to find her. She has to be alive. I was having this internal dialogue, telling myself that she'd probably been raped, might have been cut up real bad, but that was okay. Just as long as she survived, I could fix it. Somehow. But she had to be alive. I was sprinting through the woods, then a bunch of reporters from the *Seattle Times* tackled me and threw me to the ground so I wouldn't see her. The paramedics swarmed all over her. The cops covered them with their guns drawn. The TV crews filmed it. Harry Dekins took this photo. I remember it took five guys to hold me down. They told me later I was screaming the whole time."

Jack suddenly grabbed his wallet, opened it, and stuffed the crime scene photo and the other four pictures back into the secret pocket within the money fold. He unsteadily leaned left and crammed the wallet into his back pocket. He gulped down the last of his scotch. His voice became brisk, though slurred.

"The paramedics tried it all—CPR, defibrillation, IVs. Too late. I don't remember much after that until I overheard Harry talking to his assistant. He said if they'd gotten to her just ten minutes earlier, she might have lived. She bled out completely."

Jack dug in his jacket pocket and pulled out his car keys. They jangled in his unsteady hand.

"My mother took Lucy for a while. I wrote articles about the murder every day. I didn't sleep for eleven nights. I testified at his trial. He got life. I drank a lot. He got killed a year into his sentence by another prisoner. Stabbed to death in the shower. He bled out completely. Okay…I'm gonna go home now."

The designated driver with the awesome car

Thursday, March 22, 11:12 p.m.

He was astonishingly drunk. He dropped his car keys as he tried to slide out of the booth. I ducked down and grabbed them. I put them in my purse. He was so far gone that he didn't notice. He scrabbled around on the sticky carpet, hunting and cursing.

"How about I drive you home?" I said. "I've got an awesome press car this week. You'll love it. Where do you live?"

He kept fumbling around the floor until he clocked his jaw hard on the edge of the table. Stunned, he gawked at me as I pulled my coat on and beckoned to him.

"It's either I take you home or you pay for a cab," I said.

"Can't afford a cab," he sneered, as he hauled himself unsteadily to his feet. "Your paper doesn't get delivered to my home anymore. I'm an undesirable lower income household."

"Join the club," I said. "I'm parked right outside."

I started walking. To my surprise, he followed without another word. He leaned on the bar with all his weight as I paid the tab. It was a horrifying $72.19 before tax. I couldn't honorably get out of it once my credit card had been swiped by the bartender. Since I aided and abetted Jack's drinking, I figured I had to pay for it, literally and figuratively.

Out in the drizzly chill, Jack lurched along the gleaming sidewalk, trailing me to my press car. The doors unlocked automatically when they sensed I was near. The headlights and interior lights came on of their own accord. It was an awesome car. If I wasn't already spoken for, I'd have asked it to marry me. Jack fell into the front passenger seat and rubbed his face with both hands, as if washing it.

"You have no idea," he muttered.

"Where do you live?" I said.

"Ballard."

"Can you be more specific?"

"Everyone used to be a drunk Scandinavian fisherman," he said. "We bought our house cheap because nobody wanted to live around a bunch of drunk Scandinavian fishermen. Now they've got their own reality TV show and my property taxes are killing me."

"Jack! What is your address?"

Jack reclined against the plush leather headrest, his eyes closed.

"Mmm…outside your news beat, little lady."

"Little what?" I said. "Okay, just give me your driver's license."

Obediently, as if he'd been ordered to do so by many a cop over the years, Jack pulled out his wallet, withdrew his driver's license, and handed it to me. His eyes stayed closed the entire time.

"Your newspaper is probably used to wrap fish in Ballard. Do you realize that?" he murmured.

I squinted at his license, glowing pale orange beneath the streetlight outside my window. It was five years old and about to expire. Jack was an Aries. His photo appeared significantly younger than he did. He clearly drank harder than a Scandinavian fisherman.

The address was no help. I didn't know how to navigate the wilds of Ballard. Lucky for me, the car could tell me how to get anywhere. As I laboriously keyed in the cross streets of our present location and Jack's address, my passenger lamented.

"They started charging for obituaries three years ago, when the newspaper industry tanked," Jack said. "That's what I do all day now. Call funeral homes and hustle them to sell the bereaved a space in our paper. Once a day, I call the cops and write up the police blotter with whatever the rookie who answers the phone tells me. God. I was nominated for a Pulitzer Prize. Did you know that?"

"Yes," I said, pondering the map generated by the awesome GPS in the awesome press car.

"I'm an ad department tool," he moaned.

"Well, at least it's job security," I said as I started the engine.

"An intern could do it," he said.

I pulled onto the freeway and pushed the accelerator to the floor. The car was so fast! It begged me to break the speed limit. I hated to think what would happen if I got pulled over. I had scant proof of permission to be driving it, and I doubted anyone from the automotive advertising firm would pick up the phone at such a late hour of the night to explain the concept of "press cars" to my arresting officer. If I was hauled off to jail for grand theft auto, it would give me something exciting to write about in my newspaper's car section, I supposed. After uncountable articles reciting dull vehicular virtues such as horsepower, torque, and continuously variable transmission, I was almost excited by the prospect. It seemed I was an ad department tool, too.

"Lucy's gonna be so pissed," Jack said.

"She's fifteen, right?" I said.

"Fifteen. Going on fifty. She's so hard on me."

"Well, weren't we all at that age."

"She hates it," Jack said. "But if I stop, I'll die. You understand?"

"No," I said. "Jack, this is your exit, right?"

Jack didn't answer. The GPS said it was. I took the exit off the freeway, into the heart of Ballard, land of difficult parking and random intersections.

"I wish you worked at my paper," he said. "I don't talk to anyone."

"Well, you've got to make connections and all that, right? For your career. Try to extend your social network," I rambled, not listening to myself as I scanned the dimly lit street signs. Where the hell were we?

"I never do," he said. "Never. Nobody knows about me. Who are you?"

He was so drunk. I hoped the police would go easy on me when I rear-ended some plodding Nordic Ballardite as I searched for the elusive Leary Way, purported cross-street of 21st Avenue N.W. I would plead the designated, but distracted, driver defense.

"I write about dead people all day," Jack said. "My mother is dying. My father died when Lucy was a baby. I don't know why I'm telling you these things."

"You're drunk. You're chatty," I replied. "Yes! 21st Avenue N.W. It does exist! GPS, I love you!"

I turned the car a sharp right, making the tires squeal. Jack opened his eyes, one at a time. He rubbed a hand over his mouth twice. He blinked and stared out the windshield.

"Where are we?"

"Less than four blocks from your home. Isn't GPS fantastic? I love it—I'm putting it in my review for sure," I said.

Jack sat up in alarm.

"Don't drop me home! Lucy'll be so pissed. Put me out here."

"What—why?" I said.

"Stop! Stop now!"

I stopped. We were in front of a bar. Jack fumbled at the door latch.

"Jack, wait—"

He thrust the passenger door open.

"She'll raise hell. I'll sneak in. Don't tell," he mumbled.

He heaved himself out of the car and onto the pavement. He balanced himself for a moment, then turned and leaned back in, bracing his hands on the doorframe.

"Jack," I said. "You're going home, right? Want me to walk you, make sure you get inside okay? You're not going into that bar, right?"

Framed by the open car door and illuminated from behind by the retina-searing red of the neon beer signs that decorated the windows of the bar, Jack glowered down at me. His pale blue eyes were deadly. I couldn't look away.

"God," he said. "You have no idea."

He turned and veered unsteadily away from the car. He hesitated at the door to the bar. He shouldered it open and went in.

I should have gone after him. It was certain that I would be subpoenaed when he turned up dead from alcohol poisoning. The recurrent King County Coroner Harry Dekins would testify against me.

I leaned over and yanked the passenger door shut.

He was a grown man. I got what I needed for my book. More than I needed. In return, I paid his bar tab and I drove him home.

I owed him nothing.

Right?

The fabrication of our lives

Friday, March 23, 12:07 p.m.

I forgot about Jack O'Lies. Actively, with effort. Until noon the next day, that is, when the automotive advertising firm arrived to reclaim the awesome Infinity G convertible, $83,000 MSRP.

"Hey," said the driver, as he fixed to take the best car I'd ever driven out of my life forever, leaving me only my as-yet unwritten 750-word review to remind me of the joy we'd shared. "Is this a driver's license?"

He retrieved a small card from the dashboard, where I'd carelessly tossed it the previous night. He frowned at it, then handed it to me.

"You know, you're not allowed to let anyone but you drive this thing. This guy didn't drive it, right?"

I took the driver's license, glanced at Jack's face and DOB, then said, "He was drunk. I was the designated driver. Sort of."

I stuffed the license into my purse, scurried back to my office, and forgot about Jack O'Lies for three hours. However, when I dug through my purse in search of my wallet to make sure I had $3.75 in bus fare to get my carless self home, my fingers brushed a set of alien keys.

I pulled them out. I discovered a Saab car key, a brass house key, and a couple queer little keys that probably opened bank safe deposit boxes or gym lockers. They were held together by a silver, oval-shaped fob embossed with a name.

O'Lies.

Damn. I was a car key thief. I would assuredly be arrested. I'd never been arrested before. Maybe it would make a good article? Probably not. I needed to return Jack's keys ASAP. Oh, and his driver's license. And whose cigarettes were these?

I got pulled into meetings. I got drawn into conversations. I got seven phone calls. I got thirty-two emails that required immediate replies. I forgot about Jack O'Lies, his keys, his license, his cancer sticks, and my unintentional thievery. I took the bus home. I made dinner. I communed with my neglected family. I continued to forget about Jack O'Lies, without effort, until ten o'clock in the evening.

Around 10:15, I wondered...

How did he get into his house without his keys?

Did he get into his house?

Was he lying dead or delirious in some Ballard gutter?

Did he call the cops and file a report against me for stealing his driver's license and keys? I was just guessing, but it was probably some kind of felony. Some variety of identity theft.

It was late. I couldn't cart myself down to the hinterlands of Ballard at such an hour. Jack, if he was alive, was probably three sheets to the wind, anyway. I decided that I would return his property bright and early the next day.

Later, I learned that some time between when I left him Thursday night and the wee hours of Friday morning, Jack O'Lies might have killed a man with his bare hands.

Holy Redeemer Catholic School did not prepare me for this

Saturday, March 24, 4:36 p.m.

A Christian heavy metal band was screaming for Jesus on Lucy O'Lies' stereo.

"Holy, holy, holeeee! Say holy…"

"Holy!" roared an enthusiastic crowd on the CD.

"You have no idea how good it is to get away from that satanic jerk. It's like a day pass from purgatory," said Christopher, Lucy's nineteen-year-old Not Boyfriend. He lolled on her pink canopy bed in the midst of a mob of teddy bears. He was incredibly tall. His feet hung off the end of the bed a good ten inches.

Lucy gritted her teeth at the music and nodded at Christopher.

I sat uncomfortably on a grubby pink beanbag chair, clutching a glass of Hawaiian Punch and praying, secularly, that hearing damage wasn't immanent. I glanced at the stereo, then at the walls above it, which were covered with framed cross-stitch scenes of varying degrees of clumsiness, ranging from lumpy Lambs of God to a gory multi-pane of the stations of the cross complete with a gushing spear stab wound worked in three shades of red and circling vultures dripping eager threads of off-white saliva. Skeins of embroidery thread lay scattered all over the floor. A pair of wickedly sharp little scissors gleamed on the bedside table. I hoped the beanbag chair wasn't, in fact, a gigantic pincushion.

"Ave M'ria!" shouted the lead singer on the CD.

"Aaaaaaveh…Maaaaaareeeeah!" replied the crowd.

"It's effective, isn't it? I got it at work. It's the most hardcore thing they have," said Christopher.

"I'm sure," Lucy murmured, picking at a cluster of pimples at her jaw line.

My unheralded arrival chez O'Lies some twenty-five minutes ago apparently interrupted Lucy's asexual assignation with Christopher, The Future Priest. That was how she introduced him: Christopher, The Future Priest. I was handed the Hawaiian Punch, led up to her room, and invited to wait for her dad who was "out getting coffee or something." My initial chagrin at lacking Jack's cell phone number faded as I considered his daughter. I couldn't help my inordinate curiosity about fifteen-year-old Lucy, witness to her mother's kidnapping. She was a pudgy, pimply, sullen sort of teenager. She looked only a little like the photos of her mother that I saw on Thursday; much more like Jack if he put on forty pounds. She had his cold stare, though her eyes were brown and lacked his ability to hypnotize.

She was so religious it scared me.

"Where exactly do you work, Christopher?" I hollered.

"Christian gift shop at Northgate Mall," he replied.

"Ah," I said. "Could you turn it down a little?"

"What?" Christopher shouted over the holy din. "So, tell me if you think this'll work: I'm going to—"

Lucy reached out and clicked off the stereo. My ears rang and I silently blessed her. Secularly.

"I'm going to play this CD when it's just me and the Evil One. None of his freaky friends around, slurping off the bong and taking the Lord's name in vain, like they do."

"Uh-huh?" Lucy said.

"I'm sure he'll smack me on the arm like I hate when he hears it, and say something all profane, like, 'Hey Chris! You finally gone and got some fuckin' taste, man!'"

"Christopher!" Lucy's eyes bulged with shock. She made a huge sign of the cross and stared at him accusingly.

Christopher covered his long face with his hands and groaned.

"Name of the Father, Son, and Holy Spirit, forgive me," he muttered, signing the cross as extravagantly as Lucy. "See what he does to me? He's corruption made flesh!"

"So, Christopher…the Evil One? Is he your roommate, or…" I said.

Christopher nodded at me. He was as pimply as Lucy.

"I'm at the end of my rope. This CD is my last hope. If the subliminality of God's Word doesn't penetrate his thick skull and turn him into a decent Christian, I'll…I don't know. Die, probably."

I wasn't sure if "subliminality" was a real word. If so, I wanted to use it verbally and in an article right away.

"Oh, let's not die," I said. "Did you meet him through Craigslist? You've got to be careful." I almost added, "young man," but I stopped myself. I wasn't that old.

"He's the nephew of our priest," Lucy explained. "Father Bertrain."

"He's a sinner," Christopher said. "I thought I could redeem him. Then Father Bertrain would have to sponsor my seminary application."

I had no insight into the politics of seminary enrollment. But considering that Christopher, The Future Priest, was spending his Saturday afternoon in the bedroom of a fifteen-year-old girl, I would've been willing to bet the pot-smoking, profanity-saying Evil One had a better chance of getting into seminary than he did. See also the classic definition of nepotism, from the Italian "nepote," meaning "nephew."

"Ah," I said. "Maybe you could find a new roommate?"

Christopher gave me a sour look that told me how naive my suggestion was. He leaned across the bed and turned the stereo back on. My God, his arms were eight feet long!

"I wonder if he's ever going to clean up the kitchen. He had this party last night—more of a sad pagan gathering—and his stupid buddies spilled tortilla chips and beer all over the inside of the refrigerator," he complained.

"You went out with my dad on Thursday," Lucy said to me. Her voice was as flat as Kansas.

"Yes," I said. "Wait, what do you mean, 'went out?'"

"One of them stuffed chicken bones down the garbage disposal. Now the water won't go down. I'm not cleaning that mess up. If the landlord finds out—"

"I don't know all the cool teenage slang nowadays," I said, sounding like a senior citizen. "We didn't 'go out' like that. I mean…what do you mean?"

"Guess what I heard at school on Friday?" Lucy turned her attention from my slangless self to her un-boyfriend.

"I'm married!" I said. "I don't 'go out.'"

"What?" asked Christopher, The Hip Future Priest. He switched his long feet side-to-side in time to the music, his arms behind his head.

"Well, there's these—well, okay, so I was reading a back issue of Christian On Assignment in the library after school? And there was this article about these Catholics down in—was it Ecuador? Maybe Guatemala? Anyway, in Latin America, somewhere…"

Lucy had to stop talking for a moment. She was literally breathless.

"At least you still live at home. Your dad, while a drunkard and a bad Christian, isn't gonna kick you out at eighteen. 'Either get a job or go into seminary or go to college.' Huh. Thanks, Dad. The Evil One is so deaf from clubbing and the various hallucinogenic drugs he's taken over the years that I could yell, 'Jesus is here! Right here, in the living room! Welcome, Lord!' and he'd just keep sucking off the bong. Sinner. Why do I have to exorcise his satanic ways? I'm not official yet. I might screw it up."

"Are you listening? There's these Latin Americans, and they have this special ceremony for Easter that anyone can participate in. You wanna know what it is?" Lucy's brown eyes were aflame. They were aimed at Christopher.

"We were not on a date," I said. "It was an interview. Could you just give me your dad's cell phone number? I need to give him back his driver's license and keys and cig—and stuff."

"They crucify people!" Lucy exclaimed.

Christopher looked at her. I looked at her.

"They do what, now?" I said.

"They kidnap people? Torture them? That's pagan," said Christopher.

"No way! They're volunteers. They want to do it," Lucy said.

I considered this. In my idle hours, I had perused many an anthropologic publication (okay, *National Geographic*, at the dentist's office). Was this practice plausible? I wasn't sure.

"Hmm...I think it's fake. It's gotta be illegal. They could get sued big time if anyone ever got seriously injured. They probably just tie people to low crosses over, like, mattresses," said Christopher, The Future Voice of Reason.

"No, they don't! There were pictures. The priest actually nails their hands right into the wood. Not their feet, they just tie those, but still! They hang them really high above the crowd, just like Jesus," Lucy said.

"Hmm..." Christopher said. It was neither agreement nor disagreement. Mere acknowledgement. He was thinking it over. Lucy waited breathlessly for Christopher's response. I set my undrunk glass of Hawaiian Punch down on the nubby beige carpet. I sensed something significant was about to happen.

"I don't believe it," he said at last. "I don't think anyone would have the guts to do it—to let somebody actually crucify them. It's one thing to crawl a mile to church on your knees, or to fast for days. But it's something else to let someone pound nails through your hands and leave you hanging."

"But they do! People do it! I saw pictures," she protested.

"Oh, and that means it must be real. Nobody ever faked a photo before."

Christopher smirked at Lucy patronizingly. I called to mind my newspaper's graphic designer and her skill at manipulating images with Photoshop. She once manufactured an entire island and inserted it into the middle of Puget Sound. Nobody gave the image so much as a skeptical glance. I made an effort not to grin knowingly at Christopher.

Lucy scowled at her friend-who-is-a-boy.

"It's not such a strange thing at all. I'm not surprised that people would do it," she said.

She took a breath, looking down at the rug.

"I would," she whispered.

Christopher laughed.

"Oh, really? That I'd like to see! You with nails stuck in your hands. You'd scream and run off full speed into the jungle before they could get the hammer out of the toolbox."

Lucy's face went red. Her rage was sudden and palpable.

"Oh yeah?" she said, her cold, Jack-like eyes targeting Christopher.

"Yes," he chuckled, still sprawled on her bed, the picture of amused nonchalance.

"Now, kids," I said, sounding like a fuddy-duddy guidance counselor in a 1950s educational film. "Let's take a moment and calm down."

Lucy stood and marched to the bed. She reached across Christopher's whip-thin body. Before he could react, she grabbed the little needlepoint scissors from the bedside table. She flipped them open, splaying the sharp blades like legs.

She eyed Christopher, who sat up cautiously. Without warning, without flinching, she rammed the longest blade into her palm. It stuck deep. Blood began to run down her wrist. Christopher swung his mile-long legs around and stood shakily. His perpetually bored face was alight with shock. I was sure my face looked the same.

"Oh yeah?" Lucy whispered, yanking the scissors out of her palm, leaving a bloody stigmata worthy of a martyr. "You want a turn?"

Called (as I vaguely recalled)

Saturday, March 24, 11:42 p.m.

In my haste to flee Jack's house, I scrawled my cell phone number on the back of one of my business cards, thrust it at his crazy and bleeding daughter, and hotfooted it to my car. I never expected to hear from him again, though I still had his driver's license, keys, and cigarettes.

My cell rang late that night. Very late.

"Hello?" I answered suspiciously. No one ever called me so close to midnight and I didn't recognize the number. I waited for heavy breathing and a lewd proposition.

"Katherine?"

"Yes?"

"Hey. It's me."

I did not feel that Jack and I, after one whole interview—albeit a drunken one on his part—were on an "it's me" basis. Nevertheless, I knew that it was him the instant I heard his alcohol-addled voice.

"Hi, Jack. Where were you this afternoon?"

"Starbucks."

"How original."

"What?"

"Your daughter said you were getting coffee."

"I was. At Starbucks."

"For an hour and a half," I accused wife-ishly, though I was not his wife.

"Harry Dekins asked me," he said.

Ah, Harry Dekins, the quotable coroner!

"Nice," I said. "So, you want your car keys and stuff back?"

"Can we talk? Like the other night?"

"Like the other night?"

Jack let out a long sigh that vibrated through my cell phone, into my ear, and down my spine.

"Please," he said. "Just for a couple minutes."

"Well…okay," I said, settling onto the uncomfortable futon in the uncomfortable ground floor of my home. "What do you want to talk about?"

Jack sighed again, blowing my impatience away.

"I don't know," he said.

"Are you drunk right now?" I said.

"I've had a little bit."

"How much?"

"A couple screwdrivers."

"Really."

"Mostly vodka. Hard driver, light screw," he said.

"Do you mind if I tape this?" I said. "For both of our protection?"

"Why? This is a social call."

"Not for me," I said.

"How come?"

"Jack, we're not social that way. We don't know each other. I'm turning on my recorder. Okay? Jack? Okay?"

I hate how I sound on tape

Saturday, March 24, 11:48 p.m.

Transcript of recording:

Katherine: Jack? You still there?
Jack: Yeah.
Katherine: So I guess Lucy gave you my cell number.
Jack: Yeah.
Katherine: Um...I've got your cigarettes, if you want them back. And your car keys and driver's license. So...
Jack: You could've left them with Lucy.
Katherine: She was...kind of...she was...I didn't want to, just in case.
Jack: What?
Katherine: Did she tell you how she hurt her hand?
Jack: She hurt her what?
Katherine: Her hand. Did she tell you what she did to it?
Jack: No. She hurt her what, now?
(Silence for seventeen seconds)
Jack: Can we talk?
Katherine: I guess, for a few minutes. It's pretty late.
Jack: I met Harry for coffee this afternoon.
Katherine: Yeah, you said that.
Jack: He called me six times. Voicemails, y'know, the mother hen checking up.
Katherine: Is he some kind of friend of yours, or...
Jack: I guess.
Katherine: He wanted to...what? Make sure you were okay after the thing at the crime scene?
Jack: Coroner's office botched the autopsy.

Katherine: Your wife's?

Jack: What?

Katherine: They botched what autopsy?

Jack: The floater from Thursday.

Katherine: What do you mean? I don't get it.

Jack: They fucked it up. As in, Harry's assistant is a recovering meth head who chose this week to get back on the dragon, and he wrecked the body beyond belief.

Katherine: Are you serious?

Jack: Something about stuffing the abdominal cavity with inflated surgical gloves, I don't know, I was so damned hungover.

Katherine: Yeah, I bet you were! I thought you'd die or something. You got so freakin' drunk Thursday night.

(Silence for six seconds)

Jack: Why didn't you come with me?

Katherine: You told me to let you out.

Jack: I don't remember. You were there, then you weren't.

Katherine: You were plastered beyond belief. You told me to let you out, so…I mean, I had to get home. It was a work night.

Jack: You're sure you didn't follow me?

Katherine: No. I dropped you off outside the bar, then I drove home.

Jack: I think I did a very bad thing.

Katherine: What—the drinking? The pictures? What?

(Silence for eleven seconds)

Katherine: Jack? Still there? Hello? Damn, I hate this phone sometimes!

Jack: I'm here.

Katherine: It's getting late. So…

Jack: I need to tell you.

Katherine: Hm?

Jack: I already knew stuff Harry was telling me. About the body. I knew it had a word written on the left heel. "Spine." How the hell did I know that?

(Clinking sounds)

Jack: What's that?

Katherine: Hm?

Jack: Are you there? What're you—

Katherine: So I opened a bottle of wine! I'm not made of stone! You're drunk as hell.

Jack: Red?

Katherine: Yes.

Jack: Cab?

Katherine: No, gross, no. Merlot. Will you just wrap this up, please, so I can go to bed? Sorry. I...sorry. That's rude and all. But come on, Jack, I'm not following any of this, and I'm tired! I want to go to bed!

Jack: Sorry.

(Silence for twenty-three seconds)

Katherine: Jack? Still there?

(Silence for seven seconds.)

Katherine: Jack? Jack?

Jack: I don't talk to anyone.

Katherine: I'm sorry. I'm...God, I don't know. Want me to drop your stuff off tomorrow?

Jack: Okay.

Katherine: When?

Jack: Before church?

Katherine: You go to church?

Jack: Don't you?

(Silence for five seconds)

Jack: I've been getting these strange text messages. They're...I think maybe I did a really bad thing. Katherine? Katherine?

Katherine: Hm? What time is it? Jesus, it's after midnight! I've got to go.

Jack: You'll come over in the morning. Right?

Katherine: Fine, I guess, maybe.

Jack: Right?

Katherine: Yes, right, I'll come over. I've got to go. It's so late!

Jack: Okay. Good night.

Katherine: Bye.

End of recording.

The Bickering Bickersons of Ballard

Sunday, March 25, 8:18 a.m.

I drove—yet again!—south to the Norse 'hood of Ballard. It was way too early to be carting myself around Seattle proper. I longed for my suburb. I longed for my bed.

I knocked on Jack O'Lies' front door. It was army green, the paint peeling away to reveal a sickly gray undercoat. From somewhere within, his daughter yelled something.

I thought she yelled, "Come in!"

I assumed she yelled, "Come in!"

I turned the knob. It was unlocked. I came in.

I was met with the sight of worn hardwood floors and ancient throw rugs and a sagging sofa upholstered in a khaki tartan fabric that troubled me. The coffee table was littered with high school textbooks (depressing), empty vodka bottles (more depressing), and several smearily printed Catholic tracts (depressingest of all). In my current state of hungover Sunday morning blahs, "depressingest" was a word. So was "smearily."

"Hello?" I called. "Lucy? Jack?"

I heard a TV jabbering. I followed the sound.

In the kitchen, a scary-looking bald guy in a white suit was grimacing and shaking his head at Lucy.

"You out there!" he shouted from the TV screen.

"Yes," said Lucy, as she spooned cereal into her mouth.

"You witness to society's sin!"

"That's right," Lucy agreed.

I hesitated in the doorway for so many reasons; so many that it would take hours to list them all. Perhaps the top five would suffice:

1. There was a televangelist on the TV. That did not bode

well.

2. Oh, tacky gold Formica and avocado linoleum! 1970s kitchen of my childhood! I thought I had escaped you. Tasteless lower middle-class aesthetic, would I never be free of your shabby embrace?

3. Lucy was dressed in a black Italian-grandma dress with no décolletage and a ratty hand-crocheted collar. She wore four rosaries of varying weight and color around her neck. This did not bode well.

4. Lucy was eating Lucky Charms. I loved Lucky Charms. If offered a bowl, I would accept, ruining the restrictive and scientifically unfounded diet I had invented for myself.

5. I smelled not a whiff of coffee in the air. I would die without coffee.

Seriously: I would die without coffee!

"Hi, Lucy," I said, waving a limp, decaffeinated hand. "How're you?"

"Shh!" she hissed between slurps of cereal.

"You watch as society parades its perversions, its sin, its *eeeeeeevil*, and you do nothing. Well, I say, stop!" shouted the scary bald man on the TV.

"Stop!" Lucy agreed.

"Stop! Tell it, don't you come over here into my house of God! Stop!"

"Stop!" Lucy exclaimed.

"Why? You break another glass?" Jack said from the doorway.

Oy vey, he was clad in the classic open-door bathrobe! I warned him I was coming over. Was it too much to ask that he at least put on pants?

"Want me to go wait in the living room?" I blurted, shading my eyes like a Victorian damsel.

"What?" Jack said. "You had breakfast yet? Lucy, get her something."

He meandered on unsteady, bare legs to a set of folding doors at the far end of the kitchen. He sported a dark bruise on the left side of his jaw.

"That's fine, I ate already," I said. "Should I just leave your keys and stuff on the counter?"

"Calm down," said Jack, his hangover audible in every consonant and vowel. "We're almost ready. Finish up, Lucy!"

Lucy rolled her eyes, continued spooning cereal, and reached out to crank the volume on the televangelist. Jack slid the doors open to reveal a washer and drier.

Oh God, he was going to disrobe right in front of me, and I would be struck blind!

Thankfully, I heard the front door open, then slam shut. Christopher, The Future Priest, entered the kitchen.

"Hey," he said. "Ready to go?"

"Dad's still messing around," Lucy snorted, picking up her cereal bowl to drink the milk like a three-year-old. Jack, not entirely oblivious, stepped into the laundry alcove and pulled the doors shut behind him. Spared his nudity, I relaxed. I was a married woman, after all; such sights were not fit for my eyes.

From within his ad hoc dressing room, Jack called, "Hey, Katherine, you want any coffee? Lucy, make some."

"No," Lucy snapped. "You just want it for you, because you're hungover."

"We have a guest."

"She doesn't need coffee coz she doesn't drink," Lucy asserted. "Hangover, Dad—"

"Is this all there is? Didn't you throw the load in like I asked?" Jack demanded.

"Wear the good pants, Dad. I hate when you go in your work clothes. You look so sloppy."

"I hate these, you know that!"

"You look so sloppy!"

"Will you just make Katherine a cup of coffee and get yourself ready to go?"

"Hangover, Dad, is a necessary and a good thing."

"What?" I bleated.

At the moment, I was hungover as hell thanks to the glass of wine I drank to get through Jack's boozy conversation with me in the desolation of the night, and the two additional glasses I drank to force the echoes of his bleak voice out of my mind so I could sleep. I craved a cup of coffee. I would have killed for a cup of coffee. I was not in a good or necessary state!

"You see," Lucy said. "As you pour unholy poison into your body, the Lord sees and sends a pain unto you. And this pain—"

"A pain unto me?" Jack exclaimed from behind the flimsy laundry doors.

"Unto?" I repeated.

"Please tell me they didn't teach you that in English class," he said.

Bolstered by Christopher's knowing smirk, Lucy clanked her crucifix-bedecked self to the sink, where she deposited her empty cereal bowl.

"And this pain is meant to cleanse your soul, just as pain cleansed Christ on the cross," she continued. "So, when you drink of coffee, you erect a barrier between yourself and God, who wishes to help you end your drunken ways."

I felt this was a bit stagy. I felt that she was acting out for my benefit. Exactly what did she think I was doing in her house at such a raw hour of the morning?

"So, can I go? Is your church walking distance?" I asked her. "Did you really say, 'when you drink *of* coffee?'"

"It's six point eight miles away," Christopher said.

Damnation.

"Jack? Do you need me to drive you all to the *Washingtonian* to get your car?"

It was entirely possible that I actually twanged, "Dyah need me ta drive y'all?" This tasteless lower middle-class kitchen was dragging me back down the social ladder.

Jack slid the laundry doors open. I flinched.

He was dressed. I relaxed. He was in a get-up exactly like his editor would wear, unattractive pleated-front Dockers, golf shirt, and all.

"I hate this," he said. "I told you."

"And I told you!" Lucy shrilled at a gauche teenage volume, stomping her foot. "You are so embarrassing! Why can't you be normal on Sunday for once? Why can't you stop embarrassing me?"

I glanced at Christopher, hoping for an ally in my discomfort. He was smirking at Jack with his gangly arms folded across his thin chest, clearly taking Lucy's part in this father-daughter dispute. That meant I would have to side with the only other adult in the room, which was alcoholic, hungover Jack. Fantastic.

"Okay," Jack said. "Let's get going."

All three looked at me.

"Go where, exactly?" I said.

"Sacred Heart of Jesus," Lucy said.

"Pardon?" I said.

"It's in Belltown," said Christopher.

Increasingly fantastic. Belltown: a seedy neighborhood noteworthy for its impossible parking, wandering junkies, and smug IT crowd slumming from the suburbs. My second least favorite place in Seattle.

"I've got stuff to do today," I began.

Suddenly I realized that Belltown was less than a dozen blocks from *Washingtonian* headquarters. I perked up.

"So, I'll just drop Lucy and Christopher off at church, then we'll swing by your work to get your car, and I'll head home from there," I said.

"Don't forget the offering," Lucy said.

"What?" Jack said, grabbing his much-laundered Members Only jacket from the back of a kitchen chair.

"I left it on top of your wallet," Lucy said.

From the back of another chair, she pulled a black lace veil that resembled a mantilla. She swathed her shoulders and head in it, like some kind of Catholic chador.

"Are we gonna drop you two off first, like I said? What's the plan, here?" I demanded.

"That twenty-dollar bill? Forget it! I'm not dropping twenty bucks in a collection plate," Jack said, as he and Lucy motivated angrily through the kitchen towards the front door.

"Wait," I protested. "We need to figure out how we're going

to work this."

"We tithe practically nothing, Dad!"

"We tithe plenty! We tithe away your goddamn college fund."

"Don't take the Lord's name in vain!" she snapped.

"God's last name is not 'damn,'" Jack said.

"Stop it! Stop swearing!"

"Oh my God, are they always like this?" I hissed at Christopher.

"Do not take the Lord's name in vain!" he hissed back.

I haven't been to mass in nineteen years

Sunday, March 25, 8:39 a.m.

We four piled into my used Subaru. I was bereft of an awesome press car until the automotive advertising firm brought a fresh, untried specimen to my office Monday morning. Lucy groused over the grubbiness of the backseat. Christopher protested mightily at being crammed between Lucy's (seductive?) bulk and my daughter's pointy-edged car seat.

I turned to Jack, seated next to me up front.

"Okay, seriously. What's the plan, Jack?"

"Hurry up, mass starts at nine!" Lucy ordered from the back.

"Hey!" Jack turned to glare in fierce father-format at Lucy. "Do not speak to her like that."

"Fine, look, we'll drop you two off first, okay?" I hollered, as I started the engine. "Let's just all take a breath or something! You're making me so nervous, the three of you— Jesus! Jeez, I mean. How the hel—heck do we get to this Belltown church place?"

Christopher, The Expert Navigator, guided me. Jack and Lucy snapped at each other. I thought I was going to scream. Out loud, that is. I was already screaming in my head.

At last, an unendurable seventeen minutes later, I pulled up in front of Sacred Heart of Jesus Catholic Parish. The bells were tolling. Junkies, drunks, vagrants, and a few non-Lutheran Scandinavians from Jack and Lucy's Ballard environs were streaming inside. Lucy unbuckled urgently and threw her door open as I pulled to an illegal stop in the fire lane in front of the immense oak doors of the church.

"Hurry up! We're so late!" she shrilled, jumping out. Christopher, with equal urgency, launched his incredibly tall torso out of the backseat like some kind of devout jack-in-the-box. To my surprise, Jack followed suit.

"Whoa, wait—where are you going?" I said.

Jack leaned back into the car, not unlike he did when I dropped him off at the Ballard bar Thursday night.

"Find a parking place. We'll save you a spot in the pew," he said.

I recoiled. I hadn't been to mass in nineteen years! Did they really expect me to sit through their church service, kneeling, standing, kneeling again, only to be humiliatingly denied Holy Communion by the priest, like back in the good ol' days?

No way!

"Jack! No way!" I said.

Suddenly, Jack's cell phone chimed. Still leaning into my car, both hands braced on the passenger door frame, he froze. His eyes went wide and wild.

"Dad! Come on!" Lucy bellowed.

"I told you," he said to me. "I've been getting these strange texts."

From the pocket of his gray Members Only or Eisenhower jacket (depending on how old it and you were), his cell phone chimed again.

"Dad!" Lucy shouted.

"Go in," he shouted back at her. "I've got to go with Katherine."

"But I thought we were all supposed to be together today," Lucy said. "Dad, I thought she—"

"Go in. Take the bus home. Christopher, get her home afterward."

Christopher, The Perpetually Smirking, smirked.

"Dad..." Lucy said.

Jack climbed back into the front seat. He aimed hunted eyes at me.

"Drive. Please. Hurry," he said.

"Are you sure? Your daughter—"

He slammed the car door.

"She's fine. Christopher will get her home safe. You've got to help me," he said. "You owe me."

Were anyone else to make such an outrageous request from my front seat, I would have formulated a cogent counterargument. But with Jack…damn, he must have been such a good investigative reporter once. He was compelling. And I did owe him.

I was given pause. Wait…did he say "owe" or "own?"

"Where do you want me to take you?" I said.

"My office."

"Why?" I said, though I was already driving.

Jack hesitated. His cell phone chimed again. He put his hand over his pocket to smother it.

"I think I did something terrible," he said.

Flattery will get you... oh, who am I kidding?

Sunday, March 25, 9:07 a.m.

I drove Jack to the *Washingtonian* building. His car was still parked in the nearby Three Coins lot. It was untowed, patiently awaiting its rightful owner.

"So, let me give you your keys and your license," I said, digging through my huge purse, which doubled as a briefcase and occasionally tripled as a lunch box. "And your cigarettes. You ought to quit. I did. It was totally worth it. So...I guess I'll see you around, if I ever happen to find myself at a serial killer crime scene again. Fat chance, huh?" I laughed.

I held out Jack's possessions. He stared at me from the passenger seat. His cell phone chimed. He flinched. It was another text. He pulled his cell phone from his jacket pocket and held it out to me.

"They won't stop," he said. "See for yourself."

"Jack, I don't want to read your private messages, or whatever. I think...well, this is goodbye, right? Thanks for your help with the book. It's been interesting. So, here..."

My left hand gripped the steering wheel. My right hand awkwardly clutched his keys, his driver's license, and a nearly empty pack of Marlboros. Jack didn't reach for his property. He held out his cell phone, which I didn't want. Our fingers didn't brush as the turn-of-the-millennium Nokia found its way into my right hand. I didn't reach for it; I didn't want it. Reluctantly, I pressed a button with my thumb.

Letters on the small screen spelled out, "I SAW U. I KNOW WHAT U DID. U WILL PAY."

I looked at Jack. We shared a chilling of the spine in my overheated car.

"What is this?" I said.

"You tell me," he said. He fingered the dark bruise on the left side of his jaw. "Please, can you tell me? What did I do?"

"I...I don't know. The caller is listed as Unknown."

"How does that work?"

"Telemarketer?" I said.

"No," he said. "Could you check something for me? It's on my computer."

"Home?"

"No, work."

His work computer was inside the deserted building, mere feet from my car.

I sighed.

"I don't know..."

"You're young. You know more about computers than me," he said.

Flattered in two ways, I demurred—and giggled, probably.

"Okay," I said. "But I can't promise that I can do anything."

I figured, what could it hurt?

It seemed I was determined to keep learning exactly what it could hurt.

Nigerian banking email scam

Sunday, March 25, 9:14 a.m.

Jack led me through the vacant *Washingtonian* building. We took the elevator up to the third floor. It was silent and the lights were off. Weak sunlight filtered through the bank of windows along the west wall, guiding us through the rows of cubicles that stood empty like coffins at the rapture. We reached his cubicle. He stopped. I stopped.

"I'm scared," Jack said. "I don't know what I'm dealing with."

I considered his computer. It looked harmless enough.

"Turn it on and I'll have a look," I said.

Jack complied. While the machine was laboriously booting up, he said, "Someone knows."

"Someone knows what?" I said. "You mean the IT department knows? If this is some porn thing—"

Jack's cell phone chimed. He recoiled and thust it at me.

"You read it," he said.

I pushed a button and read, "I KNOW WHAT U DID THURSDAY. I SAW U. CHECK YOR EMAIL."

"What did you do?" I said.

"I don't remember."

"Do you think this has anything to do with that blogger you shoved at the murder scene?" I said.

Jack's icy blue eyes switched from side to side as he considerd this. They alighted on my face.

"No," he said. "I think I did something after you left me at the bar. I was real drunk."

Jack's computer was on. I double-clicked on his email program. It took forever to open. When it did, hundreds upon hundreds of unopened emails clogged the inbox, including all of mine from the past few weeks.

"I don't check my email," he said. "But I thought you might try to get in touch with me. My car keys and all. So I opened it."

"It" was a very phishy-looking email at the top of his digital heap. It had odd capitalization and an overall Nigerian bank fraud air.

"You've got yourself a virus," I said. "Mystery solved."

"Read it," he said.

"It's just some kind of spam," I said.

"Katherine," he said. "Read it."

He had already infected his system. What harm could it do? I opened it and read.

The subject line spelled out: "On aN ImpoRtent AnniveraarY"

The body stated: "JackOLIes, today is a signivicant One for you and I kno all about it."

"It's junk," I said.

He leaned across me and pressed his finger against the screen. His stub of a nail tapped on the icon of an attachment.

"I clicked on that," he said.

"And there's your virus," I interrupted.

"No," he said. "It was a picture. Of me. It was me standing outside that bar by my house on Thursday. It was blurry as hell, but...I was doing something awful."

"What were you doing?"

Jack shook his head.

"I don't know. The photo was too grainy. But when I woke up Friday morning there was blood on my shirt."

"Blood?" I said. "How much?"

"Some."

"A lot?"

"Some."

"'Some,' like maybe you got a nosebleed? Or 'some,' like you killed somebody?" I joked.

Jack didn't laugh. He didn't smile. He stared at me balefully.

"Maybe," he said.

My relapse

Sunday, March 25, 9:31 a.m.

On the third floor of the headquarters of the *Washingtonian* newspaper, there was a forgotten balcony that could only be reached via a cluttered janitor's closet. Jack, an old timer, was the only person in Seattle who remembered it. He took me out into the cold sunshine. I gave him his pack of cigarettes and we smoked two of them. The wind whipped my hair around my face and I didn't care if it got singed by the cigarette. I didn't care about the magnificent view of bluer-than-blue Puget Sound or the glorious golden light on my face. I didn't care that I was standing on a narrow balcony three floors above hard pavement with a possible murderer and no witnesses. How had I ever managed to give up cigarettes? The delight I felt as I inhaled was fierce and careless. A mind-killer. Jack let me float in a giddy cocoon of nicotine for a moment, then he told me that he thought he might have beaten a man to death less than four blocks from his house.

It happened Thursday night, after we sat together in the Three Coins lounge and he got completely wasted on scotch while perusing pictures of his dead wife. He told me he couldn't remember anything after he showed me the fourth photo in his awful collection.

"Well," he amended. "I remember snippets. Little flashes. I remember you. I remember you had a nice car. You said you love…Jesus?"

"GPS," I said.

"What do you love?" Jack said.

"GPS. The car had GPS. I would never have managed to find your house otherwise. You were incoherent," I said, smoke drifting out of my mouth like a belching dragon. I had forgotten how to do the smoking-while-talking thing elegantly.

Jack looked desperate.

"Were you there with me?" he asked.

"Where?" I said.

"The bar by my house. I remember there was someone with me. Was it you?"

"No," I said.

"You didn't follow me in? To check up on me?"

I turned away from Jack's searching blue eyes to search the blue water with mine. Dozens of white sailboats were drifting lazily on the glassy surface. It was a perfect day to be out on Puget Sound. They seemed so free...yet so very confined, hemmed in by the condo-ridden shoreline. If they just sailed beyond the Space Needle and went around the corner, dodging craggy islands and lesser Canada, they would have hit open ocean where nothing could hold them back. I would have loved to do that. I wondered if I would ever get the chance.

"No, Jack," I said. "I went home. It was a work night. You're a grown man. I figured you could take care of yourself."

I sounded defensive even to my own ears. I glanced at him. He had deflated. His forearms rested on the rusty iron railing that kept us from falling off the narrow balcony. His head hung low. His cigarette dangled limply between two fingers capped by horribly short nails.

"I'm sorry," I said. "Should I have stayed with you? I didn't think you needed me."

His voice said nothing, but his defeated posture said, "Yes."

It was so very sad that I, of all people, might seem like a safe refuge to him. I didn't know him. He didn't know me. He was so far beyond me in experience and talent that it boggled the mind. And yet, he thought I could have kept him safe that night? Me? Really? I took a deep drag, coughed like a consumptive, and scraped my fingers through my hair. I didn't know what to say to him. I, the relapsed smoker out on this sad excuse for Juliet's love nest, was nobody's refuge.

"I got home. I got in. I don't know how. You had my keys. Maybe Lucy left the front door unlocked? Dear God," he shuddered. I shuddered, too. His fifteen-year-old daughter, asleep in her room after midnight, with the front door unlocked? A tragedy waiting to happen…twice in Jack's life.

"I slept till seven," he continued. "When the alarm went off, I got up and my undershirt was covered in blood. And I had this bruise on my jaw. And my nails were all chipped and raw."

Jack held out a hand to show me. I didn't take it. I winced. Hard.

"You bite your nails," I accused.

"I don't know," he said. "Do I?"

"Yes. Why do you do that? Nibble and gnaw until they're raw? Don't you notice? Doesn't it hurt?"

"But," he said, his eyes confused. "I think someone punched me."

His jaw was decorated with an angry purple blot the size of a golf ball. He tilted his face down to me, as if offering it for another blow.

"You did that to yourself. You were trying to get your keys after you dropped them on the floor at the Three Coins. You hit your face on the table."

Jack ran his finger along his jaw. I did not, though I unexpectedly wanted to.

"Really?" he said.

"Yes. I saw you do it."

"And the blood on my shirt?"

I killed my cigarette with a last, lung-ruining suck. I exhaled, coughed, and exhaled more. In my louche twenties, I would have thoughtlessly pitched the butt off the edge of the balcony, or ground it out under my heel. In my non-smoking thirties, I held the spent filter guiltily.

"Do you really think you're capable of killing someone?" I said.

Jack's gaze glided to mine. His eyes were reddened by last night's liquor, cigarette smoke, and other dark things.

"You've never wanted to kill someone," he said. "You've

hated people. You've said you wanted someone dead, maybe. I used to, too. Then...during the trial, I wanted to kill him. I planned it all out. They had metal detectors in the courthouse, but they didn't search you back then. I was there every day, either covering the trial or testifying against him. I planned out exactly how I would jump him right after testifying, as I stepped down from the witness stand. He was so close, sitting right there, doodling away on a legal pad at the defense table. All I needed was a very hard, very sharp piece of plastic. Which I made in my garage from the cover of an old VCR. I could have done it."

"But?"

"But," he said. "Lucy."

Jack stared out at Puget Sound.

"So I made it all a story. I stayed objective. I wrote unbiased articles about his testimony... how, precisely, he raped my wife with a homemade bayonet over and over, then sliced her face and arms and breasts till she bled to death. And I went home and drank until I passed out every night."

"Oh Jack..."

I said nothing else as he lit another cigarette, smoked it down to the quick, and pitched it off the balcony. Jack didn't look at me. He looked at the water. So close, yet so damned far.

Based on a story

Sunday, March 25, 9:58 a.m.

"You have a computer virus. Some Russian mafia hacker thing. You got alcohol poisoning Thursday—that's why you can't remember. You hit your jaw on the table, nobody punched you. You got a nosebleed—it's your own blood on your shirt. You didn't kill anyone," I said. "Probably."

Based on nothing

Sunday, March 25, 9:59 a.m.

I did not want to write about this sad, broken man. I felt like a predator. I felt like a vampire.

I felt like a journalist.

Career Day

Monday, March 26, 8:14 a.m.

"I need a favor," said a flat voice. It took a moment for me to place it.

"Lucy?" I said. "What? Why? What? It's eight in the morning."

I was barely halfway through my first dose of coffee. I was barely halfway to work. How did Lucy get my cell number? Oh, right. I gave it to her, to give to her dad.

"I need to bring someone to school for Career Day."

"I'm confused. I'm on my way to work. What?" I bleated into my cell phone.

"I'm supposed to bring a parent or a mentor for Career Day. Can you come?"

"What? When?"

"Today."

"Today? Are you kidding?" I was driving one-handed with the cell phone plastered to my ear. I honked impatiently as my fellow motorists sought to outfox the traffic cameras surrounding my office by slamming on their brakes as soon as the light turned yellow.

"Career Day—you mean, you want to be a journalist? Why not bring your dad?"

"Hardly," she snorted. "I want to be a nun. But the only nuns I know are my teachers, and we're not allowed to bring a teacher. So…can you come?"

"A nun? You think I'm like a nun? What? I'm confused."

Lucy sighed long and loud.

"Hardly," she said again.

Yes, hardly. Oh my God, more yellow lights, more

unexpected brake lights! I would rear-end someone before the year was out, I knew it. I ought to have simply hung up on Lucy. It was illegal to talk on the phone while driving. The fine was ruinous.

"So how exactly am I your mentor?" I inquired.

Lucy sighed again, this time with the profound world-weariness of the teenager I once was. I could hear her eyes rolling.

"You're not," she said. "But you're Dad's girlfriend, right? That's close enough to a parent."

We'll gloss over my hysterical protests ("Are you kidding!? I'm married! Happily! I am not your dad's anything! We aren't even friends! I met him four days ago—professionally! I'm writing a book and I'm very married—are you kidding me!?"). The upshot: I agreed to go to Lucy's Career Day.

I agreed to go to Lucy's Career Day because I felt bad. Bad for her widowed father. Bad for her, the only witness to her mother's kidnapping. Besides, her Catholic high school was located within my newspaper's coverage area. I figured I might manage to wring a heart-warming article out of her Career Day.

As usual, things didn't work out the way I planned.

The rape of Mandy Schirmer, the whore

Monday, March 26, 9:37 a.m.

Lucy O'Lies sat as upright as a lamppost during the morning prayer. The principal of her Catholic school—a priest, as all principals of Catholic schools ought to be—intoned it in cellophane Latin over an antique intercom system.

I sat in the back of the classroom with the other parents— oh, come on!

I sat in the back of the classroom with the parents, though I was not her parent. I was not anything to her. God only knew why she had glommed onto me. I had my own daughter, thank you very much.

Lucy's hands were clasped beneath her breasts, which I noted (and cringed, but noted nonetheless) were un-brassiered. She appeared to understand the Latinate liturgy buzzing over the intercom, which was mounted on high above a cracked crucifix and the American flag. I, too, did time in a Catholic school but they didn't teach us any Latin. Even so, I could tell this was no gentle Credo, nor an abbreviated Novena to allow for lots of announcements.

"Confutatis maledictis!" the principal thundered wrathfully.

"Confutatis maledictis!" Lucy agreed a bit too loudly.

"Flaaaaamis aaaacribus! Adiiiictis!" The befuddled intercom gave a feedback-filled whine of pain.

"Voca me com benedictis!" Lucy exclaimed energetically, causing her unbound boobs to rebound.

"Know what he's saying?" whispered the man crammed uncomfortably into the desk next to mine.

"I'm not sure," I whispered back. "It's a verse from Mozart's *Requiem*, I think. It was in *Amadeus*."

"That was a great movie," he whispered.

"I know! I loved it," I said.

"I'm Mark. Greg's dad. You're Lucy's mom?" he said, offering his hand.

"No," I said, recoiling from his hand and clamming up irritably. Mark, Greg's dad, took the hint after a brief bout of puzzled staring.

"When sentence on the damned is passed and all to piercing flames are sent, amongst the blessed call my name, stupid!" Lucy was hissing at the girl seated next to her. Apparently, Mark, Greg's dad, wasn't the only one who wondered what the principal was declaiming. I felt rather proud of Lucy for knowing, then rather horrified at feeling parental pleasure on behalf of this essentially random kid with whom I shared no personal connection.

The intercom fizzled, then resumed its speech.

"You see, boys and girls, we have need of strong prayers today."

"Amen!" Lucy called out.

Her teacher frowned at her. She was a cool, jeans-clad nun in her mid-twenties with horrible acne scars. She looked like she played the guitar and wrote Catholic indie rock songs in her spare time. I imagined she and Lucy were frequently in conflict. I didn't imagine she was the type of nun Lucy wanted to be when she grew up.

"One of your companions has been tested and tried in the worst way. I speak primarily to you young ladies," said the intercom.

Lucy perked up.

"Today, on the way to school, a female student from our academy was lured away from her bus stop by a man and...rrrrrrraped!" The principal/priest trilled the *r* like a drumroll.

There were gasps, as he probably intended, and a rapid babble of speculation, which he probably wasn't after.

"All classes will be silent! This classmate of yours has survived her ordeal otherwise unharmed by the evildoer, and will return to school next week."

"Who was it?"

"Nobody in this class—we're all here."

"Was it a Senior?"

"I'll ask my brother—"

"Class—be quiet!" said the cool nun.

The box on the wall was silent for many seconds. It was very dramatic.

"You must all pray for her. She is a true martyr to chastity. Her brave resistance has made her a modern saint. That is all."

The metal box gave a static-filled death rattle, indicating that we were on our own now.

"I wonder who—"

"I bet it was Rachelle Gerhart."

"Who?"

"No way—she's just a Freshman!"

"Yeah, but she lives in a really bad neighborhood—"

"No, it was Mandy Schirmer."

"No way!"

"Yeah, it was. My cousin carpools with her. Her mom told my aunt. It's true."

It bears mentioning that more than half of the eager speculators were the parents, hemming me in at the back of the classroom with their gleeful gossip.

"Mandy Schirmer. Jeez…"

One of the boys in the back row leaned his head out the open window. "Hey, it was Mandy Schirmer!" he bellowed into the courtyard, so the boys in the back rows of all the other classrooms could spread the news.

"Greg! Get that thick skull of yours back in here right now," said the nun.

"That's my boy," said Mark. I couldn't tell if his tone was amused or regretful.

The nun fussed uneasily at her desk. She hiked up her snug jeans and scanned the prattling adults for help. None was forthcoming.

"Let's…let's all take a minute to bow our heads in prayer for this unfortunate young woman," suggested the cool nun. "One minute of silent prayer."

That did the trick. All the Catholic students and their Catholic parents automatically folded themselves over their clasped hands and closed their eyes. I glanced around. I was surprised to see Lucy was unbowed and wide-eyed.

Her mouth was open. Hot pink stained her cheeks.

"Mandy Schirmer? A martyr?" she blurted out. "Saint to chastity? That slut! She tonguey-kisses boys. She's a whore."

All heads rose. All eyes flew open and focused on her. Then the eyes shifted to me, her presumptive stepmother.

Oh, come on!

"Lucy! Class…and parents…remember to keep Mandy in your prayers tonight," said the nun. She jerked her head at Lucy. "Out in the hall. Now."

Lucy's entire body became more rigid than that of any army drill sergeant, department store mannequin, or colonial statesman statue I'd ever seen. Her lips were pressed together as thin as tissue. Her hands were clenched so tight the fists resembled the stumps of a double amputee. She stood and stiffly marched out of the classroom.

"Mrs. O'Lies?" the nun said. "Mrs. O'Lies?"

It took Mark, Greg's dad, nudging me twice before I realized she was talking to me.

Oh, come the hell on!

The Washingtonian

Monday, March 26, 9:37 a.m.

Lake Washington Killer's Fifth Victim Still Unidentified
By Jack O'Lies

Following the discovery of a recently deceased individual on the shore of Lake Washington on Thursday, Seattle law enforcement has officially classified the as-yet unidentified man as the victim of a serial killer.

Dubbed the Lake Washington Killer in early August when the third body was discovered by a group of kayakers, the assailant appears to be escalating, according to a spokesperson from the Seattle Police Department. To date, each victim has been discovered in the immediate vicinity of Lake Washington.

The unidentified victim, an obese Caucasian man, was found to have the word "Spine" written in permanent marker on the heel of his left foot. Police were unwilling to comment on the possible meaning of this mark.

Lucy's picture of heaven

Monday, March 26, 10:16 a.m.

"If anyone deserved to be called a saint, it's my mother," Lucy said, as she unlocked the front door of the O'Lies abode, then slammed it shut behind me. "It's an abomination to give Mandy Schirmer the same title as her. My mother's beyond sainthood."

What she was, exactly, Lucy couldn't say as I conducted her to her bedroom and lamely offered to a) call her dad, or b) fix her a peanut butter sandwich. I got the sense, as she ranted her way up the stairs, that in her mind her mother was something like a wronged, violated angel. What Holy Mary would have been, had she been raped, sodomized, and mutilated by the Romans at the foot of the cross.

Lucy kicked her bedroom door open and threw herself on her pink canopy bed, which had been colonized by an army of teddy bears wearing crowns of dried thorns.

"So…you okay? I need to get back to work," I said.

Lucy stared up at me. She had such compelling eyes, just like her father. Damn it. I was never going to get out of there.

"I can't remember her," she said. "But I have a photo. I cut her head out."

"Why?"

"Because," she snorted. "It was this gross shot of her and my dad. He looked like a lecher, but my mother's face was wonderful. Just like the saints in the stained glass windows at church. Wanna see?"

Before I could answer, Lucy was scrabbling under her mattress. She pulled out a 1950s-era copy of *Lives of the Saints*. I'd seen (and owned) such a book before. She paged quickly to the middle of the book and held it out.

"Look."

I took the book. The face of Saint Agnes had been decoupaged with a clumsily-cut photograph. I'd seen this face before in Jack's photos. Her eyes were delicately upturned. Her lips were half-open. She radiated serenity. Her hair glowed with what appears to be a genuine halo. She was very beautiful.

"Do you still have the photo you cut her out of?" I said.

Lucy appeared offended.

"Yeah. Why?"

"Can I see it?"

"Why?" she said.

"Why not?"

"It's in the back of the book."

It was filed right after Saint Marcellus, The Unremarkable Centurion. I pulled it out.

Jack, looking young and not remotely intoxicated, was bending a woman over just like in a romance novel. They were outdoors somewhere at sunset. There was a golden glow around them, like a genuine halo. His eyes were half-closed. His lips were half-open. He was about to kiss her. His face radiated pure happiness. Her face was a cruel hole.

Why the hell did Lucy have to disfigure this picture?

I turned back to Saint Agnes, twelve-year-old martyr and almost rape victim. Lucy had carefully glued her mother's head onto the adolescent Roman, who was dressed in an inky blue toga and was holding a dull-eyed lamb under one arm. There was an old smear of chocolate milk across her sandaled feet.

"Does your dad ever talk about your mom?" I said.

"No."

"Never?"

"No."

"Why not?"

"Because it was his fault," she said.

"Oh God, Lucy, it wasn't."

"Yes, it was. He's a drunken, remorseless sinner. He isn't a good, strong Christian. He never reads the Bible or prays. He curses and smokes and drinks. I have to make him go to mass every Sunday—you saw! It's his fault God struck down my mom, because he's a sinner."

I couldn't follow her logic, but she was near tears—the angry, hot kind that only unsentimental men tend to shed.

"Okay," I said.

I slid the ruined photo back into its forgettable hiding place. Even farther back in the book was Saint Lucy, virgin and martyr. I paged to her and sighed. Her mother bled and bled until Saint Lucy saved her. The Romans sent Lucy to a whorehouse to be raped. Lucy was stabbed to death.

And her eyes were taken out with a fork.

The green man

Monday, March 26, 12:47 p.m.

My work line rang.

"*Journal Newspapers*, this is Katherine," I said.

"I saw a green man," Jack said without preface or prelude.

"A green man? What?" I replied, attempting to type while holding the receiver cradled at a neck-cramping angle between my shoulder and cheek. My paper was set to go to press the very next day. I was kind of busy.

"He was on the bus," Jack said.

"What? I'm kind of busy," I said. "Are you at home?"

"No," he said.

"Didn't you get my voicemail? About your daughter? You probably should go home and be with her. She was pretty upset."

"In a little bit," he said.

"I read your article," I said. "I thought all you write these days are obituaries."

"It was like an obituary."

"No, it wasn't," I said. "It was exceptional."

I felt quite bitter as I typed and talked. While I coddled his daughter through her Career Day and her subsequent breakdown, he published a high-profile article that was likely to get national pick-up. And what did I get for my pains? Nothing at all!

"A byline, front page above the fold, full color photo, and everything," I said, forcing a bright note into my voice. "I'd call it one hell of an article. So...are you back, baby?"

There was a heavy silence on the other end of the phone.

It was an old TV quote. I didn't mean it like that. I felt my face turning red. Especially as the silence on Jack's end extended and extended...and extended.

"So, a green man?" I said. "Was it, like, a leprechaun decoration or something? Left over from St. Patrick's Day?"

"Do you have a minute?" Jack said. "To talk?"

"Look, I'm kinda busy, here—"

"I took the bus to work this morning."

"Right?" I said as I typed.

"There was a man in the back dressed all in green. Green jacket. Green pants. Green shirt. Green shoes and socks, even."

"So...a leprechaun," I said. "Are you sure you didn't get drunk and wake up with your face pressed against the Lucky Charms box?"

"He stared at me," Jack said.

"Right?" I said.

"The entire ride."

"Huh. Weird, I guess. Look, I've got to finish editing this article—we're about to go to press."

"I've seen him before...somewhere. I think it was Thursday night. I think I did something to him. The entire bus ride he stared at me like he knew me and wanted to kill me," Jack said.

"Where are you right now?" I said.

"Work," he said.

"Work—are you kidding me?" I exclaimed.

I had an office with a closeable door. Jack, however, was talking crazy out in the open, his three-walled cubicle providing no sound buffer at all. He would be fired in the next round of newspaper layoffs, today's fantastic front page article notwithstanding.

"Why did you write a second article about the Lake Washington Killer?" I said.

"I can't let it go. I know things—about the killer, about the victims—but I can't put my finger on why or how I know. Besides, it gives me an excuse to look into what I did on Thursday night. I've been checking police reports, hospital records, the morgue—just in case anyone was killed outside that bar. Do you think I'm capable of something like that?" he said.

Forget being fired, he was sure to be arrested before the week was out.

"Jack. Go home. Your daughter's classmate got raped today. She's extremely upset," I said.

I hung up.

When Jack was arrested for manslaughter or whatever dark deed he did outside the bar by his house, I would probably get stuck being Lucy's guardian, the way things were going. So far, I had wasted hours of my life, driven all over Seattle, and written less than 26,000 words of the book that was my sole reason for getting to know him in the first place.

I was starting to think it was time to find a way to drop this Jack character.

Blame it on the rain

Monday, March 27, 2:51 p.m.

Washington was always popular with serial killers.

Robert Lee Yates killed thirteen women in Spokane in the 1990s.

Gary Ridgeway, the Green River Killer, murdered forty-eight women from Seattle to Tacoma. In 2001, he was arrested in the very city I had moved to just a few months earlier.

The FBI's John Douglas, who profiled the Green River Killer, called our neck of the woods "America's killing fields," according to Mark Fuhrman, of O.J. Simpson fame.

Mark Fuhrman, of O.J. Simpson fame, grew up in Tacoma.

So did Ted Bundy. He killed twenty-three women, some of them in Washington.

Another Tacoma resident, John Allen Muhammad, went on a shooting spree in the other Washington (where the president lives) in 2002.

Charles Manson did time in a Washington penitentiary.

My husband had the same name as a serial killer who was incarcerated with Son of Sam, killer of six, wounder of seven, enemy of dogs. Good thing I never googled him when we were dating.

Here's the thing: I saw the green man, too. Somewhere.

Maybe I saw him on the bus.

Maybe it was Friday night, when I rode the bus home after the automotive advertising firm picked up my latest press car.

Maybe he stared at me like he knew me.

But maybe I was susceptible to suggestion. And maybe, just maybe, I should never speak to Jack O'Lies again.

Oh, Lies

Monday, March 26, 9:47 p.m.

"Hey. It's me."

A groan escaped my lips and I held my cell phone out at arm's length, glaring at it for betraying me.

Obviously the only thing to do was throw the phone away, so Jack couldn't reach me anymore. My household had at least five or six pay-by-the-minute burners that I could've resurrected. They were sitting in a box a few feet away from me, in fact, awaiting donation to the local domestic violence shelter. I'd delayed dropping them off for fear of identity theft, but I was starting to think it might be great if someone else was Katherine for a while. I needed to get off the O'Lies clan's radar once and for all.

"Hi, Jack," I replied at last. "What're you up to?"

"Nothing much."

"Drinking?"

"Yeah."

"A lot?"

"My share."

"Nice. On a work night."

"And you aren't."

"Not yet."

Given the day I'd had with his daughter, his interruption while I was on deadline, and this unanticipated follow-up call, I was sure I soon would be.

"How can I help you?" I inquired professionally.

"You still have my car keys," Jack said. "And my driver's license."

Damn it!

"Oh damn it, I forgot!" I exclaimed. "Why didn't you just take them when I kept trying to give them to you yesterday? You sure took your damned cigarettes no problem! Damn it!"

"What's the big deal? Come over and drop them off."

"That's the big deal—that right there. Do you realize how long of a drive it is from my house to your place? Why don't you drag yourself up here and pick them up? No, no, don't do that," I amended quickly.

I did not want Jack to know where I lived. He would start dropping by unannounced and drunk, I had no doubt.

"Fine, I'll drop them off. Crap. The newspaper's going to press tomorrow. How soon do you need them? Crap. Damn it!" I said.

In between one "crap" and another "damn it," I did indeed uncork a bottle of red wine and self-pityingly poured myself a glass. I detested the idea of driving to Ballard yet again, and I loathed the fact that Jack's boozing seemed to be catching.

"I need to talk to you," Jack said.

"Lucy told you what happened at school today?"

"No. She's holed up in her room with Christopher."

"She's *so* gonna get pregnant," I muttered.

"What?"

"Nothing," I said. "I'll bring your keys and license to your work. How about that? When? I need to go grab my planner."

"I looked at his autopsy file today."

"Whose?" I said.

"The floater from Lake Washington."

"Oh."

"It was right after I called you at work," he said.

"Oh. How was it?" I inquired idiotically.

"It was…the first since my wife's."

"You read your wife's autopsy file?"

"Harry let me. That's where I got the photo of her."

"Why? Why would he do that to you?" I said.

"He's my friend. I asked him to."

"There's no way I'd have given it to you," I said.

I took a drink of wine and recalled that I was not Jack's

friend. Was that what friends were for? Sharing a dead spouse's autopsy file?

"You read her whole file?" I said.

"Yeah," he said.

"Didn't they need that crime scene photo of her for the trial?"

"They had over four dozen shots. Nobody missed it," he said.

"God, Jack...I don't know what to say."

I usually didn't know what to say, but that never stopped me. My method was to babble until comprehension was achieved on the receiving end. Jack had an uncanny ability to shut me up. It disturbed me no end.

"Do you want to tell me about it? Is that why you called?" I said.

Jack audibly inhaled, then sighed.

"I don't know. No. Yeah. It's just...I knew the floater from Lake Washington would have the name "Spine" written on the left heel. It's a name. How do I know it's a name, not a word?"

I shrugged, forgetting that he couldn't see me.

"Life's been off-kilter ever since you came along," he said.

"What does that mean? I don't have time for this, Jack. It's late. My paper goes to press tomorrow. I need to get up early."

"My wife bled to death. You know that, right?"

"Yes, Jack, I know."

"He tortured her in the woods."

"I know."

"He raped her so many times. Harry couldn't even tell how many. He mostly did it with that blade he made."

"Jack—I don't think I'm the person you should be telling this story to."

"He cut her face and her body up slowly, like the old Chinese torture. The death by a thousand cuts. And...I shouldn't tell you this. Right?"

"Right. You shouldn't."

Jack sighed long and slow. Pain flowed through the phone into me.

"Will you please talk to Lucy tonight? Before you're too drunk? She was so upset about that girl from her school who got raped," I said.

"She doesn't talk," he said.

"What?"

"To me. She won't. Could you?"

"Could I what?"

"Talk to her. She really likes you."

My silence, which lasted nearly two minutes, contained several unspoken phrases, including:

1. "Jack, are you nuts?"

2. "On what planet does Lucy, the future nun, like me?"

3. "Are you really that drunk?"

I settled on a neutral query.

"What makes you think she would talk to me?"

"She took you to that Career Day thing today, right?"

"Yes, she did," I said.

And gave me no copy! No copy! I silently added. And gave me a guilty obligation to her, because I took her home, looked at the picture of her dead mom, and tucked her into bed. Damn these lies...O'Lies, I mean.

"Look. How about we just—" I began.

My cell phone's call waiting beeped. This never happened. I wasn't that popular. I glanced at the caller ID. It was Jack's home phone number. I answered it, accidentally hanging up on him.

"Hello, Lucy," I said.

She and I had such a chat. I learned so much about her, including:

1. She believed that rape was a punishment for slutty thoughts. That was the phrase she used: "slutty thoughts."

2. She believed that rape was a purifying act, like martyrdom. For the victim—not the perpetrator. The perpetrator would reunite with Satan to burn in the fires of hell forever.

3. She had been buying her own underwear since the age of eleven, when her dad had humiliated her by taking her to the lingerie department of the J.C. Penny at the mall, where he

loudly requested a training bra for her. And she had wanted to die because he made a jovial joke likening it to the bicycle training wheels he'd bought her years earlier at the same J.C. Penny. Ever since this public humiliation she'd refused to wear a bra.

4. The kids at school were making fun of her for not wearing a bra. They accused her of doing so for slutty reasons, rather than shame.

5. She had zero sexual interest in Christopher, The Future Priest. Zero.

6. She was very much ashamed of having chestile regions that required a bra. That was the phrase she used: "chestile regions."

7. She would never, ever have sex. She hated boys because they were all future rapists.

8. Could I help her buy a bra tomorrow?

Obviously the only thing to do was throw my phone away.

It's all happening at the mall!

Tuesday, March 27, 4:32 p.m.

I took Lucy, the motherless child, bra-shopping out of guilt. Catholic guilt? She was Catholic, but I was not. Parental guilt? I wasn't her parent. Professional guilt? Well...I disrupted the status quo of her home life when I tracked down her dad, extracted his sad story, and inadvertently stole assorted pieces of his property. That was certainly unprofessional of me. I felt I owed her a bra or two. Besides, my newspaper had successfully gone to press earlier in the day, and there was no better way to unwind than shopping.

We agreed to meet at Northgate Mall in Seattle, located midway between her lutefisk-loving neighborhood and the no man's land of my suburb. I knocked off work an hour early, since there was nothing more I could do once the final draft of the newspaper was sent to the printer, out of my obsessive, copy-editing red pen's reach. We convened in the food court. I bought Lucy a soft pretzel with impossibly orange "cheese" dipping sauce. She told me her bus ride north was uneventful. She didn't mention staring green men, serial killer victims, or other alarming phenomena.

"So, how come your teddy bears had barbed wire on their heads?" I asked, dispensing with the small talk. I'd been dying to ask, ever since I saw them lined up on her pink coverlet like a creepy Marilyn Manson album cover. Behold my subtle interviewing technique!

She rolled her eyes as she gnawed on the pretzel.

"They're crowns of thorns. I made them from the blackberry bush growing out in the alley."

"Why?"

"It's Lent."

I hadn't realized. I used to give up cursing for Lent. In recent years, I'd decided it was futile. My mouth was eternally dirty.

"Do you always do that? Decorate your stuffed animals for the holidays?" I said.

She glared at me scornfully and licked gobs of orange goo off her fingers.

"It's a penance. They poke in the night. See?"

She used her cleanly lapped fingers to tug down the modest white turtleneck of her school uniform. I winced. Her collarbones were raw with scratches.

"Wow. Okay. Jeez. Um…"

"I also read at least three pages from *Lives of the Saints* each night. And I got this copy of the *Apocrypha* from a yard sale. I've made it through 1 Esdras, 2 Esdras, Tobit, and the Additions to Esther."

"Wow. Okay…" I stammered.

"There's only five days left till Easter. I'm way behind because they keep giving us too much geometry homework and I suck at geometry."

"Um. Time flies," I said.

"What do you do for Lent?" she demanded.

"Ah, look, the lingerie department," I announced in the most expository manner ever. "Let's find you a bra."

I steered us through J.C. Penny, site of her preteen humiliation. I chose to stage her undergarment reclamation at this particular store not for therapeutic reasons but because it was cheap and I could get a discount if I used my store credit card.

"So, Career Day at your school," I said, as we entered a forest of metal stalks sprouting lace and elastic. "Did it give you any new thoughts about what you want to be when you grow up? Besides a nun, I mean."

I really wanted to ask about her meltdown over her raped classmate, but I chickened out. Her dad was the one who ought to do it. I was not wise to her unbalanced ways.

"I want to be a martyr. Or a saint. But I'm not sure how. Christopher's trying to help me. He's practically in seminary already. I think he might do better as a monk, though. They're more saintly, coz they aren't worldly."

"How about a friar? He could be a friar—a monk that goes out in the community and does stuff. You know, like Friar Tuck," I suggested.

She scowled at me derisively and crammed the last of her pretzel into her mouth.

"Okay, here we are," I said, to fill the void. "Discount rack. Let's load you up with a bunch of sizes and styles, and you can figure out what works."

"Nothing slutty," she said through a mouthful of pretzel.

In her dumpy white turtleneck topped with a chunky navy-blue sweater vest, grungy plaid skirt that hung in heavy woolen folds to her calves, and knee socks as thick as soccer shin guards, she was the farthest thing from a slutty schoolgirl I'd ever seen. I doubted any bra on the planet could change that.

"Don't worry, no one will see it, and if no one sees it, it's not slutty," I asserted with a logic that made sense to me, sort of.

"Sluttiness is evil because sex is evil," she said. "Those who indulge in it are evil. I want something that isn't sexy or slutty."

"Fine, fine, whatever. Did you happen to get any counseling after your mom died?"

"God is the divine counselor. Jesus and Holy Mary and the saints are the only confidants any of us need. Shrinks are the devil's lawyers."

I wasn't sure if that was a yes or a no. I grabbed an unobjectionable mom bra off a rack in lieu of responding.

"Hey, half-price! And not slutty, in my opinion."

"It's got lace."

"The lace is structural," I lied. "It keeps the garment from sluttily revealing too much."

I wasn't sure if "sluttily" was a word. I was sure Lucy would be using it for the rest of the week, however.

"All sex is evil, though a martyr can be touched by evil and be made more holy by it. No lace."

"Okay, okay, fine. Here, no lace. It's blue. Nothing slutty about blue. Mary wore blue," I said.

Lucy grudgingly eyed, in my opinion, a much sluttier bra made of electric blue satin.

"Sex is evil. You should remember that," she said significantly. Too significantly.

"You do understand that I'm not your dad's girlfriend? Right?" I said.

She shrugged.

"Has there been anyone since your mom?"

She shook her head.

Great. That meant that in her sheltered, sex-fearing, Catholic-school-attending mind, ipso facto, I was her dad's girlfriend.

"Just try it on for size," I said, pointing at the dressing room. "I'll wait out here."

I might have been spending time with Jack's daughter in the lingerie department of J.C. Penny, I might have been bearing witness to her creepy theories about rape and martyrdom and the evils of sex, but there was one intimate line I would not cross, and that was helping her try on a bra. Even I had my limits.

"Fine," she said, rolling her eyes. She held out her hand for the bra.

"Hey, what happened to your hand?" I said.

Her palm had an angry red welt in the center, which I expected. But surrounding it were at least a dozen smaller pricks, which alarmed me.

She should have snatched her hand back and hidden it.

She should have snapped that it was none of my business.

She should have hastily changed the subject.

Instead, she gave me a smug smirk, stood up straighter, and held her hand out with the fingers spread, like a statue of the Blessed Virgin offering a benediction.

"Christopher came over last night," she said. "He was supposed to stay, but he left early. I tried to tell him about

Mandy Schirmer, the whore, but he kept going on and on about that stupid roommate of his. He left because he'd bought beer and a new rock CD and was gonna try to convert his roommate."

Lucy let out a snort that indicated the sort of lie she believed this to be: far beyond white, almost at the level of courtroom perjury.

"He really left to drink of alcohol and pollute himself with rock music and partake in the unholy companionship of a pot-smoking pagan," she continued. "He isn't so pure of heart after all. He's as bad as Dad. I'll never drink anything ever!"

She didn't stomp her sensibly-shod foot, but I could tell she wanted to.

"So I did this," she said. "I was working on my cross stitch. I had lots of needles threaded with different colors. I pushed one into my hand. Then the rest, one by one. It was like Christ's blessed blood in a painting, flowing in a rainbow from my hand. And then the rainbow mingled with my blood. It was very holy."

"Where was your dad during all this?"

"Talking on his cell phone," she said.

To me.

Now I had this psychotic shit to feel guilty about, too. Wonderful. I didn't think an electric blue bra was going to absolve me after all.

On the couch

Tuesday, March 27, 5:17 p.m.

"Jack?" I hollered into the silent kitchen.

Nothing.

"Go put hydrogen peroxide on your hand right now, or you'll get lockjaw," I hissed at Lucy.

Lucy produced a scoffing little "Pfft!" sound and tossed her bookbag onto the chipped Formica table.

"Go on, do it! You'll wind up with tetanus or something. Jack? Are you home?" I called again, as Lucy slouched off to the bathroom, slamming the door behind her.

I found Jack seated on his living room couch, his feet up on the coffee table. A yellow legal pad was perched on his knees. He had exchanged his standard-issue reporter's sports jacket for an ancient University of Washington sweatshirt. He was so focused on what he was writing that he didn't notice me until I slapped my hand over the page.

He flinched and looked up at me.

"Oh, you're home," he said, as if I lived with Lucy and him, all cozy. "Did you girls have fun shopping?"

"Your daughter is seriously messed up," I said. "You need to take her to a psychologist or psychiatrist or something, like today, Jack!"

Retroactively, I hoped Lucy wasn't standing horrified in the doorway. I glanced over my shoulder, found it mercifully empty, and turned back to Jack.

"Lucy's very religious," he sighed. "Probably picked it up from her grandmother. I never encourage her."

"This isn't some Catholic thing," I said. "She's weird as hell!"

Again, I glanced over my shoulder. Striving for tact, I lowered my voice.

"She's the psychologically-damaged kind of weird. You need to get her professional help or something bad is going to happen," I said.

Jack shook his bristly head dismissively.

"She'll outgrow it. Want some coffee?"

I wasn't surprised he tried to distract me with a drink. But I was surprised he didn't offer me a real drink. Something destructive, like vodka or scotch.

"Sure, I never say no to coffee," I said automatically. "But seriously…your daughter…aren't you going to do anything?"

Jack gently pulled the legal pad from under my splayed fingers. I retracted my hand before it could land on his knees. He stood and scratched his fingers over his short-stubbled scalp.

"Let's go out on the porch. Want a smoke?"

"No, I do not want to smoke, Jack. You know I don't smoke anymore. You shouldn't keep trying to get me to."

"Come on," he said. "It's a beautiful sunset."

Before I could respond, he had shambled off to the kitchen. Unsure what to do, I went outside to wait for my cup of coffee, which I knew I would eagerly drink, and my cigarette, which I vowed I would not smoke. I took a breath of salt-saturated air. Jack's neighborhood was practically waterfront, but it was rundown. Because it was located in Seattle proper and not one of the unstoried suburbs, its rundown state would've been described as "classic" or "historic" by a real estate agent. But it was trashy to my eyes. And believe me, I knew trashy.

I sat on the moldy couch on Jack's front porch (trashy!) and gaze at the rusted-out 1960s-vintage pickup truck on cinderblocks in his next-door neighbor's muddy front yard (trashy!). I shiver. It's getting cold. Jack emerges from the house bearing two steaming mugs of coffee and a pack of Marlboros (trashy as hell!)

"I'm not smoking," I reiterated as I accepted the hot cup.

"You shouldn't try to make me. Do you have any idea how hard it was to quit?"

Jack sat next to me on the couch. Not too close. But sort of close. He lit a cigarette, took a long drag, and sighed. He stared at the reddish-gold light that bejeweled his neighbor's roof as the sun slowly died behind it. It was pretty. I stared at it, too. We clutched our steaming coffee mugs, not touching, not talking. What a picturesque white trash couple we must have made.

"I'm gonna get laid off soon," Jack said.

"Probably," I said.

"Newspapers aren't hiring."

"Nope," I said.

"There's no way I can freelance."

"It's a horrible lifestyle. I hated it," I said.

"Too uncertain. Too much hustling. I'm too old."

"Yeah," I agreed. "Me too."

He turned his face to mine.

"You're getting laid off?"

He appeared genuinely concerned. I'd never seen him look at me, at anyone or anything, like that. His ice-blue eyes were clear as they searched mine. His hands were steady on the coffee mug and the cigarette. His body radiated the coiled, tense patience of a snake. So this was Jack sober. He must have been an incredible reporter.

"You never know," I shrugged. "Maybe it's time for a change. I've had three different careers so far. Maybe I'll become a baker or something this time."

"How do you do it?" he said.

"Dunno. I've had to reinvent myself every four years or so. You just fully commit to changing who you are, I guess. What will you do?"

He took a sip of coffee, took a drag off his cigarette, and shrugged.

"Die out?"

"Oh come on, Jack. Don't be like that."

He turned the unintoxicated version of his basilisk stare on me. It was overwhelming. I was paralyzed by his eyes. My God, he must have been such a good reporter once.

"Don't be like what?" he said.

"I don't know. Self-pitying," I fumbled, taking a drink to avoid his gaze. "Just...clean house, man. Know what I mean? Your daughter's screwed up. And you're...look, I don't know you. I'm getting over-involved, overstepping boundaries and all. I should get going."

He held out his hand. He didn't put it on my forearm, or wrist, or shoulder, or any of the usual places a man puts his hand when he wants to stop a woman from standing up and walking out.

He put it over the top of my coffee cup.

"Any progress on the book?" he asked.

I sat back down on the couch next to him. I shrugged.

"Can I ask you something?" he said.

"Sure," I said.

He hesitated. He looked at me, looked away at the fading sunset, then looked back at me.

"Will you..." he began.

He hesitated again, and I knew that he wasn't going to ask me what he really wanted to. Not unless I forced him to.

I didn't want to force him to.

I didn't want him to ask me.

I didn't want to be part of his life, part of his story.

"Jack," I heard my voice saying, before I could stop myself. "Ask me."

Jack's yellow legal pad

Tuesday, March 27, 5:37 p.m.

TO DO:
- Research homicides involving buses/public transit—any connection with Lake Washington murders?
- Call Katherine tonight. Ask her.
- Request police records for individuals with surname/nickname "Spine"
- Buy beer
- Buy vodka
- Buy scotch
- Call Katherine tonight. ASK HER!

Jack pops the question

Tuesday, March 27, 5:38 p.m.

Jack finally asked me after finishing his cigarette but before finishing his coffee. The setting sun dyed his face orange and gold. He didn't make eye contact with me.

"Will you help me?" he asked in a voice so soft I could barely hear it. "Please, will you?"

"With Lucy?" I said.

He shook his head.

"I did something Thursday night," he said. "I can't remember. But I think I did something terrible after you left me."

And there it was: the guilt trip, pulling up to the curb and asking me to go for a ride. I left him that night. I was stone sober. He was drunk as hell. He told me to let him out of the car. And I did. I drove away. I left him.

"What can I do to help you?" I said. My voice was a tight braid of apology, shame, and defensiveness.

Jack slid his cold eyes to mine. In the ebbing light they weren't their usual blue but copper, like pennies on the eyelids of a dead man.

"Will you help me find out?" he said. "Will you tell me the truth?"

"The truth?" I echoed. "What do you think you did?"

Jack inhaled, cigarette-less. He pulled another out of the pack, stuck it between his dry lips, lit it, and sucked in hard.

"I think I left the bar late Thursday night. I think someone approached me. I think it was a man. I think he was dressed in green. All in green. I think I hit him. I think I hit him over and over and over. I don't know why I would do that. Maybe he was trying to mug me. Or maybe I was fucked up in the head because of what you and I did."

What he and I did was peruse photos of his dead wife on the anniversary of her murder. I liquored him up and drank nothing myself so that I could maintain control of the situation. Then I abandoned him in the street. Could a woman be a bastard? If so, I was a total bastard.

"Oh God, Jack…I'm sorry," I said. "I'm so sorry. I should have stayed with you. But…are you sure you really remember all that? Are you sure you didn't just imagine it?"

Jack considered. He continued to consider through three drags on his cigarette.

"You're all I remember—really, fully remember—from that night. I remember I got out of your car, and you said…" He closed his eyes, his voice morphing into the staccato chant of a schoolboy reciting a poem. "You said, 'Jack? You're going home, right? Want me to walk you, make sure you get inside okay? You're not going into that bar, right?'"

That sounded like me. He had a good memory.

"And I said…'God…'" he trailed off.

"'You have no idea,'" I supplied.

"Yeah."

We sat in silence. Jack's cigarette burned out. The sun vanished behind his neighbor's roof. It grew so cold.

"I know cops," Jack said at last. "If I went to the local police station and told them half of what I've told you, I'd be charged with all the unsolved murders currently on the books. Maybe even the Lake Washington Killer cases I've been covering. I need you to help me."

"How?"

"I'll die in prison."

"Jack…"

"Who would take care of Lucy?"

Please don't ask me to take her! I shrieked silently.

"How can I help you?" I said. "I don't understand what you're asking me."

"You've been investigating me for months, right?"

"No, I haven't," I protested.

"Did you read my old articles?"

"Yeah," I said. "Some of them."

"Which ones?"

"A few before your wife was murdered, to get a feel for how you used to work. All the ones you wrote about her killer's trial. And a few after. There weren't many after."

"You talked to my boss, you kept calling and emailing me, you followed me to work, you yahooed me—"

"If you mean googled, yes, I did that. And other stuff too, I guess. So what?"

"So keep doing it and tell me what you find out."

"I'm not an investigative reporter, Jack. I'm just a small-time newspaper editor. I didn't know what I was doing, to be honest," I said. "Why don't you apply your own journalistic talents and investigate yourself, um, yourself?"

"No one can be that objective," he said.

"I don't know. You of all people could probably pull it off," I said.

"I'm too old," he said. "I'm done being objective."

Jack took a last drag off his cigarette, then pitched the butt into his sodden front yard (trashy!)

"I miss being married," he said. "I miss her like hell. But I miss the whole wedded bliss racket worse. Being a couple, you know? Being...accountable?"

"I know," I said. "Speaking of accountable, I should probably go. It's getting late."

"Will you do it?"

"Maybe. If you tell me exactly what you want me to do," I said. "Maybe."

Jack didn't praise my innate journalistic talent, nor my Lois Lane-like tenacity, nor my searing intellect. He simply said, "You're the only person who knows me. Keep investigating me and tell me what you find out. Tell me the truth."

I didn't want to go poking around Jack's life anymore. I didn't want to help him. I didn't want to tell him the truth. I wanted to go home to my un-murdered husband.

I set my coffee cup on the porch next to the wobbly leg of the couch and began to dig through my purse.

"I need to get home."

"Katherine," he said. "Don't go yet."

"It's cold," I said.

"Please stay?"

He held out his hand.

The sky had gone navy. The stars would pop out any minute. In the compelling half-light, his eyes were the sky…navy-blue with sharp stars shining in the pupils.

I sighed.

I reached out my hand.

I dropped his car keys and driver's license into his waiting palm. Our fingers did not touch. I stood, turned away, and left him.

The Washingtonian

Wednesday, March 28, 10:55 a.m.

Another Body Discovered
Near Lake Washington
By Jack O'Lies

A body was discovered by Seattle Police early Wednesday morning in a condo located on the shore of Lake Washington. The victim, tentatively identified as female, was extensively mutilated. The name "Spine" was found on the bedroom wall, written in the victim's blood.

Jack's email inbox

Wednesday, March 28, 10:58 a.m.

From: Unknown
To: Jack O'Lies
Subject: Another Body Discovered Near Lake Washington
Attachments: JackOLies8.jpg, JackOLiesHome.jpg

Dearst Jack! Hi! Great article. But it needs a picture. Maybe u can use one of these? Check em out:
Another picture of u from Thursday nite.
U and your girlfriend at your house yesterday nite.
Ta!

My recollection, unreliable at best

Wednesday, March 28, 11:09 a.m.

A call was transferred to my office at ten-ish. Or maybe it was eleven-ish. It was before noon, I was sure of that. Fairly sure. I hadn't had lunch yet and I was hungry.

"*Journal Newspapers*, this is Katherine," I answered mechanically.

A heavy, shaky exhalation made the phone buzz against my ear.

"Hello?" I said.

"Did you get an email from him?" a voice said. It was a man's voice. It was a voice that I didn't immediately recognize.

"Excuse me?" I said.

"Are you okay?" the man said.

"Who is this?" I said. "Are you trying to reach the sales department? I can transfer you."

I wasn't paying attention. I was fiddling with my newspaper's Twitter feed, which I had forgotten to attend to until that very moment. And I was pondering lunch.

"Katherine! Tell me you're okay," the voice rasped.

"Jack?" I said. "Is that you?"

Now I was paying attention. He was breathing hard, like a person coming straight off a hundred-yard dash. I stopped playing with the tweets and kicked my office door shut.

"What's going on?" I demanded.

He said something. He was breathing too hard for me to understand a word.

"What?" I said. "I can't understand—mind if I tape this? Mutual protection and all?"

He said something. It made no sense.

I turned on my recorder.

Transcript of recording

Wednesday, March 28, 11:11 a.m.

Katherine: Jack?

Jack: Are you there?

Katherine: What's wrong?

Jack: Did you read my article?

Katherine: Which article?

Jack: I filed it at ten. The tech kid posted it on the *Washingtonian* website a couple minutes ago.

(Clacking sound. No speech for forty-six seconds.)

Katherine: Is it "Another Body Discovered Near Lake Washington?"

Jack: Yeah.

Katherine: No, I didn't read it.

Jack: Did he email you?

Katherine: Who?

Jack: I got an email. There were pictures. Check.

Katherine: Um…

(Clacking sound. No speech for fourteen seconds.)

Katherine: I got a couple pitches from foodie PR firms. One's got a photo of some kind of lamb dish. Looks tasty.

Jack: Nothing else?

Katherine: Fries…yam fries. I love those—oh, now I get it, "The Lamb 'n' Yam Festival." Clever-ish.

Jack: Katherine! Check and see if there's a picture of us.

Katherine: Us? What? Us when?

Jack: Yesterday. On my porch.

(Clacking sound. No speech for six seconds.)

Katherine: Nope. Are you sure you didn't imagine it?

Jack: It's us last night. I'm looking at it right now.

Katherine: Who could've taken our picture? Lucy?

Jack: No. No way. I'll forward it to you.

Katherine: Wait, no—do not forward me some weird, virus-having email, Jack!

Jack: I already sent it.

(Clacking sounds. No speech for six seconds.)

Katherine: I deleted it.

Jack: Did you see?

Katherine: No, I said I deleted it. I marked it as junk and deleted it. I'm not infecting my office with your Eastern European malware.

Jack: *(Inaudible)* frustrating as hell, you know that? You're the most stubborn woman I ever met.

Katherine: What? Calm down. It's nothing—just spam. Probably.

Jack: I—Jesus, I've got to get out of here. Can he see me? Through the computer or something?

Katherine: You mean some kind of keystroke capture program? I think a virus can do that.

Jack: I mean, can he *see* me? I feel like he's watching me.

Katherine: Who? You've got to get it together! Nobody can see you through your computer. That's ridiculous.

(No speech for four seconds.)

Katherine: Although…do you have a webcam? What if the Russian mafia could hack it, like in a spy novel? I never thought about that. How cool a plot twist would that be?

Jack: I'm leaving. I've got to get away, this damned computer is spying on me. Can you meet me at home? No, he knows how to find us there. Shit!

Katherine: Who is "he," Jack? There is no "he." "He" is some precocious teen in Moscow or Vladivostok, cruising the dark web and stealing your credit card information. Go to the bank and cancel everything, but calm the hell down!

Unidentified: Hey, did you get a chance to look at that yam festival press release I forwarded you?

Katherine: What? Sorry, I—hang on. Jack? I've got to go. Sorry, what did you forward me?

End of recording.

Your public library: where reading is FUNdamental!

Wednesday, March 28, 3:09 p.m.

I couldn't resist the idea once it occurred to me. Granted, it took several hours and a dose of lunch, along with a couple shots of espresso, for it to occur to me. Still, it was irresistible.

Jack was very upset over the Baltic phishing email. I doubted it was anything serious. I doubted there was a photo of us attached. "He," whoever "he" was, had sent nothing to my work email, so I doubted "he" really photographed Jack and me together. However…

I had a personal email account.

I'd been busy lately. I hadn't checked it since the previous morning. What if "he" sent the putative photo of Jack and me not to my work email, but to my personal account?

Or accounts.

I had three. Not counting two I shared with my husband and never checked, one I set up for junk mail, and a university account I hadn't used since graduating but never bothered to deactivate just in case…of what, I wasn't sure. A crucial History 241 syllabus update? Some people collected baseball cards or stamps or failed relationships. I collected email accounts. And dead pay-by-the-minute cell phones.

I didn't dare open a potentially infected personal email at work. How would I explain that? So I took a fifteen-minute break and drove to the public library a few blocks from my office, where the internet firewall was notoriously sturdy. I snagged a free computer, logged in, and checked my primary personal email account. Nothing. I checked my secondary account. Nothing. In the third, I found it. And reality suddenly shifted to a very bad spectrum.

My email inbox

Wednesday, March 28, 3:14 p.m.

From: Unknown
To: Katherine Luck
Subject: Jack OLies
Attachments: JackOLies8.jpg, JackOLiesHome.jpg

Hi ya! So your Jack OLies's new drug of choice? Watch out. He's bad news.

Have u seen what he's been up to lately? Here's a picture of him in action last Thursday. Consider it a warning. Friendly warning :-)

And here's a shot for the stepfamily album.

Ta!

Phishing for answers

Wednesday, March 28, 3:16 p.m.

There were two photos attached to the email.

I didn't understand the modus operandi of computer viruses, spam, spyware, malware, and other digital rogues. I didn't want to open the photos. I didn't want to see them. I had seen so many bad pictures lately.

I didn't have to look at them. I could just delete the email, log out, go back to work, and forget all about them.

Right?

Adult subjective matter

Wednesday, March 28, 3:17 p.m.

I opened the photo of Jack first.

It was blurry, low-resolution, and terribly pixilated. I squinted, zoomed in, and was able to make out a brick wall in the background, splashed by the orange glare of a streetlight. In the foreground was a spectral, underexposed face. It was Jack's face. He was hunched over, his posture like that of a cobra. He appeared to be caught in the act...and not the act of kindness. Maybe he was reaching for something he had dropped. Or maybe he was lunging at a shadow-shrouded lump that might have been a sack of garbage or an abandoned duffle bag or a person, which lay on the sidewalk at his feet.

Good God...

I clicked on the second photo. I expected another low-res snapshot. The photo took its sweet time opening. When it finally revealed itself, I gaped at the ultra-sharp, high-resolution image, which had clearly been captured by an expensive camera wielded with true skill.

Jack and I were sitting on a moldy old couch on a shabby porch in a rundown section of Seattle's historic Ballard neighborhood. Night cocooned us in soft shades of sapphire and cobalt. Luminous starlight was poised to shower us from the vault of heaven. He was holding a coffee cup in his right hand. I was holding the thick strap of my purse in my left hand. As for our unoccupied hands...they seemed to be entwined. We were looking at each other with great intensity. Our eyes shone like pools of still water at dusk. What a pair we were.

I stared at the photo, aghast. We weren't holding hands. I

was dropping his driver's license and car keys into his upturned palm. Our fingers never even touched. We weren't a pair of anything.

The digital camera I used for work wasn't powerful enough to produce an image like this. Not in such low-light conditions. Smart phone cameras and mid-range DSLRs couldn't do it, unless the photographer had been standing in the soggy front yard, obvious to Jack and me, and let the flash rip.

The photo was taken by a pro. A photojournalist.

Or someone with a really expensive camera and a serious grudge.

Jack's panic began to seep into my bones.

Eight facts, eight questions

Wednesday, March 28, 3:19 p.m.

1. "He" had one of my email addresses, but not my work email or my primary personal email.

This particular address was almost completely inactive—how did "he" get it?

2. Jack was freaking out.
How could he not, given the circumstances?

3. I was freaking out.
How could I not, given the circumstances?

4. I had been photographed with Jack at his home; photographed at a tricky moment that created an unfortunate tableau, for those who choose to interpret it wrongly.
What was the purpose of this incriminating photo?

5. I had been cyberstalked. And real stalked.
Why?

6. "He" thought I was Jack's girlfriend. "He" didn't know that I most certainly was not, that I was married, and that I had only known Jack for one day shy of a week.
How had these crucial details escaped "his" notice?

7. "He" had been stalking Jack for days, texting and emailing him, and following him to his neighborhood bar and his house. But this was the first time I had been contacted.
Why now?

8. "He" didn't know how to find me. Yet. When would that change?

Stop this reality, I wanna get off

Wednesday, March 28, 3:21 p.m.

I stood outside the library, my face dappled with yellow sunlight and chilled by the early spring wind. I called Jack's cell number. Apprehensively, I scrutinized everyone that passed me. I was scared as hell.

Jack picked up on the second ring.

"Katherine?"

"Yeah."

"Are you okay?" he said.

"I checked my email," I said.

"Are you safe? When I called your office a minute ago, they said you left work. Where are you?"

"Where are you?" I countered. "You're not at some bar, are you?"

"Are you okay?" he cried. His voice was unsteady, his breathing uneven. He sounded like someone was strangling him.

"Yes."

"Good...good. God, I think I'm having a heart attack."

"You're fine. Jack? You're fine, right? Jack?"

"Yeah...I guess. You saw the pictures?"

"Yes," I said.

"Was I right?" he asked.

I took a breath, then I said the words I knew he needed to hear.

"Yes, you were right. I believe you."

He let out a long, ragged exhalation.

"Who's sending these emails? The texts? Who took our picture?" he said.

"Shouldn't you go pick Lucy up?"

"Someone was watching us yesterday," he said.

"Yeah, and what if he's watching us now? I gonna go get my daughter. You ought to go get yours. Jack? Jack! Are you going to get Lucy?" I might have been yelling. I didn't know and I didn't care.

"Someone's following us, watching us, stalking us, just like twelve years ago. Both of us."

"Screw this, Jack! There is no 'both of us!' We are not a 'we!' I have my own life and my own family, and I don't need this. I am not part of your life, you hear me?"

"Can we get a drink?" he pleaded. "Can we please go get a drink and figure this out?"

"Goodbye, Jack."

Eureka

Wednesday, March 28, 3:38 p.m.

Reckless and panicking, I sped up the freeway in this week's automotive advertising firm offering, an uninspiring Volkswagen Jetta. I was heading north to my child's daycare, to snatch her safely away from the clutches of cyberstalkers, uncanny photographers, and other terrors. Suddenly, as the speedometer hit seventy-four, it came to me in a heart-stopping flash...

I knew exactly who sent us the emails.

theseattlecrimeologist.com

Wednesday, March 28, 11:19 a.m.

Another Body Discovered
Near Lake Washington
By The Seattle Crimeologist

A body was discovered by Seattle Police early Wednesday morning in a condo located on the shore of Lake Washington. The victim, tentatively identified as female, was extensively mutilated. The name "Spine" was found on the bedroom wall, written in the victim's blood.

Acording to an anonymos source, the victum was a lawyer with ties too a recent assalt on Seattle Metro Bus line 15 that runs thru the Ballard neighrborhood. An unidentified man wearing green clothes was sited at both crime scenes.

Got a hot tip? Email me!
theseattlecrimeologist@gmail.com

Nobody needed this aggregation

Wednesday, March 28, 4:48 p.m.

I emailed The Seattle Crimeologist as soon as I got home. I used the compromised email account, just to keep things neat.

From: Katherine Luck
To: theseattlecrimeologist@gmail.com
Subject: Hot tip about Jack O'Lies
I've got a hot tip about Jack O'Lies at the Washingtonian. *Answer your phone when I call you.*
- Katherine

It took me barely seven minutes to discover a phone number for Leo Krakowski, The Seattle Crimeologist. He was interviewed six months earlier by the *Seattle Times* as a blogging "expert," then was re-interviewed this week regarding his altercation with Jack at the Lake Washington Killer crime scene. I dug around the internet and found an old web-archived version of his blog from a year ago. He used to list his phone number on the contact page. I dialed it from my cell phone. I wished I'd resurrected one of my old untraceable phones, but there was no time to spare. He'd surely read my email by now.

He answered promptly.

"The Seattle Crimeologist," he said.

"Leo?" I said.

"Yeah…are you Katherine?" he said. He sounded all of nineteen years old.

"You sent a couple very threatening emails today," I said.

"Whoa…back up on this a second."

"You recently had an embarrassing run-in with Jack O'Lies in front of the entire Seattle media. You have a really expensive camera," I said. "You took a photo of Jack and me at his house last night, didn't you?"

"Hey," he said. "Is this some sex thing? Are you on the police force? Are you sleeping with a crime reporter—is that it? Did you tip him off about that dead body in the Lake Washington condo this morning?"

"Oh my God, seriously? I'm married!" I exclaimed.

He chortled with delight.

"Oh, hell yeah! What precinct are you with? Is it South Seattle? There was a big sex scandal down there last year that I was *this* close to breaking, but the freakin' police union lawyers shut me down. I've got to interview you. On the record. We should talk in person. How's now? Where should we meet? Hello?"

I sighed. Captain Overeager here could not possibly be my cyberstalker. Damn. I was so sure.

"I can't meet you," I said.

"Sure you can! Let's pick a place. I'm in Capitol Hill. Where are you?"

I sighed again. He *would* live in the Capitol Hill neighborhood. Of course. My number-one least favorite place in Seattle: land of jaywalking club kids, illogically meandering streets, and zero parking.

"I'm north of you," I said. "We can't meet."

"I'll come to you! What bus line are you on?"

I sighed a third time. I was *so* sure. But this panting puppy was harmless. I was wasting my time.

Then I reconsidered. Jack asked me to investigate his life. Where better to start than with his nemesis?

"I can meet you around seven-thirty tonight," I said. "But I'm not dragging my carcass down to Capitol Hill."

"Sure, that's fine, sounds great! Wherever you want," he said.

I meanly considered making sex-scandal-seeker Leo bus it through two county transit systems, four city routes, and at least three local transfers to my neck of the woods.

But I was not made of stone.

"How about Northgate Mall?" I said.

"Is there a Starbucks? I'll buy you a coffee," Leo said.

I never said no to coffee.

Why I never did an internship

Wednesday, March 28, 8:09 p.m.

"Jack O'Lies is an alcoholic waste of skin who deserves to die," said Leo Krakowski, a.k.a. The Seattle Crimeologist. His long fingers encircled and worried the Starbucks cup, which was the same pasty hue as his complexion. It was his third latte in forty minutes. And I thought I had a caffeine addiction.

"But you already know that, right?" he added, sneering at me.

"He's a very good writer," I replied lamely.

"He's a hack! An ad department tool! He's a complete space suck," Leo retorted. "I can't believe he's still got a job."

Leo Krakowski, professional blogger and crimeologist (whatever that is), was not at all what I expected. I remembered seeing his distorted image in the now-iconic news footage from the Lake Washington murder scene, in which Jack shoved him and he fell down in the mud. I didn't know what happened between them to provoke the shove, but there was clearly bad blood between the two. Could it be professional jealousy?

Besides the genuine reporter's notebook he carried, available at any office supply store, there was very little about young Leo that convinced me he was a real journalist. He was twenty. He was scrawny. He jittered to and fro on his café chair like a cokehead. He wore second-hand combat boots, fingerless motorcycle gloves, and a voluminous black trench coat. He looked like a Columbine killer. Maybe he would shoot me, right there in the Northgate Mall Starbucks. Nah, the post-adolescent dork didn't have the balls to kill a story, much less me. He was a journalism school dropout turned full-time crime blogger. The little bastard made a hell of a lot more money than I did.

I was beginning to understand why Jack shoved him.

When we'd met less than an hour earlier, The Seattle Crimeologist was all smiles. Upon learning that I was not, in fact, a policewoman engaged in a torrid affair with *Washingtonian* crime reporter Jack O'Lies, Leo's disappointment was profound. His response could be summarized as "Are you freakin' kidding me?!" but seeded with epic profanity. After I'd assured him that I was merely a newspaper journalist who had interviewed fellow newspaper journalist Jack O'Lies for a book I was working on, he threw his head back and covered his eyes with both spindly, leather-encased hands.

"Oh, come the crap on!" he wailed. He then chugged the entirety of his first latte, jumped up, and huffed off to buy another. I remained at our little circular table, my hands protectively clutching my cappuccino, which Leo had insisted on buying me. He was embarrassingly ostentatious about it, as all twenty-year-old boys are when buying a drink for a woman. I knew I would have to make the $4.49 beverage last, since it was clear we were now going Dutch.

"What a waste!" he lamented upon returning. "I was sure I'd finally nail that miserable a-hole!"

He slugged back half of the latte, bemoaned his long bus ride from Seattle's awesome Capitol Hill neighborhood to the lame remoteness of Seattle's crummy Northgate neighborhood, then drained the latte.

When he returned with his third drink, he appeared resolved that he would make hay of his fruitless sex scandal quest. He had an hour to wait until the next bus back to Capitol Hill; he decided to spend those sixty minutes unloading an internship's worth of resentment on me. It was an internship suffered two years ago under the inebriated aegis of Jack O'Lies, *Washingtonian* crime reporter.

Leo's grievances, in order of their appearance in his apprentice-who-resented-his-master jeremiad, were:

* Jack's unprofessional hungoverness at work

- Jack's lack of sympathy for Leo's cool, totally justified hungoverness at work
- Jack's acerbic insistence that "hungoverness" was not a word
- Jack's endless nitpicking over petty details of journalism, such as spelling, grammar, punctuation, and the accurate representation of facts
- Jack's ad department tool tasks ("writing stupid obituaries for stupid old white people from stupid bourgeois neighborhoods like Magnolia, Queen Anne, and Ballard"), many of which he foisted off on Leo
- Jack's lazy habit of calling the public information officers at the various police agencies and asking, "Is there anything I should know?" once a day, instead of downloading the police scanner app to his (nonexistent!) iPhone and sallying forth to get the story firsthand
- Jack's lameness at coming in second for a Pulitzer Prize
- Second!
- Jack's inexplicable tenacity when it came to holding onto his job

"That was the worst thing about him," Leo railed. "I had to watch, like, forty-five brilliant investigative reporters get axed, while Jack just kept on doin' his thing, writing pay-per-line obits and helping the marketing department sell ad space to mortuaries. The man has no journalistic ethics."

"The *Washingtonian* fired forty-five investigative reporters? How many did they have to start with?"

"I don't know, a lot, whatever! The point is, he's a tool. In all five senses of the word."

Where had I heard that before?

"He's got post-traumatic stress disorder or something," I said. "And he's an alcoholic. I'm not apologizing for him. I don't really know him. But it's pretty obvious, don't you think? After what happened to his wife..."

"And boo-hoo, let's keep him on staff forever, drawing sixty-five grand a year for whoring himself to the advertisers and regurgitating the B.S. that the cop mouthpieces feed him,"

Leo retorted.

I was given pause.

"He makes sixty-five thousand dollars a year?" I said.

Leo's sneer bloomed into a grin. He leaned back in his chair and nodded slowly at me. He had me by my Achilles heel: unequal compensation. I made half as much. Half!

"Are you sure?" I said.

Leo nodded again, very slowly. Then he winked at me, even more slowly. He looked like an anorexic Cheshire Cat. He was trying to work me. It was working. Indignance flooded my chakra centers and flowed along my chi pathways. It wasn't fair!

"I had a friend in HR. I got a look at his employment file," Leo said. "Do you know how many times he was disciplined for showing up drunk at the office around the time he lost the Pulitzer?"

Wrong tactic. Suddenly I felt sad rather than righteously outraged.

"His wife had just died," I said. "She was murdered by the serial killer he was covering."

"Oh, cry me a river!" said heartless, hyper-caffeinated Leo. "It's not like the killer targeted Jack specifically, like in a bad novel or something. It was just stupid bad luck."

"Exactly!" I said. "It was a coincidence. It wasn't his fault, but he blamed himself. I can't believe you don't get it."

"Whatever," Leo said. "She died. Everybody dies eventually. She could've been taken out by a drunk driver or cancer or anything at all. Does that give him license to wallow in some third-rate depression and get drunk every night for the rest of his life?"

The blogger's words gave me pause. Maybe I shouldn't have underestimated young Leo. Maybe he had a point.

"He's depressed because he's trapped," I suggested. "The newspaper industry's dying and he's over-specialized. He can't change careers at his age."

"He's, like, forty-five, right? Yeah, that's old, but it's not like he's some broken-down seventy-year-old trying to score a

Walmart greeter job just to pay for his blood pressure meds. He's got no hustle. He's gotten away with being a drunk slacker for too long. He's gonna wind up a homeless wino before he's fifty, mark my words. And it'll be his own damned fault."

The Seattle Crimeologist was remarkably insightful.

"You really are obsessed with him, aren't you?" I said.

Leo set his latte down on the little table too hard. He folded his trench coat encased arms over his trench coat encased chest. He attempted to glare at me penetratingly, like Jack often did. Jack saw through me without effort; Leo without success.

"And, seriously, *seriously*, what's that supposed to mean?" he said.

"I'm not being sarcastic," I said. "You seem to know a lot about Jack. I want you to tell me everything you know. Everything."

My stalker/protector

Wednesday, March 28, 10:07 p.m.

It took me an hour and a half to extricate myself from Leo's bloggerly bitchfest, which furnished me with far more than I ever wanted to know about the workaday peccadillos of *Washingtonian* crime reporter Jack O'Lies. When I finally got home, my house was dark and silent. The exact moment I turned the deadbolt on my front door, my cell phone rang. I recognized the number: Jack's cell phone. After listening to a litany of not entirely unfair complaints about him, I was tempted to ignore it and let it go to voicemail. After four rings, I reluctantly answered.

"Jack?"

"Why haven't you been answering your phone? Where are you? Are you okay?"

In the hushed darkness, I said, "Hold on."

"What? You're okay, right? Katherine? Katherine!" he sounded panicked.

"Will you chill out?" I hissed. "I'm going downstairs. My husband and kid are sleeping."

"You're home?" he said.

"Yes," I said, stepping into my laundry room slash writing studio (home of the uncomfortable futon) and closing the door. "For God's sake, Jack, calm down. Everything's fine."

Jack's breath went out long and slow. And hot, I imagined. My left ear, plastered to the cell phone, was cold from the great outdoors.

"How about you?" I said. "Are you okay? I'm worried about you."

"You are?" he said.

"Well, yeah, you know. You're at home, too?"

"Yeah."

"Drinking?" I said.

"No."

"Really?" I said.

"No," he said. "I'm too scared."

"Because of the picture of us?" I said.

"No. I went to the morgue after I called you."

"Why? What happened? Is Lucy okay?" Now I was the one who sounds panicked.

"Sure, she's upstairs. Blaring some kind of Christian heavy metal, doing homework, you know teenagers."

"Why did you go to the morgue?" I said.

"Harry Dekins called me right after you hung up on me," he said. "The Lake Washington condo murder."

"Can I record this?" I said.

"Why?" he said. "Don't say, 'For our protection.' What are you planning to do with this?"

I didn't answer.

"Why can't we just talk?" he said.

When I still didn't answer, he said, "Why do I want to talk to you?"

"I have no idea, Jack. Why do you want to talk to me?"

"I think about what I want to say to you all day long. I don't get it," he said.

"Well, neither do I. Maybe you've been bottling stuff up and you finally want to let it all out," I said, as I hunted through my purse for my elusive recorder.

He didn't agree or argue. There was nothing from his end of the line for a long time.

"Jack? You still there? I hate this phone, I swear—Jack? Hello?"

"Still here," he said. He sounded like he was coming up from the deepest fathoms to gasp for air.

"Did you just take a shot or something?" I said.

"Yeah. A double. It was so bad today. Can I tell you?" he said.

"God, Jack, is this going to freak me out and give me nightmares?"

Again, there was nothing from his end of the line for several seconds, then the gasp for air.

It must have been so bad.

"I'm turning on my recorder," I said.

Transcript interrupted

Wednesday, March 28, 10:24 p.m.

Jack: What?

Katherine: Nothing. Are you going to tell me what you saw at the morgue?

Jack: Did you just turn on your recorder?

Katherine: Yes.

Jack: I don't want you to record this.

Katherine: But—well, see, I'd just really rather—

Jack: What?

Katherine: So, are you going to tell me or what? It's getting late. I've got work tomorrow—

Jack: I don't want this conversation recorded, I said.

Katherine: But—

Jack: But nothing, Katherine! Turn it off.

Katherine: But—

Jack: You need two-party consent to record phone calls in Washington. You're an editor—you know that.

Katherine: But you know I'm recording. That's implied consent.

Jack: I'll hang up and then I'll call back, and if you start recording again, I'll hang up again. I'll keep doing it until you stop.

Katherine: Oh, come on, Jack!

Jack: I'm hanging up.

Katherine: Okay, okay, Jesus freakin' Chr—

End of recording.

My reporter's notebook

Telephone interview with Jack O'Lies
Date: 3/28
Time: 10:26 p.m.
Subject: Trip to the morgue

Preliminary notes:
Three minutes of back-and-forth between Jack and me about whether the recorder was off.
I informed Jack I was taking notes.
Jack laughed.
I threatened to hang up and go to bed.

Interview notes:

Jack: Sorry. Don't do that. Sorry.
Me: What happened at the morgue?
Jack: Harry called and asked me if I wanted to take a look at the crime scene photos from the condo murder and watch the autopsy.
Me: Why did he invite you?
Jack: He knows I'm working on the story. Wanted to throw the old dog a bone, I guess. I don't know.
Me: Why are you still working on it?
Jack: Something about it is *(lost quote—Jack was talking too fast)*. It's just so damned familiar. Know what I mean? It's like something I already know, like a *(lost quote—Jack was talking too fast)*. Does that make any sense?
Me: What were the crime scene photos like?
Jack: Horrible. Brutal. Worst I've ever seen, frankly. Worse than my wife's. I mean, hers were worse for me personally, but

Jesus Christ. Intestines strung out all over the living room, draped over the sofa and the curtain rails. Face cut off and her fingernails pulled *(lost quote—Jack was rambling/words unclear)*. And the name "Spine" again. Written in her blood—

Me: I think we should stop now.

Jack: Then Harry started the autopsy. Absolutely grotesque. So much worse than the pictures. So much—

Me: Jack! Stop.

Jack: I've got to tell you. Please. Because you're *(lost quote— Jack was talking too fast)*.

Me: No, I'm not, Jack.

Jack: I think you are. I don't know why.

Me: I think we should end this interview.

Jack: I got more of those texts today. And more emails. Did you?

Me: I don't know.

Jack: Did you check?

Me: No.

Jack: Why not? Where've you been today? I've been trying to get ahold of you for hours. I thought something happened to you.

Me: I was getting coffee.

Jack: Where?

Me: At Starbucks.

Jack: For an hour and a half?

Me: How drunk are you right now?

Jack: Not drunk enough. Jesus, not nearly drunk enough. I left you eight voicemails. You scared the shit out of me. You always leave me.

Me: Where's Lucy? Are you sure she's really up in her room?

Jack: *(Lost quote—Jack was incoherent/drunk).*

Me: Jack! Where is Lucy?

Jack: Upstairs. She and her boyfriend or whatever he is had some kind of fight. She's moody. Moodier than usual. Could you come over?

Me: What? Come where? What?

Jack: Come over.

Me: To your place?

Jack: Yeah.

Me: At this time of night?

Jack: Yeah.

Me: What for? For Lucy? Are you that drunk? Deal with her yourself!

Jack: I can't.

Me: Why?

Two pages torn from notebook.

Jack: I'm scared as hell. I *(lost quote—Jack was incoherent/drunk).* Don't ever leave me like that again, Katherine. I have to be able to find you. To save you.

Me: This is exactly why I wanted to tape this!

Jack: We're both in danger. I can feel it. He's out to get us both. You have to let me save you. Promise you'll let me.

Me: This is getting weird.

Jack: Please, Katherine. Promise me. Promise?

Me: Okay, okay. I promise. I have to go.

Jack: Leave your phone on. Katherine?

Me: Bye.

Jack: Katherine?

End of interview: 10:47 p.m.

You and me and the devil makes three

Thursday, March 29, 10:05 p.m.

Jack made me call him every hour on the hour, from the moment I got up until I went to bed, to let him know I was safe. Words could not express how much fun it was to explain this to interested parties (my co-workers, my kid, my husband).

Even with all the calls, he left me four voicemails and sent me seven texts, all grammatically flawless and written in AP style.

Good Friday, Part 1

Friday, March 30, 7:43 a.m.

From: theseattlecrimeologist@gmail.com
To: Katherine Luck
Subject: Re: Hot tip about Jack O'Lies
Attachment: A-holeFiles.zip (2.3 MB)

Here's everything I've got on teh A-hole. Let me kno if u need anything else.
Leo K.

Got a hot tip? Email me!
theseattlecrimeologist@gmail.com

Good Friday, Part 2

Friday, March 30, 8:12 a.m.

My cell phone's text inbox:

8:12 a.m.
I'm going to Everett. It may take all day. Can we get a drink afterward? I'll come over to your place.
Jack

8:16 a.m.
Stay home — do not go to work today! Call me!
Jack

8:21 a.m.
STAY HOME! LOCK THE DOORS! I'll come over tonight. Do not let anyone else in! CALL ME!
Jack

Good Friday, Part 3

Friday, March 30, 9:11 a.m.

Note left on my desk by the *Journal Newspapers* receptionist:

Phone call from: John Whiteclay of the *Washingtonian*
Time: 9:09 a.m.
Message: Call him back about Jack O'Lies. URGENT.

I, oblivious

Friday, March 30, 10:51 a.m.

I had a pair of interviews to knock off bright and early down in Seattle. The traffic report on the radio warned of major backups on Interstate 5; instead of going into the office, I drove straight downtown from my house. Given Jack's free hand with my phone number over the past day, I turned my cell phone off before venturing into the formidable gridlock. I needed to concentrate.

Standing in the overpriced Seattle Center parking lot in the shadow of the Space Needle after wrapping up my second interview, I turned my cell phone back on. It immediately began to ring. Startled, I dropped it. It bounced on the hard pavement, with the sound of an egg cracking. It was sturdy, however. It continued to ring as I picked it up.

"Hello?" I said.

"Katherine?"

"Yes, who is this?"

"John Whiteclay. From the *Washingtonian*. We met last week—"

"Oh, sure!" I said. "Hi, how're you doing?"

"Could you and I have a conversation about Jack O'Lies? In private—not over the phone. It's urgent."

For an eternal moment, I thought my heart had stopped. A frightening enervation percolated within my chest, paralyzing my arms and legs and brain.

"What happened?" I said. "Is he okay?"

"Are you available right now?" he asked.

"Actually, yes. I'm not that far from you. I'm at Seattle Center. Is he okay?" I repeated.

"Let's meet at the Three Coins. It's a restaurant about two blocks west of the *Washingtonian*. It's—"

"I know where it is. I've been there before. Give me ten minutes. Is Jack hurt or in jail, or…" I said.

"Let's talk in private," he said.

As print lay dying

Friday, March 30, 10:55 a.m.

At stop lights, illegally, I checked my text messages. As soon as I pulled into the Three Coins parking lot, I dialed Jack's cell number. My hands were shaking so severely that I nearly dropped my phone again.

No answer.

"Jack. Are you okay? Call me—I'm okay, I'm safe. I'm sorry I didn't answer my phone. What happened, where are you? Call me," I rambled into his voicemail.

I got out of the Volkswagen. I checked my watch. I had to return to work by two o'clock to relinquish this less than awesome press car to the automotive advertising firm. As I locked up, one of my rare moments of—dare we say brilliance?—struck me. My weekly car-swapping might have been the very thing that kept me off the radar of anonymous texts and threatening emails and live stalkers. Unlike Jack, with his unswerving daily commute from Ballard to the *Washingtonian* to the bar in his decrepit yellow Saab, I was hard to follow in my ever-changing rides.

I went inside the Three Coins, which was just as gloomy at lunchtime as it'd been the night I met Jack. Had it really been just eight days? It felt like years.

I found John Whiteclay seated at a two-person table close to the entrance. He looked nervous. I felt frantic. Put the two of us together and we were a wreck. I slid into the seat opposite his.

"Thanks for coming," he said. "I'm very concerned. Very concerned."

The table was without menus and he was without preamble.

That couldn't be good.

"Me too," I said. "Did something happen to Jack? Did he...do something?"

"I'm not sure. I found this on my desk this morning."

He handed me a light blue Post-it note.

Call Katherine at the Journal if anything happens. Ask her to get Lucy.
Jack

"And then there was this," he said, passing me a pink phone message slip.

Date: 3/30
Time: 8:52 a.m.
To: John Whiteclay
From: Jack O'Lies
Message: Call Katherine at the Journal immediately.

"And under both, I found this," he said.

He offered me a manila folder labeled "Celeb Obits."

"What is it?" I said.

"We keep prepared obituaries of famous people on file, just in case," he said. "Open it."

I placed the folder flat across my empty place setting and let it fall open. A stack of at least sixty single-spaced printouts were stacked inside neatly, unbound. I glanced at John Whiteclay, then began to leaf through them. Britney Spears, Tiger Woods, Barack Obama, Madonna, Charlie Sheen...Jack O'Lies.

I pulled out the sheet and stared at it. I glanced at Jack's editor, who nodded.

"Read it," he said.

I scanned the text. Born, raised, schooled, married, child, employed. Nothing I didn't already know, either from talking to Jack himself, from Leo, or from my pal Wikipedia. The peculiar thing was, the obituary ended with his wife's murder.

There was nothing else in his bio—not about the trial or his Pulitzer Prize nomination or any of the other milestones he must have reached during the dead-drunk years of his widowerhood.

Was "widowerhood" a word? It ought to be. I considered asking John Whiteclay, editor extraordinaire, but decided against it. It really wasn't the proper time to indulge my dumb diction.

"Oh God," I sighed. "He's so messed up."

John Whiteclay impatiently rifled through the pages.

"That's not all I wanted you to see," he said.

He grasped a page and thrust it at me.

It was my obituary.

I liked to think of myself as an articulate person.

"What the hell!" I cried. "Why? What—why is this—what the hell is this shit?"

Articulate in print, at least.

"What is this thing?" I demanded.

"You tell me. I don't know," he said.

"Jack told me not to leave my house today. He texted me. Did he plan to come up to my place and kill me? Murder-suicide style? Is that what you're telling me?"

Even as I said (shrieked) this, I didn't believe it. But the automatic novel plot generator in my head demanded that I momentarily consider whether Jack might be the very killer he had been writing about.

John Whiteclay, age twenty-nine, looked at me with serious, blacker-than-black eyes as I attempted to rake my scattered wits back into a rational pile. I realized that he was as profoundly disturbed as I was; he was just far, far better at containing it.

"Jack's been writing a lot lately," I said.

His editor nodded vigorously.

"Yes, and I don't know why. I've been pushing him for months to file something besides the obits and the police blotter," he said. "And now, all of a sudden—"

"Now he's filing articles every day," I said.

"And they're good," he said. "Was he playing some kind of game with me before? Testing me?"

"No," I said. "He's investigating. He told me he's worried that he might have done something."

I hesitated. I wasn't sure I trusted Jack's editor, who looked at me with those steady, falsely calm eyes. I couldn't tell what he was thinking.

"What are you thinking?" I demanded.

"You just seem to know him a lot better than I do," he said. "I've been his editor for five months. You met him, what? A week ago? Do you always figure people out this easily?"

"No," I said.

"Did he tell you where he was going today?" he asked.

I shook my head.

"He just...he texted something about...something about going to Everett."

"Everett? What could he be doing way up there? That's the *Herald's* coverage area—well outside Jack's beat."

I opened my mouth.

Everett was the largest city in the county north of Seattle.

Everett was less than half an hour from John "The Chief" Whiteclay's former Indian reservation stomping grounds, home to the slaughterhouse where young Jack and his young family used to feed the ducks, blissfully ignorant of the wretched future that awaited.

Everett was a stone's throw from my house.

I closed my mouth. I stood. I hoisted my oversized purse onto my shoulder. John Whiteclay stood as well.

"I'll pick his daughter up from school," I said. "If Jack calls, tell him."

"Will you call me? When you get ahold of him?" he asked.

"Sure," I said.

John Whiteclay took out a business card and scrawled a number on the back. He handed it to me. He had cast all caution from his eyes, leaving them raw and unguarded.

"Any time," he said. "Three in the morning, I don't care. Call me and tell me if he's all right. I don't think I'll be able to sleep until I know."

This was why he was a far, far better editor—and person—than I would ever be.

Jack's voicemail inbox

Friday, March 30, 12:14 p.m.

12:14 p.m.
"Jack? Are you okay? Call me. I'm on my way to get Lucy."

12:15 p.m.
"It's Katherine from the *Journal.* You probably already knew that. Um…call me, please?"

12:18 p.m.
"Hey Jack, will Lucy's school let me pick her up? I'm not a parent or an emergency contact or anything."

12:20 p.m.
"I'm not an emergency contact, right? You didn't go and list me without telling me. Right?"

The storage closet where they keep
the Christmas decorations

Friday, March 30, 12:39 p.m.

Lucy eagerly consented to leave her Catholic school and come with me. Her school eagerly consented to release her to me without consulting my ID or ascertaining whether her father had given permission for me to take possession of his only child. Lucy's teacher, the cool jeans-wearing nun, said she remembered me from Career Day and called me "Mrs. O'Lies." Only the urgency of the situation kept me from energetically contradicting her.

"Where's Dad?" Lucy asked, as I hustled her out of the school and through the parking lot.

"I was hoping you might know," I said, hunting for the press car. I was constantly losing those temporary rides of mine, their unfamiliar shapes and colors blending into a deceitful background of strange vehicles.

Lucy shrugged.

"He said he'd be home late tonight," she said. "He told me he's gonna go out with you after work."

"Oh my God, he did not say that!" I exclaimed, suspending my search to round on Lucy. "He absolutely did not say 'go out.' He didn't. Did he?"

Lucy shrugged.

I spied the press car over her shoulder, bit my bottom lip, and hoisted my purse purposefully.

"Come on, I need to drop you home, then get back to work. The ad firm guys are coming to pick up the car in an hour," I said.

Lucy was infuriatingly slow as she dogged me to the Volkswagen. She took long minutes to put her backpack, and then herself, into the front seat. I was already in the driver's seat, the engine running, my hands squeezing the steering wheel like I was trying to wring water from it.

As she buckled her seat belt in slow motion, she said, "I met a priest yesterday."

"Oh yeah?" I said, whipping the car out of the parking lot. "I don't have GPS in this damned Jetta. Remind me how to get to your house."

"Could we go to the mall first?"

"No, Lucy, no way. I have to get back to work. Left or right?" I said.

"Left," she muttered, folding her arms across her as-yet unharnessed bosom. I still owed her a bra. I'd forgotten.

"Maybe I can take you shopping this weekend," I said.

She brightened. For Lucy, brightening involved little more than ratcheting her scowling eyebrows up half a centimeter.

"Where's Dad taking you tonight?" she asked.

"Lucy, listen to me. I am not, never have been, and never will be your father's girlfriend," I enunciated. "We do not 'go out.' We are professional acquaintances and that's all. Understand?"

"Whatever," she said.

"So, what's that you said about a priest?" I said, to prevent myself from swearing at her willful density.

Lucy brightened yet more, which meant her arms unclenched and settled at her sides, her hands coming together to clasp piously in her lap.

"It was at Bible Study at the church. Christopher was supposed to go with me, but he called and he's such a jerk because he wanted to try to convert his roommate again. Again! Last time, the Evil One made him drink a whole six-pack of beer and eat a whole large pizza and watch some stupid movie about I don't even know what gross stuff with girls in bikinis. And by the time the Evil One was willing to hear the Good News of Our Lord and Savior, it was two in the morning and Christopher had to go to bed, coz he had to be at work by eight."

"I take it young Christopher plans to succeed in failing again,'" I said sagely. I felt quite mature and wise. "I presume there will be more beer and pizza?"

"Exactly!" Lucy said, throwing her hands up. "He just wants to sin, so I told him to go to hell."

"Wow," I said. "So, we're swearing now?"

She rolled her eyes at me.

"It's not swearing. It's where he's headed if he keeps drinking and watching unchristian movies with that pothead."

"Ah," I said. "Straight through the stop light?"

"Right," she said.

"Right, I should go straight? Or right, I should turn right? Quickly, Lucy—come on!"

"Go right, turn, jeez!"

I jerked the wheel hard to the right, making the tires squeal on the rain-slicked pavement. Instead of apologizing for snapping at her, I said, "So, some priest was teaching your Bible class last night?"

"Well, Father Bertrain was teaching it like always. But there was this other priest I've never met before."

Lucy's normally flat voice had grown curves. I glanced at her. There was color in her pasty cheeks.

"Was he cute?" I said.

She turned to me and glowered.

"That is irreverent," she said.

"Sorry," I said.

I could tell from the way she twisted her fingers around each other in her lap that he was indeed cute. I sensed a juicy scene straight out of *The Thorn Birds* was a-coming.

Salaciously, I prodded, "So…?"

"I had to go to the bathroom," she said, staring at her fingers. "I thought I was the only one on that side of the building. The church is pretty deserted that time of night."

"How late at night was it?" I said.

"Six-thirty," she said. "When I came out, he was standing in the hall. I didn't notice him at first. I bumped right into him."

Lucy's voice was soft. I'd never heard her sound like this. She sounded like a real, live girl.

"It was so embarrassing! I knocked him down. I was in a hurry to get back to Bible Study and I didn't see him when he came around the corner. I felt so bad," she said.

"You knocked him down? Actually down to the ground?" I said.

She nodded.

"I felt *so* bad! I tried to apologize and help him up, but he said, 'No need, Sister.' Like I was a real nun."

Lucy sounded flattered beyond words.

"Just how old was this guy?" I said.

She shrugged.

"Pretty old. Thirty. Thirty-five maybe. Not as old as my dad."

If she had added, "Or you," I would've put her out on the side of the road right there and let her make her own way home through the Norwegian backwater overrun with bad drivers darting to and fro in their kitschy Volvos. Fortunately, she lowered her gaze to her lap and continued.

"So then, he said, 'Actually, maybe I could use a hand after all.' And…so…I…"

She fell silent. I peeked at her. She was studying her hands.

"What? You helped him up?" I said.

Lucy nodded mutely, her pale face turning a genuine shade of pink.

"He held his hand out," she nearly whispered. "And I…took it."

Wow, he must have been so goddamned cute! A handsome thirty-something priest gazing up at her from the floor, offering his hand. Their hot palms touching…"palm to palm is holy palmers' kiss" and all that.

"I helped him up and he smiled at me, even though I'd profaned him," Lucy said.

I started to reply, then realized that I was puzzled by precisely how she "profaned" him. Was it the blundering bump that knocked him to the floor, or the evidently erotic touching of hands?

"He said his name is Father Anthony and he's new at Sacred Heart of Jesus. When I told him my name, he said...he said that he was looking for me," she said.

"Whoa," I said. "Hold on. What do you mean, he was looking for you?"

"I do a lot of volunteering at church. I know where everything is. Father Anthony said that the moving company made a mistake and his stuff got stashed in the basement. He said someone at the rectory told him to get me to help find it."

Lucy was positively beaming.

Suddenly, this hot, young Italian stallion priest was making my skin crawl ever so subtly.

"Who told him to get you, exactly?" I said.

Lucy shrugged.

"So anyway, I told him they probably stuck his stuff in the basement storage closet where they keep the Christmas decorations. They're always sticking random stuff in there," she said.

"Who's 'they?'" I demanded.

"Y'know, stupid people," she said.

"So you and the priest went into some storage closet together?" I said. "Alone? How much did that profane him?"

Lucy shot a hostile glance my way.

"We did not go into the closet together," she said. "Only bad kids from the weekend catechism class do that."

I could imagine.

So I did: Catholic schoolgirl skirts skidding up under eager, groping teenage hands. Tongues sliding over braces. Awkward, dusty fumbling in the dark under the benevolent eyes of the Three Wise Men from the Christmas crèche.

I must have been smirking, because Lucy's eyes widened in horror.

"I just took him to the basement and showed him around!" she exclaimed. "It's huge, you can get lost real easy if you don't know where you're going. There's all this stuff—old pews and broken pianos and these giant paintings of the Madonna that got water damage and this massive bronze bell that used to be in the tower before they put in that mechanized chime thing. I checked the storage closet where they keep the Christmas decorations—by myself! But his stuff wasn't there. He waited while I looked."

"Where did he wait?" I said.

"He sat on this bale of tracts the church had printed in foreign languages for mission trips," she said.

"He sat there watching you dig through the closet?" I said.

Her Catholic schoolgirl skirt riding up before eager, priestly eyes?

"You have a dirty mind!" Lucy cried.

My God—she could read my thoughts!

"He talked to me," she said. "He was nice."

"Sorry," I said.

And I was. Given how instantaneously she'd latched onto me, it was apparent that this socially awkward teen was starving for attention from an adult—any adult. Considering Jack's habit of neglecting her so he could drink himself into oblivion every night, was it any wonder she would gravitate toward a father-figure who actually had the title "Father?"

"What did you two talk about?" I asked.

"My mother," she said.

I was surprised.

"Really? You told me you can't remember her," I said.

"I can't," Lucy said. "But I read Dad's articles about her getting killed."

I felt like I was sinking down to the darkest depths of the ocean.

"Oh Lucy, why did you do that?" I said.

She shrugged.

"And then Father Anthony told me why he decided to become a priest," she said.

"What did you tell him about your mom?" I persisted. "Did you tell him about your book, where you pasted her face onto the saint's body? What did he have to say about that?"

Lucy lost a bit of her preternatural pink.

"That's private," she said. "You can't tell anyone about that."

"Have you told Christopher?"

She hesitated, then slowly shook her head.

"Your dad?"

"No!"

"Anyone?"

She shook her head.

I should have felt honored to be her one and only confidant. Instead, I felt a squirmy, uncomfortable sensation that always came over me when I sensed that someone was trying to become intimate against my will. I often felt this sensation with Lucy's dad. I couldn't handle both of them at once. It was time to cut these lies out of my life.

O'Lies, I mean.

"He told me why he became a priest," Lucy said again. "It was really interesting. Wanna hear?"

"Left on Leary, right? I mean, I should go left on Leary, correct?" I said.

"Left, yes, turn left," she said. "Are you coming over for Easter dinner this Sunday? I can make a ham. I know how, with pineapple and cloves. I make one every year for me and Dad. We don't eat much, so we end up having ham sandwiches for weeks."

"I've got an Easter egg hunt thing with my daughter at the park. Sorry," I said.

Lucy looked stricken.

"But I'll take you to the mall Saturday to get you a bra. Several. You should have several bras. Okay?" I said.

She shrugged.

"So, the cute priest had an interesting reason for becoming a priest?" I said.

"Turn left here," she said.

I turned. The silence stretched taut between us

"Could you maybe stay for dinner after the mall on Saturday?" she said. "With me and Dad?"

I sighed.

"I don't know. I've got a family of my own," I said. "I kind of want to spend time with them, if you understand."

I didn't dare look at her. I felt like the wicked stepmother rejecting Cinderella. Now she would go use meth and get pregnant. I would forever represent the degenerative turning point in her life. She would always recall my closed, unaccepting face. At least I'd be remembered.

"So...why'd he become a priest?" I said into the awful silence.

"Here's my house," she said.

She grabbed her backpack as I braked.

"So, I'll come by Saturday to take you shopping, maybe noon? Maybe two or three? I don't know, I've got a lot of stuff to do this weekend. Can I call you?" I said. "Maybe next weekend would work better."

Lucy didn't answer. She opened the car door and got out. She hefted her backpack onto one shoulder and turned back to me. She leaned into the car, bracing one hand on the door frame exactly like her father did the night I encouraged him to bare his soul to me and then left him. Exactly like I was now doing to his daughter.

"He said it was Easter. He was my age. He wanted to feel what it was like to be crucified. He took his uncle's drill and ran the bit through each hand and each foot. He said it didn't hurt at all. It felt good. Holy. That's when he knew he had to give his body to God, like the martyrs," she said. "He was nice. He wore a funny-looking cassock, though. Green. Evergreen, with a mint-green collar. I've never seen one like it. His shoes were green, too."

As if from far, far away, I heard a faint buzzing sound in my ears. Something was terribly, terribly wrong.

"Lucy," I said. "What did you say the priest's name was?"

"Father Anthony," she said.

"Father Anthony what?"

"Spine."

Occasionally, disparate details assemble themselves in my

mind and I achieve overwhelming comprehension. At this particular moment, the pieces of the puzzle violently came together in my stunned brain, making me jump as if jabbed in the temple with a darning needle.

The priest was the man in green.

The priest was the Lake Washington Killer.

The priest was coming for Lucy.

Lucy could not stay in her insecure Ballard enclave tonight.

"Lucy, get back in the car," I barked. "Now!"

My "mom voice," generally ignored by my kid, shocked Lucy and impelled her back into the passenger seat with alacrity.

"You can't stay here alone," I said. "I don't know for sure if your dad is coming home tonight. Is there someone else you can stay with? Not me! Maybe Christopher?"

Lucy recoiled in virginal horror. Her hand went to her throat. What a great saint she would make.

"Okay, not Christopher. But a relative? An aunt or uncle, maybe?" I said.

She shook her head.

"Or a girlfriend—a friend who is a girl?" I said.

She shook her head again.

"Grandparents?" I said.

"My grandma," she said eagerly. "Can I?"

"Yes, let's do that, let's have you stay with her for a night or two," I said. "Where does she live?"

"Real close," Lucy said with more excitement than I've ever heard in her voice. "Go to the end of the block and turn right. What's wrong? You look mad."

"I'm not mad," I said. "Nothing's wrong, everything's fine. But don't tell anyone where you're staying tonight, okay? No texting or emailing or Facebooking or whatever you kids are doing nowadays."

My God, I sounded like I was old enough to be her grandma myself! Maybe I should've been the one to stay in whatever active senior lifestyle community she occupied. I'd fit right in.

"I haven't seen my grandma in so long!" Lucy enthused,

grinning and glowing and looking nothing like her usual dour self. "This is so great! Can I stay all weekend? Can I? Dad never lets me stay at her place. This is so cool!"

Her rapture and Jack's reported reluctance did not bode well. My uneasiness proved to be well-founded as I pulled into the parking lot of the Ballard Memory Care Center.

Alzheimer's. Lucy's grandmother had Alzheimer's.

"Okay," I said. "Maybe this won't work after all." I took a deep breath, drawing on all my internal reserves. "Maybe...maybe you can stay with me. God, what will my husband say?"

When Jack turned up dead or arrested, I was going to end up her foster mom by default. Crap. If I'd wanted a fifteen-year-old daughter, I would have had oodles of pregnant-making fun in high school instead of being a dull grade-grubber.

"No, no, it's fine, they have guest rooms. This is so cool! This is so cool!" Lucy said.

She bounded out of the press car and jogged to the entrance, which was dominated by thick, frosted glass and neutral beige siding. I followed, utterly ill at ease. Even if Lucy could be safely stashed in this asylum for the elderly, where would Jack hide out tonight, now that his home was compromised? Not with me, that was for sure! God, what would my husband say?

Lucy pressed a red button on a dingy metal intercom, gabbled at some unseen receptionist, and gained admittance.

"Come on!" she urged. "I haven't seen my grandma in ages and ages!"

The door buzzed, granting us entry into a realm of urine and excrement odors, blaring TVs, and wandering old folks. I tightened up inside. Lucy appeared to be in heaven.

Grandma O'Lies' nursing home, like Lucy O'Lies' Catholic school, was unconcerned with who I was and why I had Jack's daughter in my clutches. The nurse at the duty station waved us by, recognizing (or pretending to recognize) Lucy, all grown up since she last visited. We walked down a fetid hallway that masqueraded as sterile with white tile, white paint, and white fluorescent lights, until we came to a door labeled, "O'Lies, Marion. DNR."

I remembered that acronym from my hospital volunteer days back in high school. DNR: Do Not Resuscitate. Jack's mom, never to be revived. Oh God…poor Jack.

Lucy yanked on the ergonomic stainless steel door handle with one hand and beckoned at me to follow with the other. I did so apprehensively. Maybe if I pretended I was reporting a story for my newspaper, the unpleasantness might recede into the background a little.

Grandma O'Lies lay in a hospital bed replete with bags and tubes and electronic monitors. Her face was slack, her eyes taped closed. A feeding tube snaked down one nostril. She was dead to the world. Lucy was oblivious. She eagerly grasped her grandmother's skeletal hand and commenced an animated, one-sided conversation. Jack told me his mother kept Lucy for "a while" after his wife died. I'd naively assumed it was for a couple months, at most. Was it longer? A year? Two? More? How long did Jack spend sunk in alcohol-soaked grief, dead to the world? When did he finally pull himself together, miss his child, and come to collect her?

And where the hell was he now?

Mrs. Kennedy's rosary

Friday, March 30, 1:01 p.m.

Jack's mother was a vegetable. A very Catholic vegetable. The walls of her room were paneled with framed photos of Pope Francis, Pope Benedict, and Pope John Paul II. There was a classic long-haired Jesus with mournful eyes, and a nice shot of Mother Teresa with some cute Indian kids that evoked late-night appeals to sponsor a child for pennies a day; less than the cost of your weekly Starbucks addiction. Mother Teresa was originally named Agnes. She ought to have been Mother Agnes. Or maybe Saint Agnes. Was that why Lucy was drawn to paste her murdered mother's face on the body of Saint Agnes in her copy of *Lives of the Saints*?

Lucy was jabbering at her unresponsive grandmother, her hands clasping the limp, arthritic paw she'd plucked from the bedcovers. A catheter bag hung from the side of the hospital bed. The room stank of urine and bleach. Monitors beat rhythmically. I peered uneasily at the five crucifixes on the wall, ranging from bloody Jesus-mounted models to glitter-ridden Popsicle stick creations evidently made by Lucy in her younger years.

"This is Katherine, she's Dad's friend. He likes her and you'll like her, too, Grandma," Lucy was saying. "Can I show her your rosaries? She's not Catholic, but it's okay, right?"

Lucy abruptly jumped up, having received a telepathic go-ahead, apparently.

"Look, wanna see?" she said to me. "They're amazing. Some of them are over fifty years old."

I glanced at Mrs. O'Lies, then gingerly approached a tatty velvet jewelry box on the oak dresser. Lucy was digging through it with both hands. She held up three rosaries, her eyes alight with religious fire and something more. Love? Yes, burning love. I'd seen pale sparks of this love directed at her dad, as well as a few incongruous embers shot my way. But here, with her empty sock puppet of a grandmother, she was aflame. Her face was aglow with the radiant joy of being accepted, cared for, and utterly at home.

Poor Lucy. Poor Jack. If the murder hadn't fractured their family, would they be effortlessly happy, like the households of the 1980s sitcoms I was weaned on? Or would Jack be a divorced alcoholic, his daughter just as screwed up, and his mother still a Do Not Resuscitate Alzheimer's case?

And most important of all, to me at least: Would I be exactly where I was now, reaching out to touch a particularly attractive onyx rosary of luxurious luster?

"That was Mrs. Jacqueline Kennedy's," Lucy said reverently. "Presented to her by the pope in 1963 when she and President Kennedy went to the Vatican."

"Seriously?" I said.

Lucy nodded.

"Grandma's friend gave it to her," she said.

I ran the rosary skeptically between my fingers. On second inspection, there was a plastic sheen to the onyx. The weight seemed to come solely from the cross, which looked more like chrome than silver. I was willing to bet Grandma O'Lies' friend included a toaster oven if she was one of the first hundred callers.

"It's very nice," I said, as I handed it back to Lucy.

I glanced at my watch. It was nearly one-thirty. If I didn't get the press car back to work by two o'clock on the dot, the automotive advertising firm would probably report me to the cops for grand theft auto. I enjoyed my zero-arrest criminal record. I preferred not to join the ranks of debauched citizens who had been booked for a vehicular offense. Lucy barely acknowledged me as I waved myself out of her grandmother's room. She was reading aloud from a chubby Bible with a cracked white cover, her face as lively and animated as a preschool teacher reading Dr. Seuss.

The nurse at the duty station confirmed that the facility did indeed have guest rooms for family members to stay in. Lucy was more than welcome. The bill would be sent to her father. I silently questioned the wisdom of allowing an unaccompanied minor to stay overnight in a nursing home filled with Alzheimer's patients, then I left my cell phone number, as well as Jack's, with the nurse. In case of an emergency.

As I walked myself out of the nursing home, breathing shallowly to keep the unpleasant smells of toileting and semi-solid foodstuffs out of my nostrils, I extracted my cell phone from the depths of my trench coat pocket. No calls. No texts. I called Jack. It went straight to voicemail.

"Jack? It's Katherine. I got Lucy from school. She's staying at your mom's place. They said it's okay. Where are you? Call me. Please call me. I'm really worried about you."

theseattlecrimeologist.com

Friday, March 30, 3:29 p.m.

Possible Connection: Condo murder Victim & man Named Spine
By The Seattle Crimeologist

The body discovered by seattle Police on Wenesday morning in a Condo located on the shore of Lake Washington has been posibively Identivied as Madeline Connor, Seattle Corporate attorney/lawyer.

A man in green, with the name of "Spine" has been implecated in connection with her murder, acording to The Seattle Crimeologist's <u>EXCLUSIVE SOURCES</u>.

Got a hot tip? Email me!
theseattlecrimeologist@gmail.com

Texting…texting: 1, 2, 3

Friday, March 30, 5:17 p.m.

My text inbox
5:17 p.m.
I'm leaving Everett now. Are you at your place? I'm coming over.
Jack.

Jack's text inbox
5:18 p.m.
@ work. Dropped Lucy @ your mom's. About 2 catch th bus. R U
OK???

My text inbox
5:18 p.m.
DO NOT GET ON THE BUS!
Jack

Jack's text inbox
5:19 p.m.
Dropped off press car. Gotta take the bus home. WTF, Jack?

My text inbox
5:20 p.m.
I'm on the freeway. I will pick you up in 20 minutes. Stay in your
office. Lock the door.
DO NOT GET ON THE BUS!
Jack

Investistalked

Friday, March 30, 5:39 p.m.

Jack pulled into my newspaper's parking lot precisely nineteen minutes after sending his last text. It had started to rain. Twilight was gathering in the black puddles, making me glad I didn't have to schlep myself home via my suburb's notoriously laggard public transportation system. Nevertheless, I was confused and annoyed by his insistence on picking me up. Jack's beat-up yellow Saab, the perfect car for a Ballard dweller, came to a hard halt directly in front of the main door. I scurried through the chilling drizzle to the passenger door. He leaned across the seat and thrust it open.

"Thanks," I said, settling on the ripped upholstery and yanking the door closed. The car smelled exactly like the couch on Jack's front porch: mildew mingled with cigarette smoke.

"Let's go get a drink," he said.

His voice was tight. He sounded pissed off. At me?

"What's going on, Jack?" I said. "What happened to you today?"

His face glowed dead white in the streetlights that refracted through the rain-spattered windshield. His knuckles were bloodless, every tendon in his hands sharply delineated through his skin as he clutched the steering wheel. His eyes were wide, the arctic blue of his irises nearly swallowed by the red-webbed whites. He abruptly accelerated out of the parking lot, squealing the tires and jouncing me against the door.

"You scared the hell out of your boss, going AWOL this morning like you did," I said. "And what's the deal with those obituaries you left on his desk? Jack?"

To my surprise, Jack exploded.

"Why didn't you stay home like I told you?" he shouted. "What the hell is wrong with you?"

I shrank against the cold passenger door. His voice was so loud, so harsh. I instinctively made myself small, cringing away from him.

"It was so simple—stay home! Lock your door! Why didn't you listen to me?"

He was breathing hard. He jerked the steering wheel too roughly. He sped through three intersections, ignoring red lights. We were going to get into an accident.

"You don't listen," he said. "You're the most stubborn woman I ever met."

"You don't know me, Jack," I retorted, anger replacing fear. "We met eight days ago—you don't know me at all! Screw this, let me out. Stop this car! You let me the hell out!"

He swerved illegally across traffic, setting off a chorus of horns, and pulled onto the freeway. He cut across four lanes to the carpool lane on the far left, where he could speed with relative impunity. I continued to rail at him.

"You have no right to talk to me like this! Don't ever yell at me, Jack, you hear me? You let me out of this car! Let me out!"

I was stubborn.

I didn't listen.

He did know me.

Jack proved himself to have been a husband for over a decade and the father of a teenage girl by masterfully tuning me out. Five miles flew by, then he veered across the freeway, taking the exit that led to my house. Just off Interstate 5 was the world's nastiest Irish pub. The one and only time I'd eaten there, I found a hair in my french fries. Not the kind of hair that came from a head. Jack cut into the pub's parking lot at forty-five miles an hour. The Saab bottomed out and the undercarriage scraped shrilly against the wet cement. He slammed on the brakes, sending us careening into an empty parking space at a wild angle. He killed the engine.

He turned on me, pale, panting, and wild-eyed. The fire went out of me, replaced by cowering cowardice.

"Calm down," I said.

"You're so damned stubborn!" he hissed.

For a moment, I was certain that he wanted with all his heart to do something bad to me.

Grab my shoulders and shake me?

Slap me?

Crush me in his arms and smother me against his wrinkled Members Only jacket?

His glacial eyes were not seeing me right now. Had I been replaced by a vision of his endangered daughter? Or maybe the specter of his raped and murdered wife?

"Lucy's safe," I said. "I got her. Jack? I got her, like you asked me. Jack…say something."

He blinked. He blinked again, then took a deep breath. He exhaled shakily. His hand came up to scrub across his mouth. He turned away from me. He stared at the raindrops making snail trails down his window. Three minutes passed, according to the digital clock in the battered dashboard. The only sound in the car was Jack's unsteady breathing.

"I need a drink," he said at last.

"Not here. Trust me," I said.

Another minute passed. I watched the clock so I wouldn't meet his cold eyes.

"You know where I live, don't you?" I said.

He didn't reply. I looked at him. His eyes were on the window, the pupils following the rivulets of water gliding down the glass. He nodded.

"How?" I said. "Did you investigate me?"

He nodded again.

It had taken me barely seven minutes to dig up The Seattle Crimeologist's phone number. It probably took Jack all of thirty seconds to discover my home address, social security number, and legal name.

"Why?" I said.

Jack didn't answer me. He didn't look at me.

"Jack?"

I'd never touched him. He'd reached fruitlessly for my hand

once, the night he got drunk and showed me his pictures of hell. Our fingers appeared to be entwined in that unfortunate photo of us on his porch. But he had never so much as grazed a strand of my hair; I'd never brushed so much as a fingernail against his skin. I reached for his shoulder. He flinched away before my hand could make contact. Our eyes met instead.

"Can we go to your place?" he said.

"No."

I wasn't about to take Jack home, introduce him to my husband and kid, and complicate things further. There was no way I was setting foot inside the pubic pub, either. But I would sit out here in his dank, uncomfortable car for as long as it took.

"Tell me what happened today," I said.

He deflated. His hands gripped the wheel like a shield. His neck bowed until his forehead touched his knuckles.

It must have been very, very bad.

The one thing Jack needed to hear

Friday, March 30, 6:13 p.m.

The rainfall grew steady as I sat with Jack in his car, both of us gazing through the water-streaked windshield at the gaudy neon lights that clotted the windows of the Irish pub. Neither of us said a word for a long time. This must have been what the Sunday car picnics with his wife were like, back when they were having problems.

"Yesterday," he said at last. "After the autopsy, I went back to work. I put my notes in my desk drawer and went to the bar. I got pretty drunk. I left my car in the lot and took the bus home."

"That was smart," I said. "Taking the bus, I mean. You shouldn't keep getting drunk after work."

I knew about his two DUI arrests. They were in a file from the *Washingtonian* human resources department, which vindictive Leo emailed me early this morning. From the way Jack's pale blue eyes slipped over mine with the speed of a snake's flicking tongue, I knew that he knew I knew.

"I called you when I got home," he said.

"And told me you hadn't been drinking," I said.

"I don't remember," he said. "I had some vodka while we talked. A couple shots. It felt so good to talk to you. That's all I remember. Then suddenly I wasn't on the phone anymore and the bottle was empty. It was pretty late, I think. I remember I took out my cell phone to call you again, but then it was morning and I was lying on the couch. I was still holding my cell phone."

"Nice," I said. "Did your daughter see you passed out on the couch like that?"

Jack shrugged, his shoulders lifting asymmetrically exactly like Lucy's.

"I got Lucy onto her school bus. I took a shower, shaved, caught the bus to work. I sat in one of the handicap seats. You know, the ones that're turned sideways instead of facing front?"

"You're not supposed to do that," I said.

"I sent you a text," he said. "When I looked up, there was a man sitting across from me. All in green. Green jacket. Green shirt. Green pants."

"Green shoes?" I said.

"You've seen him," Jack said. His eyes burned into mine. "You have, haven't you?"

"Maybe," I said. "I'm not sure."

"On the bus?"

"Maybe. I think so. But maybe not. I'm suggestible," I said. I didn't tell Jack that Lucy had seen him, too. Had spoken to him and touched him. I didn't want to scare him. Not yet; not until he had calmed down.

"He stared at me like he knew me," Jack said. "I sent you another text."

"Telling me to stay home," I said. "Why?"

"Because I knew," he said.

"You knew what?"

"That he was looking for you," he said.

I didn't know what to say. So I said the one thing Jack needed to hear.

"Thank you for trying to protect me."

He let out a shaky sigh and closed his eyes. His right hand reached for my shoulder and it was my turn to instinctively shy away before he could touch me. He opened his eyes and put his hand back on the steering wheel.

"His eyes were dead. There's something horrible about him…can we get a drink? Please? Just a beer?" Jack implored.

I shook my head vigorously.

"That pub is nasty," I said. "I won't set foot in there after what I found in the fries. Just talk to me, Jack. What happened after you sent me the second text?"

"The man stared at me. He never blinked. Not once. Then he smiled at me. An awful, grotesque smile. And a name came into my head: Spine."

The drafty Saab felt much colder all of a sudden.

"When we got to my stop, I jumped off the bus and ran flat out until I made it inside the *Washingtonian* lobby," Jack said. "I sent you the last text. Then I went up to my cubicle, grabbed my notebook, wrote a note to The Chief, and left the obit folder on his desk."

"Yeah, with your obituary in it. And mine," I said. "What the hell, Jack?"

He looked at me. Like the man in green, he didn't blink. Not once.

"I left our obituaries with my editor because you wanted me to."

A slight revision

Friday, March 30, 6:46 p.m.

"No," I said. "That's wrong. That's not why you did it. Tell me what really happened."

Jack blinked. Once, twice. He gripped the steering wheel and shook his head, perplexed.

"I thought you...didn't you?" he said slowly. He rubbed his forehead.

I didn't like where Jack was going with this. Not a bit. I needed to regain control of the narrative.

"Tell me again what happened," I ordered. "Start over."

"I fell asleep on the couch last night," Jack repeated.

"You passed out drunk," I said. "And?"

"I had my cell phone in my hand. I was going to call you again," he reiterated. He hesitated, then continued cautiously, as if mentally fact-checking each word before he let it out of his mouth. "It woke me up this morning. It was going off."

"It was ringing?" I said.

"No. I got a text," he said. "No words. Just a picture."

Jack reached into his jacket pocket and withdrew his cell phone. He fumbled with the buttons, then handed the phone to me.

On the small screen was a photo of Jack standing outside the Ballard bar not far from his house. The image was nearly identical to the one his cyberstalker sent me on Wednesday: blurry, low-resolution, and terribly pixilated. But the lighting was better. And that made all the difference. I was able to make out a brick wall in the background, splashed by the orange glare of a streetlight. In the foreground was a spectral, underexposed face. It was Jack's face. He was hunched over, his posture like that of a cobra. He appeared to be caught in the act...and not the act of kindness. His fists were balled. His shoulders were tensed. He was leaning over a man who lay supine on the sidewalk. The old mnemonic from school ran through my head...

Supine: on the spine.

The man was wearing a dark green suit. Evergreen, I'd call it. And a mint-green shirt. On his feet were a pair of green suede dress shoes. His face was obscured by shadows. And by blood.

"As soon as I got to work, another text came in," Jack said. "It said, 'Everett. 12th Street and Hope Avenue. Or I'll get her.'"

"Get who?" I said.

Jack didn't reply.

"Jack? Who?"

"Does anyone know you're with me? Your husband?" he said.

"No," I said.

"Could anyone find you?"

"No," I said.

"Good," he said.

I wasn't sure whether I found this comforting or unsettling.

"So...you went up to Everett?" I said. "Where, exactly? 12th Street is north of the naval base, right?"

"I think so. I could see the water," Jack said. "It was chilly out. Real rundown neighborhood. Broken glass, graffiti. Everything smelled like the ocean. No one was around. There was a closed-down bar. I peeked in the windows, but it looked like the place had been sealed up for years. Dust everywhere. No chairs or tables. Broken stuff scattered around."

"What did you do?" I said.

"I sat down on the sidewalk and waited," he said.

"You just waited?" I said. "I called you over and over. I was scared to death something awful had happened to you. Why didn't you answer?"

"I don't remember the phone ringing," he said.

I scrolled through his call record, then held the phone up.

"See? And your editor called you eight times. We both texted you dozens of times. What were you really doing?" I asked.

Jack frowned in confusion.

"I just sat and waited."

"Don't give me that, Jack."

"Maybe I sort of nodded off. I was kind of hungover," he said.

Just hungover. Sure.

"Any hair of the dog this morning?" I said.

"No," he said.

"So you just nodded off right there on the sidewalk, leaned up against some derelict bar? Is that what you're telling me?" I said.

"Yes," he said.

Leo was right: Jack was within shouting distance of being a wino.

"You've got to dry out," I said. "Can't you get into that detox place they're always advertising on TV?"

Jack yanked his cell phone out of my hand. I thought he was going to stuff it back in his jacket pocket and order me out of his car into the pouring rain. Instead, he began to scroll through the menu.

"Can't work this damned thing," he muttered. "There! Look."

He thrust the phone back into my hand.

I stared at a blurry photo of downtown Everett. The view of the water just north of the naval base and the desolate urban landscape were unmistakable. In the background was an abandoned bar with filthy windows and a boarded-up front door. In the foreground was a man dressed all in green.

I had to hold the cell phone with both hands to keep from dropping it. My fingers were numb and my hands were shaking terribly.

It was him.

"He was at the bar in Ballard last Thursday. I remember. He

was inside the bar. He followed me out. I hit him," Jack said. "I knocked him down and I hit him. Over and over."

"Why?" I said.

"I don't know. Today, when I was sitting outside the bar in Everett, all of a sudden I snapped to. I think I heard something. Or maybe I...sensed something. When I opened my eyes, there he was. I think he was hiding behind the building, waiting for me. I didn't see him when he came around the corner."

"I didn't see him when he came around the corner," Lucy said.

The man in green had been waiting for her, too. And she, like her father, knocked him down. I inhaled unsteadily, struggling to maintain my composure.

"He stopped dead in front of me. He looked down at me. Then he smiled, so horribly. I jumped to my feet, snapped the picture, and ran like hell."

I rubbed the cell phone screen with my finger. The image did not fade. It was all too real. Numerous responses floated through my mind. Among them:

"Is the man in green going to kill you? Is that why you left your obituary with your editor?"

"Is the man in green going to kill me? Is that why you left my obituary with your editor?"

"How did you manage to find out enough about me to write my obituary?"

"Can I get out of your car and forget I ever met you?"

I didn't know what to say. So I said nothing.

I'd always wanted to see someone
I knew on "Cops"

Friday, March 30, 7:24 p.m.

There was a low-to-middling quality motel just across the freeway from the Irish pub. I coaxed Jack into driving us there by promising him a mini-bar stocked with booze. I checked him in on my credit card and hustled him up to his room. The universal anonymous motel smell pushed us out of the elevator and down the deserted hallway. I slid the keycard through the electronic lock, opened the door to the room, and clicked on the lights. Jack trailed me inside.

"This is nice," I said doubtfully.

Jack sat on the bed and looked up at me.

"Will you stay?" he asked.

"Nope. And there's no mini-bar, either," I said. "I'm gonna use the bathroom."

When I came back out, Jack was sprawled across the bed. He was asleep.

For a moment, I wondered if I ought to stay after all. He tried to protect me today. I felt like I should protect him in turn. I felt like it was my duty to keep him from wandering out into the night and across the freeway overpass in search of filthy Irish comfort. I felt like I owned him.

Owed.

I quickly decided against it. I could explain most of the irregular things I'd done lately to interested parties (my husband), but not spending the night in a low-to-middling quality motel room with another man.

"Hey Jack," I said. "Jack?"

I considered shaking him. I leaned down instead and peered at his slack face. He was breathing lightly and evenly. His face was utterly peaceful. I'd never seen him look like this before. He looked like a dead man.

I unearthed a piece of motel stationary and scrawled him a semi-legible note.

I borrowed your car to get home. I'll bring it back tomorrow morning. We'll get breakfast.
- Katherine

I took his car keys. After a moment of reflection, I took his cell phone as well. I left my cell phone in its place. I didn't get many calls after hours, and I didn't want to leave Jack without a portable telecommunication device while I was snooping through his text and call records. I crept out of the room, turning off the lights as I went, leaving Jack shod and uncovered on the bed.

As I drove home, I pondered the impending karmic joke at my expense. Jack's car was a manual: the most objectionable form of transmission on the market. Despite the diversity of my weekly press car usage, I had operated a stick shift exactly once in all my years as a driver. With less than stellar results.

I lurched, swerved, and stalled. I ground gears while swearing flamboyantly at the engine through the Saab's open window. I would surely be pulled over for erratic driving mere miles from my house. I'd always wanted to see someone I knew on "Cops." I'd seen a cop I knew (and in whose cop car I once rode while working on an article about women in the police force), but that didn't count. I wanted to see a criminal I knew. Preferably someone I went to high school with.

When the cops pulled me over in Jack's cruddy car, and the "Cops" camera crew shone their bright lights in my face, I knew I would spout the same bullshit line uttered by all grand theft auto suspects on the show: "This car? It belongs to a friend of mine."

Oh Arturo, god of irony! The person I knew on "Cops"

would be me!

Somehow, I made it home without being scooped up by the five-O. I parked several blocks away from my house, just in case Jack came to, was unable to decipher my bad handwriting, and called the police to report his car stolen. I ate a late dinner, then settled on the couch to pore over the digital contents of Jack's cell phone. It was a bare-bones old-school model. In his photo app, I found the two shots of him outside the Ballard bar, the picture of us on his porch, and the image he snapped in Everett today. Nothing else. Nothing taken for work. Not a single photo of his daughter.

In his inbox were several unread texts from me, as well as eleven from his editor. The most recent had been sent eighteen minutes ago. I opened it.

Are you OK? Give me a call.
John

There were dozens from "Unknown." I didn't want to open any of them. Jack had already shown me enough. I knew they were scary, and I'd been scared enough today.

I opened his phone app and scrolled through his list of saved contacts. It was sparsely populated:

"Home"

"Work"

"Lucy's cell"

"Katherine's cell phone"

"Katherine's work phone"

"Katherine's home phone"

What the hell, Jack!

Unsettled, I put his phone down, grabbed my laptop, and opened my email to review the dossier sent to me by Leo, The Seattle Crimeologist. It was awfully comprehensive; obsessively so. It comprised ninety-eight pages, single-spaced, with photos. Among the highlights:

- Jack's two DUI arrest records and mug shots
- Every article Jack wrote while covering the trial of his

wife's killer

- Jack's human resources file from the *Washingtonian*, filled with write-ups for drunkenness at work, action plans, official reprimands, and AA referrals
  - A long list of regional journalism awards Jack had won
  - A long list of national journalism awards Jack had won
- A copy of the notice of nomination from the Pulitzer Prize committee
- A copy of the letter from the Pulitzer Prize committee awarding Jack second place
- An official report, written by a *Washingtonian* human resources rep, describing the incident between Jack and Leo that resulted in Leo's summary firing from his newspaper internship
  - The address of Jack's church
  - The address of Lucy's school
  - Jack's home address
- Several high-resolution photos of the exterior of Jack's house (I wasn't in any of these, thank God)

The photos gave me pause. They were identical in quality, style, and framing to the picture of Jack and me on his porch. That meant it was Leo who took the photo of us that night. Did that also mean he took the photos of Jack attacking the man in green outside the bar? Had Leo sent Jack the threatening emails and texts? Or had he released this investigative file to someone else?

I didn't know, and I didn't know how to find out. So I went to bed. At three in the morning, I awoke suddenly. My heart was pounding. I listened intently. Before I went to bed, I'd leaned several bags filled with cans destined for the recycling bin against the front and back doors. If a murderer tried to enter, he would knock them over and the clattering cacophony would alert my family, allowing us to flee for our lives.

The house was silent. But my heart continued to pound. I realized it was pounding in the urgent manner that signaled the recollection of an unfinished task.

The Chief.

I staggered out of bed, wandered through the dark house, and located Jack's cell phone. I scrolled to the "Work" listing, hit the dial button, and blinked in drowsy bafflement when I was sent to voicemail.

I was not very sharp at three a.m. I hung up and dug through my trench coat pockets until I found the business card with The Chief's cell phone number written on it. I dialed. I was sort of awake by the time it began to ring; The Chief was not when he answered.

"Low?" he murmured groggily into the phone. "Jack? You okay? What happened?"

"It's Katherine from the *Journal*," I said, my voice robotic in the wee hours.

"What…is he with you?"

"He's okay," I said. "He's staying at a motel tonight. I'm still trying to figure out what's going on. But he's safe. His daughter's safe, too. You can stop worrying."

"Okay. Thank you. Katherine?" Jack's editor murmured in his bedroom voice. "Is there anything I can do?"

Half-asleep, yet still so professional! Was he alone? Was he shirtless?

I was so immature.

The Washingtonian

Saturday, March 31, 8:01 a.m.

Girl, Age 15, Found Dead in Ballard

The body of a teenage girl was found in the Ballard neighborhood of Seattle late last night. Police have ruled the death a homicide and are currently canvassing the area for suspects. Sources close to the investigation confirmed that the unidentified girl may be the latest victim of the Lake Washington Killer.

Holy Saturday

Saturday, March 31, 8:02 a.m.

Jack's voicemail inbox:

8:02 a.m.
"Ephesians 5:18. 'Be not drunk with wine, wherein is excess, but be filled with the Holy Spirit,' Dad! You better not have gotten drunk in front of Katherine last night. She took me to stay at Grandma's. And I'm never coming home!"

Leaving myself a voicemail

Saturday, March 31, 8:14 a.m.

"Hi, this is Katherine. Please leave me a message," my voice, in recorded format, said to me.

"Jack?" I said into my cell phone's voicemail. "It's Katherine. Our cell phones got switched last night. Lucy's okay. She left you a voicemail just a minute ago. She's not that dead girl in Ballard—don't freak out on me. But I think she's in danger. Are you up? I'm coming over. Don't open your door to anyone until I get there. We need to talk about Leo. I think he's your stalker. I think he's the Lake Washington Killer."

The Lake Washington Killer

Saturday, March 31, 8:32 a.m.

I knocked on Jack's motel room door.

"Jack?" I called. "It's me. Sorry, I didn't bring your car back. I drove mine. I hate stick shifts. Why do they even make them anymore? They're impossible. Jack? You up?"

The door opened. I was yanked into the room.

By Leo.

He kicked the door closed. He leaned against it, trapping me. Leo wasn't pointing a gun at me, but he acted as if he was. He loomed over me like an enforcer from the Trench Coat Mafia. I couldn't be sure whether I yelped in terror or just goggled at him in mute shock.

"About time you got here," he said.

"Where's Jack?" I cried.

"How the crap should I know?" he said. "You've got to help me. I pissed him off. He's on his way here right now!"

Leo sounded utterly panicked. I was utterly confused.

Leo stalked Jack. And me. He followed us and photographed us. He sent us intimidating texts and emails. He tracked Jack through two counties to this obscure motel, and deftly took me prisoner. Why did he sound as frightened as I felt?

"Jack's coming here?" I said.

"No! *He* is. *Him.*"

"Who? What did you do with Jack?" I said.

Leo clawed impatiently at his floppy hair.

"Nothing! I haven't seen that worthless S.O.B. since…wait. Are the two of you staying here together?" Leo cocked his head at a lascivious angle, his fingers meeting to twiddle under his chin. "I thought you were married."

"I am!" I said. "Jack's staying here. Alone."

"This is Jack's room?" Leo queried. His anemic forehead creased in confusion.

"Yes."

"But you paid for it with your credit card," he said.

He hacked my credit card account! That's how he tracked us down. Now I'd have to cancel everything. What a hassle.

"And your cell phone's here," he said, pointing at my phone, which sat abandoned on the bedside table.

"Our phones got switched last night," I said.

"But his car isn't here," said Leo. "Yours is."

"I stole—borrowed it. His car's at my house. Where is he?" I demanded.

"I don't know, I said! I don't care! He's useless—you've got to help me."

I knew I ought to fear for my life. I knew I ought to cower and plead. Instead, I rolled my eyes and huffed over to the bed, where Jack lay sprawled the last time I was in this room. I sat and glared at the postpubescent blogger with his baggy black coat and his tattered goth gloves and his ironic Trix cereal T-shirt. The only thing stone-cold killer Leo, the murderer of my hypothesis, was able to kill was the mood.

"You're a stalker," I accused. "You investigated Jack."

That was supposed to be my job!

Leo, still barricading the door with his redoubtable scrawniness, let out a snort.

"Big deal. He's an ass. He deserves it."

"You sent him all those creepy texts and emails," I said.

Leo hesitated.

"Technically," he replied.

"You took that photo of us on his porch," I said.

Leo grinned.

"Hell to the yeah I did!" he chortled salaciously. "Seriously—I thought you said you were married."

"I was handing him his car keys, pervert!"

"Whatever."

"So, that means you also took the pictures of him outside the bar in Ballard," I said.

Leo blanched. The color in his already pasty face actually drained, like a weird species of chameleon turning white to match the door he was leaning against.

"Yeah," he said.

"But," I said. "In the pictures, Jack's standing over a man in green. I thought you were the man in green."

"No!" Leo choked. "No way. He's…I made him mad. He's coming for me. You've got to help me."

Despite Leo's essential dorkitude, my skin crawled.

"What do you mean?" I asked.

Leo sank to the floor, his back still pressing hard against the door. He wrapped both arms around his knees. He wasn't trying to keep me in, I suddenly realized.

He was trying to keep someone out.

Do not get on the bus!

Saturday, March 31, 8:37 a.m.

My voicemail inbox:

8:37 a.m.
"Katherine? It's Lucy. Could I talk to you for a minute? I'm
still at Grandma's. Christopher did a very bad thing last night. I
want to go to confession. Could you drive me? If you can't, I'll
take the bus."

Leo explained himself

Saturday, March 31, 8:40 a.m.

"I never stole Jack's car," Leo said. "It was all a big misunderstanding."

Had I not recently stolen/borrowed Jack's car without permission myself, I would have had a lot less sympathy for former *Washingtonian* newspaper intern Leo Krakowski. His tale of misuse at the perpetually hungover hands of Jack O'Lies sounded plausible, however.

One drizzly morning two years ago, after abandoning his battered Saab in the parking lot of the Three Coins lounge the night before to avoid a third DUI, Jack inappropriately ordered fresh-faced journalism student Leo to go fetch it. He instructed young Leo to move it all of two blocks to the *Washingtonian* parking lot so it wouldn't get towed. After weeks of aggravation from Mr. O'Lies, Leo impulsively decided to exact a bit of petty revenge by taking the Saab on a joyride.

He drove Jack's car around Seattle from ten in the morning until noon, blasting the radio and running the gas tank dry and feeling vindicated…until he was pulled over on Interstate 5 by three state troopers. The Saab had been involved in two DUIs. Leo was dressed in his juvenile delinquent uniform of black trench coat, blacker fingerless gloves, and blackest aviator sunglasses. And he was speeding.

"And, okay, so maybe it was closer to five o'clock," Leo said. "Or maybe six. Anyway, the cops agreed to call Jack's editor to, like, confirm that Jack had given me permission to drive his car, coz the a-hole wasn't answering his cell phone. That damned lush was off the clock, drinking it up as usual! Jack's editor told them, yes, I was an intern there. And yes,

Jack had asked me to move his car, and gave me the keys and all. It wasn't that hack from that pathetic reservation weekly—this guy was old-school, had been at the *Washingtonian* for, like, thirty-two years. The cops had the car towed back to the *Washingtonian* parking lot, Jack's editor got him to agree not to press charges against me, and I was fired on the spot."

Leo radiated unresolved bitterness.

"The state troopers handcuffed me in front of all the evening commuters crawling along at, like, three miles an hour, staring at me. Locked me in the back of a puke-smelling patrol car for over an hour. I almost ended up a felon because of that miserable a-hole. He ruined my career!" Leo said.

This little bastard with the ruined career made a helluva lot more money than I did.

I limited myself to grunting, "Ah. I see," which seemed to satisfy him.

"That's why I keep tabs on him," Leo concluded. "If he ever does anything wrong, I'm *so* gonna break that story! After he bitch-shoved me at Lake Washington last week, I figured here's my chance. Simple assault of a member of the press with video evidence, sure, but I needed more. After I uploaded the footage of him doing the deed, I camped out across the street from that dive bar by the *Washingtonian*."

"It's an historic restaurant," I said.

"Whatever," Leo said. "I figured I'd get some juicy pictures of him staggering out drunk. But when I saw you and him leave together, and watched him get in your car, I thought, even better! I had a feeling you were taking him home. I took a chance and jumped a bus to Ballard. I was right. I can't believe I actually beat you there."

"I don't navigate well in Seattle," I said defensively. "What happened after I dropped him off? He doesn't remember."

Leo smirked.

"He went into that little hole-in-the-wall tavern by his house. He drank. And drank. And then, he drank. And then, do you know what he did? He drank. But around one in the morning, he went outside."

Leo suddenly shuddered, hugging his knees to his thin chest. He looked like a frightened ten-year-old.

"I didn't notice at the time," he said. "But I wasn't the only one in there watching Jack. There was a man sitting in the back corner. A dude dressed in weird, all-green clothes. When I got up to follow Jack, the man in green was already out the door."

Leo swallowed, slow and hard.

"I heard shouting. I found Jack out in the alley behind the bar. The man in green had jumped him, but the ol' booze hound's a hell of a lot stronger than he looks. Jack had knocked him down and was punching him."

"Who?" I said.

"Him," Leo said. "Mr. Spine."

Supine: on the spine.

"I didn't know what to do. I pulled out my phone and took a couple pictures real quick—click, click, click. Jack went all deer in the headlights and ran."

Leo shut his eyes, gripping his knees tighter.

"I helped him up. Mr. Spine. He was grateful. We went back into the bar, he bought me a beer, and we got to talking. About Jack."

"Who is he?" I said. "What does he want?"

Leo opened his eyes and shook his head slowly.

"Don't find out," he said.

A keycard rattled in the keycard lock

Saturday, March 31, 9:11 a.m.

The door, against which Leo was leaning, beeped suddenly.

We both froze. The door swung inward an inch, bumping against his back. Out in the hall, there was a masculine grunt.

"It's him!" Leo gasped.

"What the hell?" a voice muttered just outside the room.

Leo jumped up and dashed into the bathroom. He slammed the door with a staccato *wham!* as Jack shouldered the motel room door open and entered.

He saw me sitting on the bed. He stopped short.

"Hi," he said. "Did you lock it?"

From the slight redness of his eyes and his difficulty with consonants, I could tell he'd had his breakfast, and it had consisted mainly of whiskey. Oh Jack...getting in touch with your Emerald Isle heritage before noon!

"Where were you? Did you go to that nasty pub across the freeway?" I accused. "I warned you about it."

"What happened to my car?" he countered, setting his keycard on the table beside my cell phone.

I sat primly at the foot of the bed. The pillow was dented from his head, the blankets twisted into a hectic tangle. I considered them casually while I considered my response.

"It's at my house," I said.

"What's it doing there?"

"I had to get home last night, didn't I?" I said. "I left you a note. I thought we were going to get breakfast. Why didn't you wait for me?"

"I got hungry," he said.

He sounded like a defensive husband. I sounded like a

shrewish wife. But he was a widower and I was someone else's spouse. I suddenly felt petty and deceitful. Especially given the fact there was a young man hiding, commedia dell'arte style, in the bathroom.

"I talked to someone who knows what happened outside the bar by your house," I said.

Jack recoiled. He collected himself almost instantly and leaned against the cheap armoire that concealed the TV. He folded his arms across his chest. His face assumed the skeptical lines of an unflappable crime reporter. He pierced me with his frigid eyes. But I could tell he was terribly anxious.

"Oh yeah?" he said. "Who?"

"A reporter. Of sorts," I said.

"Of sorts?"

"Yes."

"You mean a blogger?" he said.

"Maybe," I said.

Jack pondered this for a moment. I could chart the course of his comprehension as it crawled across his face.

"You don't mean...that little bastard!"

Jack's face went purple. Cords stood out in his neck. His hands balled into fists that resembled a pair of sledgehammers.

I rose.

"Before you freak out—do not freak out, Jack!—will you let me tell you the most important thing he had to say?"

"That horrible little punk!" Jack shouted.

"You didn't kill anyone! Isn't that great?" I said, spreading my arms wide and forcing enthusiasm into my voice.

Jack's pale blue eyes flamed like the gas burners on my stovetop back home. He looked as enraged as he'd been in the shaky video from the Lake Washington Killer crime scene, right before he pushed Leo into the mud.

He crossed the room and put his face too close to mine.

"Let me tell you," he hissed. "Exactly what that miserable little bastard is capable of."

Jack's complaint

Saturday, March 31, 9:19 a.m.

Jack endured much in his role as supervisor of Leo Krakowski, erstwhile *Washingtonian* newspaper intern. His primary grievances, in no particular order:

- Leo was always late to work.
- Leo always left early.
- Leo was never at his desk, instead spending hours hustling the flunkies in HR for a job or trying to get a piece of ass down in the all-female Arts and Entertainment newsroom.
- Leo fact-checked nothing—he preferred to check his email, Facebook, Twitter, and "I don't know what-all."
- Leo was a car thief who could not be trusted to move a fellow journalist's vehicle a mere two blocks from one parking lot to another.
- Leo was a terrible writer.

"That was the worst thing about him," Jack railed. "He couldn't write a coherent sentence to save his life."

The bathroom door flew open.

"Yeah? Really?" Leo barked.

Cue the melodramatic music.

Fights of fancy

Saturday, March 31, 9:29 a.m.

Jack said, "What are you doing here?"

Leo said, "The same thing you're doing here, idiot!"

Jack said, "This does not go on your pathetic blog. None of this, you hear me?"

Leo said, "You can't suppress the press, man."

Jack said, "You're not the press. You're barely literate."

Leo said, "Says the guy who hasn't written an article in a decade!"

Jack said, "You aggregated my articles on the Lake Washington Killer. You're a car thief and a plagiarist, you little bastard!"

Leo said, "So, you read my 'pathetic' blog after all! You're a freakin' hypocrite."

Jack shouted, "You're not a journalist!"

Leo shouted, "You're an a-hole!"

I interjected, "Guys! Can we just calm down for a minute here?"

Leo and Jack turned on me.

Leo said, "Wanna talk car thieves? Right there: She stole your car last night!"

Jack said, "Jesus Christ, what's the matter with you? First my driver's license, then my keys. And my cigarettes! And what the hell did you do with my cell phone?"

Leo said, "You think you're so much better than me because you work at some lame monthly newspaper!"

Jack said, "You only care about that book you're writing."

Leo said, "Your stupid newspaper sucks! You're no better a blogger! You're worse! Worse!"

Jack said, "You're the most frustrating woman I ever met!"

Jack glared at me. Leo sneered at me.

I shrieked, "Way to gang up on me! I thought you two hated each other. But the minute you get a chance to lay into a woman, suddenly you're on the same team—aren't you, frat brothers? To hell with you both!"

I snatched up my purse and marched myself to the motel room door. Neither of them lifted a finger to stop me. I seized the door handle, yanked it, and stalked out into the hall. They let me go without a word. I stomped down the hall toward the elevator. They didn't come after me. At the end of the hall, I realized the elevator was located in the opposite direction. I turned around and walked less and less assuredly as I approached the closed door to Jack's room. It didn't open as I passed by. I reached the elevator and pushed the down button. I glanced back at the empty hall. I was deeply hurt. How could they insult me like that, and not come after me to apologize?

Clearly they were not gentlemen.

I got on the elevator, punched the down button, and meanly took solace in the possibility that they were too busy beating the shit out of each other to bother with me.

The coroner called

Saturday, March 31, 9:38 a.m.

I got in my car, which sat slicked with rain in the motel parking lot. As soon as I put the key in the ignition, my trench coat pocket began to jangle a tune that sounded like Janis Joplin's "Ball and Chain." Mystified, I reached inside and pulled out a cell phone. It wasn't mine. It was Jack's phone—I forgot to give it back to him.

The caller ID read, "King County Coroner."

My stomach seized in a sour clench. Had something terrible happened to Lucy after all?

"Hello?" I said.

"Hello?" said a man whose voice was completely unfamiliar to me. "I'm sorry, I'm trying to reach Jack O'Lies?"

"He's not available right now," I said. "Did anything happen to his daughter?"

"Who is this, please?" the man said.

"A friend of his," I said, though "friend" was too strong a word for our vague acquaintance, in my opinion. "We switched phones last night."

"Are you Katherine?" he said.

"Yes," I said. "Who are you?"

And how do you know my name? I silently demanded.

"I'm a friend of his, too. Were you with him last night?"

"Yes," I said. "For the most part."

"Good, because I went by his house yesterday and nobody was home. I got concerned," he said.

"You're Harry, Jack's coroner friend, right?" I said. "His daughter's visiting her grandmother this weekend. He's staying up here near Everett."

"With you?" he asked.

"No! No way!" I exclaimed.

"I see," he said slowly.

A long, weird silence stretched between us. I wasn't sure what it signified.

"Could I talk to Jack for a second?" he said.

"He's not here," I said.

"When do you expect him back?"

"I don't. He's not staying with me," I said.

The weird silence fell again.

"Would you be available for a brief chat? Over coffee, maybe?" Coroner Dekins inquired.

Déjà vu. But I never said no to coffee. Even with someone who cut up dead bodies for a living.

Coffee with the coroner

Saturday, March 31, 10:08 a.m.

I met the coroner at a Starbucks equidistant from our respective homes. It was crammed into a small storefront in a nondescript strip mall just off the freeway. It looked exactly like every Starbucks I'd ever been in, which rendered the peculiar rendezvous a bit less remarkable. The coroner was waiting for me at a little table next to a picture window that looked out on the parking lot. When I saw him, I instantly remembered him from the crime scene at Lake Washington. Nine days later and without the authority of his dark blue King County Coroner windbreaker, he seemed to have aged. His eyes were weary. He looked ready for retirement.

The coroner and I had such a chat. He told me more than I ever wanted to know about Jack O'Lies. He began nearly every sentence with the phrase, "I'm not sure I should share this, but..."

These sentences ended, in chronological order, thusly:

"...Jack's an alcoholic."

"...I think Jack's in the middle of a sort of prolonged nervous breakdown that started with his wife's murder twelve years ago."

"...Jack's wife died horribly. I had nightmares about that crime scene for months."

"...Jack read my report on his wife's autopsy. Cover to cover. I would never have released the records to him, but he went all Freedom of Information Act on me, got a court order. He was so unhinged after she was killed. Sometimes I can't believe he's still alive."

"...Jack's never going to get over her murder. He loved her, but he could have gotten over her death. If she'd died the natural way, I mean. He could have eventually moved on. But he's going to blame himself for what happened to her till the day he dies."

"…I'm not sure if Jack can emotionally connect with anyone ever again. On a relationship level, I mean."

Finally, I interrupted the coroner.

"Why are you telling me all this?" I asked.

He gazed at me steadily. He had great eye contact for a guy who worked with dead people.

"I'm worried about him," he said. "Hell, I'm scared to death. I think he's finally skidding off the rails for real. But when he met you, I thought maybe…"

He trailed off into the weird silence that marked our introductory phone conversation.

"You thought what, exactly?" I said.

Coroner Harry Dekins held up his palms placatingly. I must have sounded mighty hostile.

"Look, I don't want to overstep here," he said. "But there hasn't been a woman in Jack's life since his wife died. So…"

"Oh good God!" I cried. "I'm married! I barely know him! I got his name off the internet. I met him, like, a week and a half ago after I set up an interview through his editor for a book I'm writing. You're as bad as his daughter. Why—what did he tell you? What the heck did he say about me?"

I was a conflicted amalgam of grossed out and flattered. I was married…but I wasn't dead. The thought of Jack talking about me with his friends and family in romantic terms made my skin crawl. However, I liked the idea that I still had it after all these years—and without even trying.

Coroner Dekins watched me with neutral eyes that plainly indicated he was able to track each and every thought as it registered on my face. One of these days, I had to learn how to hide my emotions.

"I understand; it's none of my business," he said. "It just seemed like he came around the corner when he met you."

Déjà vu again. Where had I heard that before?

The greatest plot twist ever

Saturday, March 31, 10:46 a.m.

I dialed my cell number as soon as I concluded my rendezvous with the coroner. Outside, hunched against the chilling rain, I held Jack's cell phone to my ear. After three rings, just as I reached my car, he answered.

"Katherine?" he said. "Where are you?"

I cut him off curtly.

"You gave me permission to investigate you, right?"

"Yeah," he replied.

"Did I give you permission to do the same to me?"

Silence flowed from Jack's line to mine.

"But you did, didn't you?" I said.

I fumbled my car keys out of my purse and opened the driver's door.

"You found out where I live. You wrote my obituary before the fact. And now, your coroner friend tells me that the two of you have been talking about me. Your *coroner* friend! What the hell, Jack?"

Another fathoms-deep silence gushed out of the cell phone into my ear. I climbed into my car and slammed the door. Rain pattered on the roof. I opened my mouth to say, "Care to explain, Jack?" when suddenly I froze.

It all made sense.

"I didn't see him when he came around the corner," Lucy said.

"When I opened my eyes, there he was," Jack said. "I didn't see him when he came around the corner."

"It just seemed like he came around the corner when he met you," the coroner said.

The corner wasn't a literal corner, but the thin veil between life and death. And the man in green wasn't a regular fella with a thing for green outerwear, but the grim reaper. The solution to the mystery I'd been wrestling with for the past week was...

I was dead!

Wait.

No. That didn't make sense. I had gone to work. I had driven press cars. I had bought groceries. I had interacted with my family. My coworkers had spoken directly to me during meetings. There hadn't been one mention of my funeral, or a single comment upon the sad absence of Katherine while I was standing right there, wailing, "Look at me! Why can't anyone see me?"

Still...

"Am I dead?" I whispered. "Please, Jack. You can tell me. Is that why you wrote my obituary? And talked to the coroner about me?"

Jack was speechless for a moment, then he let out an elephantine snort that dispelled any further melodrama I might have planned.

"Jesus Christ, Katherine," he muttered. "For the love of God."

"Well," I said defensively. "It was a very good obituary. Very accurate."

"I'm thorough," he said.

"I guess you just stalked me on the down-low and wrote a summary of my life story for the hell of it—is that it?" I said.

His silence was brief, broken by a world-weary sigh.

"Things have been so mixed up since the day we met," Jack said. "Sometimes I wonder if you're out to get me."

"Don't turn this around on me, buddy. You stalked me," I said.

"I did no such thing," he said.

"You investigated me, then," I said.

Jack, the investigative reporter, hesitated.

"Possibly," he said.

"Why?"

"You were trying to interview me," he said. "For some book

225

you're writing. Why the hell wouldn't I?"

He knew who I was and what I wanted from the start. He'd acted so obtuse when I introduced myself nine days ago. What a liar. He must have been an incredible journalist once.

"So, how boring does my story seem to you?" I said.

"What?"

"You got everything right about me. Boring birthplace, boring childhood, boring college, boring first career, boring second career. Marriage and a kid—very bourgeois and boring. Third career as a third-rate journalist. You're a very good writer, but even you couldn't make my story interesting," I said.

"Can we get a drink?" Jack said.

"You always say that," I said.

"Then say yes, for once," he said.

I sighed. I wasn't dead, so why not live a little?

The nastiest Irish pub outside Dublin

Saturday, March 31, 11:12 a.m.

We met at the nastiest Irish pub I'd ever set foot in. And I'd set more than a foot in more than my share. He was waiting for me. He was so gray. Gray Members Only jacket, gray pleated-front Dockers his daughter bought for him, button-down shirt gone gray from too many washings, graying close-cropped hair and five o'clock shadow. The only color came from the highball glass on the table, which glowed amber with what was probably scotch. And from his eyes, half-closed until I said his name, which glowed ice-blue with what may have been anger or sadness or any of a number of dark sentiments.

I sat primly across from him, clutching my purse on my lap like a Midwestern schoolmarm.

"So," I said. "Are you pissed off at me, or what?"

"Diet Coke, right?" he said.

"This place is nasty," I replied. "I won't order anything here."

Jack sighed. He turned his face away, scanning the crowded pub for the waitress.

"You're the most stubborn woman I ever met," he said.

"You *are* pissed off at me," I said. "Well, I'm pissed off at you. I'm not happy about the stalking, or the investigating, or whatever you want to call it. And you and your blogger bro said some pretty unforgivable stuff back in your motel room."

"You shouldn't have stormed out like that," Jack said. "Leo warned me the man in green knows about us. And he's planning to—"

"He knows what about us?" I said. "What 'us?' There is no 'us,' Jack!"

Distracted, I allowed my purse to fall to the pub floor, which probably hadn't been cleaned in months. It would become encrusted with liquor and pubic hair. How would I ever explain that at home? I plucked it from the floor and stood.

"This is getting out of control," I said. "It feels like the structure's falling apart. I think this is a good point for us to part ways. Before it's too late to change things."

Jack rounded on me, abandoning his hunt for the absentee waitress. His cold blue eyes stabbed through me.

"Don't go," he said.

My left hand was clenched in a fist on the grimy tabletop. My right hand was fishing through my purse for my car keys.

"I don't want to do this anymore. It wasn't supposed to turn out like this," I said.

"You always leave me," he said.

I couldn't look at him. This was the turning point. It was critical that I disconnect our lives, our stories, once and for all.

"Stay."

Jack reached across the table and almost...

Almost...

Almost covered my hand with his.

His hand hovered over mine, his fingers spread wide like the talons of a hawk descending upon a vulnerable nest. I felt the warmth of his palm radiating into my cold fingers.

He withdrew his hand just before it could touch mine.

"Stay," he said again. "I need to keep you safe."

"Oh God, Jack," I said. "You can't..."

But I had already sat back down; had already missed my chance to put an end to this series of events, which I'd hoped would be a thrilling adventure but was swiftly turning into a tragedy.

The proposal

Saturday, March 31, 11:14 a.m.

The waitress arrived with my Diet Coke just as Jack started talking about murder.

"Leo knows the man in green. The Lake Washington Killer," he said. "They had an arrangement. The man gave Leo exclusive information about the murders so he could write about them on that crime blog of his. In return, Leo gave the man a dossier on me."

The waitress nearly dropped the plastic cup of soda, sloshing a great puddle onto the tabletop. She beat a hasty retreat.

"Do you believe him?" I said, brushing futilely at the spreading lake of brown fizz.

Jack shrugged. He grabbed a handful of greasy napkins from an abandoned table and sponged patiently at the soda. I waited impatiently.

Finally, I blurted, "Well? Do you trust Leo or not?"

"I don't know," he said. "Some of what he told me rings true. But...no, I don't trust him."

"Who do you trust, Jack?" I asked.

He tossed the sodden napkins onto the opposite table, then leveled his eyes at me. They were so cold and so compelling.

"I don't trust you," I said, before he could say it himself. "You've lied to me."

He exhaled. It was not exactly a sigh.

"But I've never lied to you," I added.

Even as I said it, I realized it was a lie. But I didn't correct myself.

"I trust you," he said.

"Leo's telling the truth about the dossier. He sent it to me, too," I said.

"Why?" Jack said.

"Because he hates you," I said.

"What's in it?" he said.

"All the dirt that's fit to dish," I said. "Your DUI records. Your—wait. First, you tell me how you found out I went to Catholic school for three years. Then I'll tell you."

Jack eyed me appraisingly for a moment.

"Did the dossier change your opinion of me?" he asked.

"Sort of," I said. "I understand you better now, if you know what I mean."

"Finding out that you went to Catholic school for three years made me understand you better," Jack replied. "If you know what I mean."

I bit my lip and shook my head and gave up.

"Fine," I said. "Fair enough. Whatever—we're even, I guess."

"Leo said the man in green is after me," Jack said.

"I bet you wish you'd killed him in that alley after all," I joked halfheartedly.

Jack did not look amused.

"Do you actually believe that Leo knows him?" I said. "He's been known to exaggerate."

"He's a miserable little punk," Jack said.

"Sure he is," I said. "But is he a liar?"

"Yes, he's a liar," Jack said. "His reporting at the *Washingtonian* was full of factual errors and misquotes. And his blog is a plagiaristic disaster."

"But?" I said.

"But..." Jack said. "He reported details about the murders that the police didn't release to the media. I checked with the cops, with Harry Dekins. They confirmed it's all true."

"Are you sure Leo's not the man in green?" I said.

Jack hesitated.

"He can't be," he said.

"So..." I said.

"So...someone's after me," he said.

I nodded.
"And you," he said.

Screw you, Truman Capote!

Saturday, March 31, 11:18 a.m.

"No one's after me," I said.

Jack's ice chip eyes made me shifty. I wished he would drink more. When he was drunk, the pale perception of his gaze was veiled. Did that make me a classic enabler?

"You were right," Jack said. "I've lied to you."

"White or bald-faced?" I said.

"I've been keeping something from you," he said.

From under the table, he pulled an innocent-looking manila folder. I'd learned through bitter experience that manila folders were almost never innocent. He set it on the table. It was as thick as an old timey department store catalog. Or an issue of *Vogue* magazine during fall fashion season. They said that print was a dead medium, but I always ended up buying—

"Katherine?"

"Hm?"

"Open it."

I flipped the folder open and my heart stopped.

"I found this on my desk Thursday morning," Jack said.

It was another dossier. A dossier on me.

"I asked The Chief about you when you contacted me about the book. And I read a couple of your articles," he said. "But I never investigated you. This is where I got the information for your obituary."

"Where did it come from?" I whispered.

"There was no return address. It was mailed from Seattle. The postmark on the stamp was 98122."

The Capitol Hill neighborhood. Leo.

I glanced at Jack. I could tell he'd sussed it out faster than me. I closed the folder and shoved it at him.

"He does love putting together dossiers, doesn't he?" I managed, my voice shaking. "Leo told me he made the man in green mad. Because of this?"

Jack nodded.

"Leo had a lot to say. I took notes," he said.

He reached into his jacket pocket and withdrew a reporter's notebook. He flipped it open and began to read aloud.

"Leo: 'He wanted to kill you that night. Knock you out behind the bar, drag your drunk ass down to Lake Washington, and carve you up in the dead of night. But after he and I hooked up...change of plans. I gave him the dossier on you. He came up with the idea of sending the texts and emails and photos. To, like, torture you. Then he found out about her.'

"Me: 'How?'

"Leo: 'I'd put together a dossier on her after I met her for coffee that time. Just for my own information. He saw it. He wanted me to give it to him, but I told him hell no. She's nosy as hell, but she's a neutral party as far as I'm concerned. He got pissed at me. Really, really pissed. Now he's coming after me. And dossier or not, he's coming after her. She's perfect.'

"Me: 'How is she perfect?'

"Leo: 'Coz it'll hurt you when he kills her. That's how he does it. The fat guy in the lake, the lawyer in the condo, that fifteen-year-old kid in Ballard this morning—they're all people someone cared about. Killing's just half the fun for him. The real thrill comes from watching the people who cared about the victims suffer. Sick fuck.'

"Me: 'Why would he want to kill Katherine?'

"Leo: 'She's your girlfriend or whatever, right?'

"Me: 'What makes you think that?'

"Leo: 'Oh gee, Jack, let me see—that photo of the two of you on your porch? All the texts you send each other every freakin' day? All the phone calls? How she's constantly carting your kid to school and the mall and your mother's place? And then there's the time the three of you went to church together, family-style. Oh, and where are we right now? A motel room she paid for. Less than five miles from her house. For you both—'"

"Whoa, whoa! Hold on!" I blared loud enough to turn heads in every Celtic cranny of the pub. "Are you kidding me, Jack? What is this sick fantasy you're reading?"

"It's what Leo said," Jack replied.

"Gimme here," I said, snatching his reporter's notebook from his hand.

I scanned the pages, flipping from front to back. They were filled with the pretending-to-write squiggles of a toddler. I felt ill.

"Okay," I said, dropping the skinny notebook on the table. "I'm leaving. You are not to contact me ever again. I'm serious. I have to go…"

"Look, Katherine, I have no control over what that little bastard said—"

I shoved the notebook at him.

"He didn't say any of that!" I exclaimed. "There are no notes in this thing."

There was an odd silence from Jack. I'd had this kind of silence directed at me about a thousand times since I learned to talk. It pulled me up short, signaling incomprehension from my communicatee.

"You do realize this is shorthand?" he said slowly.

"What?" I said. "No—I mean…what?"

Nobody used shorthand anymore. I'd been accused of using it once or twice, but that was because my handwriting was abominable. The last person—the only person—I knew who wrote in shorthand was my grandmother. A former secretary straight out of the 1950s, she used it to take minutes at meetings of the secretive, quasi-Masonic women's group she belonged to. She showed me her notes once. They were a tangle of pretending-to-write toddler squiggles.

"Um…" I said. "I don't know. I mean…"

"You tape all your interviews, right?" Jack said.

"No. Not all. Not when it's noisy or I'm outside," I said.

"You take notes?" Jack said.

"Yes."

"So…show me yours," he said.

I hesitated, then I fished my identical reporter's notebook from my purse. I handed it over. Jack flipped it open and frowned.

"My God, your handwriting is horrible," he said.

"No shit, Sherlock," I snapped.

"You think you're accurate?" he said.

"Pretty accurate," I said.

"But you think I'm not," he said.

"I…I don't know," I said.

"Talk," he said.

He flipped to a blank page, pulled a pen out of his jacket pocket, and observed me expectantly.

"Oh come on, Jack!" I said. "This is stupid. Will you just— quit writing, come on! Will you stop that!"

Jack ignored me, busily writing in my notebook.

"Look, I really think we should go our separate ways and, you know, leave things the way they are…crap, I don't know. Will you quit writing, please!" I said.

He stopped writing. He regarded me for a moment, then read aloud, "'Oh come on, Jack. This is stupid. Will you just quit writing, come on. Will you stop that. Look, I really think we should go our separate ways and, you know, leave things the way they are. Crap, I don't know. Will you quit writing, please.'"

"Screw you, Truman Capote!" I said. "Don't you dare write that down, too!"

Jack frowned at me. I glared at him.

Oh damn…I started to laugh. And for the first time since we met, Jack smiled.

He held out my notebook. I took it and shoved it into my purse.

"So…" he said, still smiling.

"So…" I said, still giggling.

Oh God, he was so appealing when he looked like that! His smile gave me a heart-wrenching glimpse at the carefree man in the photo Lucy destroyed. This was the man who radiated pure joy as he bent his wife over before deeply kissing her in the warm, golden sunset. This was the man who took his wife and child on picnics where they fed friendly ducks, never realizing they were at a slaughterhouse. This was the man who was blissfully oblivious that, as bad as life could be, there were vast continents of misery yet to be explored all alone.

Both of our faces fell in unison, like mirror images.

"Leo has a point, no matter how big a liar he is," Jack said. "You're the perfect person to kill. It would destroy me."

Way to kill the mood, O'Lies.

In a guarded tone

Saturday, March 31, 11:29 a.m.

"I want you to come stay at the motel with me," Jack said.

"Why?" I said.

"It's safer."

"I doubt that."

"Just for the next twenty-four hours. Maybe forty-eight. Leo and I agreed it's the only way to protect you. We can't go back to my house. Spine knows about it. He has pictures of both of us there, thanks to Leo."

"You can hole up at the motel," I said. "Until I cancel that credit card Leo hacked, at least. I'll hide out at my house."

"Absolutely not," Jack said. "You're not leaving my sight."

"I appreciate the impulse, or whatever, Jack. But—"

"But nothing. You're staying with us at the motel."

"'Us?' You actually told Leo he could stay with you? You're one tolerant man, that's all I can say. Look, how about if I promise to call you every couple hours to let you know I'm okay? Or I'll text you—"

"No!" Jack's voice was loud. Too loud. Heads and eyes turned toward our table.

"Jack, calm d—"

"You always leave me!" he said. "You're not going anywhere without me this time."

"People are staring. Can we please not discuss this in public?"

"Fine with me. Let's go to my motel room."

"Oh Jesus," I muttered.

Jack tugged his wallet from his back pocket and began counting ones into an estimation of what we owed.

"We'll barricade the door," he said, as he laid the bills on the table. "Leo and I will take turns keeping watch. Spine can't dodge the cops forever. We'll wait him out."

"I'm not doing this," I said. "No way. Not happening. I'm going home."

Jack stopped counting his money. He stared at me with deadly eyes. I glared back at him. I saw the future he was prognosticating all too clearly. A day or two spent hunkered down in a low-budget motel room with an alcoholic crime reporter, a paranoid post-adolescent blogger, and no room service would without question result in murder. But I'd be the one who emerged with blood on my hands.

"I'm going home," I repeated. "You can't stop me. You know you can't."

Jack's jaw worked as he ground his molars together in frustration.

"Is your husband home?" he asked.

"I don't know," I said. "It's Saturday—he could be anywhere."

"Then I'm staying at your place until he comes back."

"No!" I exclaimed. More heads turned and more eyes stared.

"You can't stop me," Jack echoed infuriatingly. "You know you can't."

I opened my mouth to begin a long and shrill rant. Like a snake striking, Jack thrust his face within an inch of mine.

"Just try to stop me, Katherine," he sneered. His breath was hot and smelled of scotch. "Just try it."

I leaned back in my chair and shook my head. So this was what "exasperated" felt like.

"You're the most stubborn man I ever met," I said. "How the hell do you suggest I explain this? Serial killer after me, some random reporter sitting around my house half-drunk before noon—yes, you're a sheet and a half to the wind, I can tell! A charge for a motel room on my credit card, and your car parked a few blocks from my house all night. How exactly do I explain this?"

"To who?"

"To my husband, for Christ's sake!" I said. "Forget it, Jack. I'm not going along with this insane plan of yours."

Jack slammed his palm down on the manila folder, making the empty glasses dance on the table.

"You are not going to get yourself killed, do you hear me? I'm not leaving you—not for a goddamned minute!"

Now everyone in the pub was staring at us.

"Will you please calm the hell down!" I hissed. "You can't come to my house. It would be too weird."

"Weird?" he said with the bitterest sarcasm I'd ever heard.

"Yes, weird!"

It would have been beyond weird. I didn't know if there was a term in English, or any human language, for what it would have been if his world and my reality were to collide. Everything would implode.

"Look, wouldn't it be safer if the three of us split up? You, Leo, and me, I mean. Spine can't come after all of us at once," I said.

"You're not leaving my sight," Jack insisted.

"You're not setting foot inside my house," I countered.

Jack slumped in his chair. He pressed his forehead into his hand, his elbow resting on the tabletop. He dug his fingers into the stress lines that were permanently carved into his brow. His other hand balled into a fist on his thigh. His shoulders were up around his ears. I'd seen him look this frustrated once before. But only in a photograph.

"All right," he finally said, his voice weary. "You win. Go home. Lock all the doors. Open the drapes in every window. I'll sit in my car and keep watch."

"What?" I said. "But...why?"

Before he could answer, before I realized that he couldn't answer, I understood. He had always sat in his car and kept watch over his wife. While she did her shopping, he had watched her every move through the store windows. If anyone had tried to hurt her, he would have rushed in and saved her. But the one time—the only time—she needed him, he wasn't watching.

Twelve years later, he wanted to sit in his old yellow Saab, his eyes fixed once again on unshaded windows, patiently waiting to save the day. He wanted a second chance.

"The neighbors are gonna call the cops when they see you parked out there, staring at me through the windows like some kind of perv," I grumbled.

Jack was already on his feet.

"Give me my car keys," he said.

The ways we didn't touch

Saturday, March 31, 12:01 p.m.

Exiting the pub, our shoulders didn't graze as Jack held the door open for me.

Out in the parking lot, my hair didn't brush his face as it whipped wildly in the wind.

In my car, our elbows didn't jostle as we buckled our seatbelts.

As I gave him his cell phone and he gave me mine, our fingers didn't meet.

When I dropped him off at his car several blocks from my house, we didn't hug or shake hands.

I waved. He raised his hand slightly.

He got in his beat-up old car. In the rearview mirror, I saw him pull out onto the road and begin to slowly follow me home.

"What're you wearing?"

Saturday, March 31, 12:21 p.m.

The first thing I did when I got inside my house was open the drapes. I glanced outside. Jack's battered Saab was parked across the street from my home. He was smoking a cigarette. Even from a distance, I could tell he was staring at me intently. I settled onto my couch where I was clearly visible to him, took out my cell phone, and checked my voicemail. I discovered a message from Lucy. I listened to it and immediately began to panic.

"Katherine? It's Lucy. Could I talk to you for a minute? I'm still at Grandma's. Christopher did a very bad thing last night. I want to go to confession. Could you drive me? If you can't, I'll take the bus."

I dialed her cell phone number. She answered on the second ring.

"Katherine?" she said in a voice that was flatter than usual, as well as wobbly and as thin as tissue paper. "Can I talk to you?"

"Yes, yes, of course! What happened? Are you okay? What did he do?" I said.

She inhaled wetly.

"Something bad," she said.

"Did you go to his apartment last night?" I said.

"No."

"He didn't come to the nursing home, did he?" I said.

"No."

"But you met him somewhere? And he raped you?" I said.

"No," she said.

"Well, what happened, then?" I said.

She inhaled again and let out a soggy sigh.

If she told me he broke up with her or some such teenage irrelevance, I would reach through the phone and smack her but good for scaring me.

"He called me. Last night. Really late," she said.

"And?" I said.

"He said stuff to me," she replied.

"Stuff? What? You mean sex stuff?" I demanded impatiently.

"Yeah," she said.

She sounded like she was crying. I lost a bit of my righteous anger. She was only fifteen, after all. Her first heavy-breathing pervert call; I felt so nostalgic all of a sudden.

"He was probably drunk," I said. "Don't take it personally."

"He *was* drunk!" she sobbed. "Drunk on beer fed to him by the Evil One. They'd been watching some dirty movie. He told me."

"Well, that's gross and all, but I wouldn't get too worked up about it," I said. "Perhaps you ought to find some friends your own age. And gender."

She didn't answer, unless the snuffling sobs just barely audible through the phone could be considered an answer.

"Was it totally dirty, what he said?" I inquired.

I imagined that nineteen-year-old wannabe priest Christopher could conjure some truly obscene scenarios to describe in slurred tones late at night.

"No," she said.

"Then why are you so upset?" I asked.

Then it dawned on me.

"You said dirty stuff back to him, didn't you?" I said.

She openly sobbed.

"Y—y—yeah," fifteen-year-old wannabe nun Lucy hiccupped. "I wanna go to confession! I'm despoiled!"

"You're not despoiled," I said.

"I'm on the bus right now," she said.

My heart went cold.

"Lucy. Get off the bus. Get off now!"

She let out another little sob and hung up on me.

I ran to the window and peered out. Jack's yellow Saab was gone. I dialed his cell phone number. It rang and rang, then sent me to voicemail. I hung up and grabbed my purse.

Was it a sin to double-park
in front of a church?

Saturday, March 31, 1:14 p.m.

I pulled up in front of Sacred Heart of Jesus Catholic Church, inconveniently located in a part of Seattle that boasted the worst parking I had ever encountered. For blocks upon blocks, the curb was solidly bricked in by Detroit steel and Japanese innovation. I gave up, put on my hazard lights, and abandoned my vehicle in the middle of the street. I jumped out. Lucy was nowhere to be seen.

Standing on the stone staircase leading up to the church entrance was an impossibly tall young man.

"Christopher!" I shouted. "You stay put. I need to talk to you."

If he was guilty of violent crimes against Lucy or other unsuspecting innocents, I assumed he would bolt. I pulled out my cell phone and dialed Jack's number. Christopher stood obediently on the stairs, waiting for me.

I was dumped yet again into Jack's voicemail.

"It's me," I said. It seemed I'd finally accepted that we were on an "it's me" basis. "Lucy took the bus. I'm scared something happened to her. I'm at your church. Christopher's here, too. He did something to upset her. Call me back."

I hung up. I approached Christopher. If he tried to attack me, I wasn't sure which of us would emerge the victor. He was at least a foot taller than me, but I doubted he weighed more than I did. He had no muscle mass whatsoever.

"What did you do to Lucy last night?" I demanded.

Christopher retreated a step up the staircase. His expression was horrified.

"Nothing!" he bleated. "Why? What did she tell you?"

"Booze and a porn video, which led to late-night drunk dialing. Then you pulled the inevitable 'Are you naked?' routine," I said.

"I did not...I would never...it wasn't a porn video, exactly. I...oh, Lord Jesus!"

Christopher turned as pink as Barbie's Dream House and covered his face with his spidery hands.

"I'm such a sinner!" he moaned hollowly between his stick-like fingers. "I said unholy things about her body—a future nun's body. How will I ever get into seminary now?"

There was no way this gangly kid was a rapist/kidnapper/killer. And he wasn't wearing so much as a green sock or scarf. He continued to moan. I considered patting him consolingly on his bony shoulder, but I didn't want to give him any ideas, seeing how all it took was a couple beers and a "Girls Gone Wild" DVD to push his repressed self over the edge.

"Has Lucy called you? Or emailed or texted?" I asked.

He shook his head miserably.

"Will you take your hands down, please?" I said. "She called me. She said she was taking the bus here so she could go to confession. Have you seen her?"

Christopher clasped his hands uneasily at belt level and shook his head, his face still alarmingly pink.

"Has the bus come?" I said.

Christopher nodded.

"It only runs once every three hours from Ballard on Saturday," he said.

My heart, already beating fast, accelerated.

"Let's go check her house," I said. "Maybe she changed her mind and got off."

As we jogged to my car, I dialed Lucy's cell phone number. It went directly to voicemail.

"Lucy?" I said. "If you're on the bus, get off! There might be someone dangerous on it. Get off and call me."

Seattle Police Department media credentials were good for three years

Saturday, March 31, 1:31 p.m.

As we drove through Ballard, Christopher called the nursing home where Jack's mother lived. I was dismayed to learn that Lucy had left hours ago, informing the nurses that she was not coming back.

We pulled up in front of the O'Lies homestead. It was dark and deserted. I called Jack again. No answer. Christopher called Lucy. No answer. I called Lucy.

She picked up on the fourth ring.

"Hello?" she said.

"Lucy? Thank God—where are you?" I said.

"Katherine?" she said. She sounded small and far away. "Where's Dad?"

"I don't know. I'm trying to reach him. Where are you?"

"I don't know," she said. "There's ducks all around."

"What?" I said. "Lucy, where are you?"

Suddenly, there was a bumping sound on her end, punctuated by a voice in the background—male, jabbering incomprehensibly, and laughing with a glee that was not quite human. Lucy's line went dead.

I called her back five times. She didn't answer. So I called 911.

I was put on hold three times. The operator cited the seventy-two-hour rule for missing persons. I was dismissed. I called back and asked if they could issue an Amber Alert. I was dismissed again. Why oh why didn't I get media credentials from the Seattle Police Department when I had the chance?

Then I would have been taken seriously. All I had to do was get my newspaper's publisher to write a letter stating that I was a real, live journalist, then cart myself downtown to police headquarters to file it and receive a crummy plastic ID badge bearing my mug and moniker. Media credentials were good for three years.

"You call," I ordered Christopher.

He dialed 911 and for whatever reason (sexism), they believed him.

The cops arrived three hours later. In the meantime, I got to know Christopher so well.

First of all, he was quite the nineteen-year-old gentleman. As we sat side-by-side on the chilly front steps of Jack O'Lies' drab home, Christopher insisted upon draping his coat over my shivering frame. Not at all what I expected from the midnight phone pervert Lucy described.

Second of all, he was Catholic.

Third through seventeenth, he wanted to be a priest more than anything. Or maybe a monk. But there were temptations! They included—oh hell, you know what they included. I tuned him out as he recited, "Beer and girls and video games and pornography…"

Eighteenth, he kind of liked Lucy. But not that way.

Nineteenth through thirty-first, he was terrified that he wouldn't get into the seminary of his choice. He had doubts about his Latin. He needed to find a tutor. But there was no one in Seattle who spoke fluent Latin and was willing to take less than fifty dollars an hour for private lessons. How would he ever ascend to the rank of archbishop—his fondest dream!—and work in Vatican City if his Latin was subpar? "Even their ATM machines are in Latin," he groaned.

Thirty-second, he kind of liked Lucy…that way.

Oh God, he was going to confess the lascivious details of last night's phone sex with Lucy! I squirmed away from him. Ew…what if he'd been wearing this very coat at the time?

"You should open your mind to other career paths," I rambled, to keep him from telling me all about it. "Take me, for example. When I was your age, I thought I was going to become a surgeon. Instead, I became a journalist, and I get to talk to interesting people and tell their stories. I've interviewed the Duchess of York, Elvira Mistress of the Dark, Carrie Fisher—you know, Princess Leia from *Star Wars*—oh, and the guy who created 'CSI.' Man, he talked fast! Man, I love that show!"

Christopher gaped at me. Had I shocked him with my worldly ways?

"No way! You talked to Princess Leia? What was she like? Was she still hot? What was she wearing?" he gushed.

At that very moment, the cops rolled up: one whole cop car containing one whole cop. Our statements were taken. The cop's face registered no interest whatsoever...until I mentioned that Lucy's father was a reporter covering the Lake Washington Killer case. Like some kind of human search engine that had received the right keyword, the cop's eyes became alert. She blathered a few coded phrases into her radio, then made us give our statements all over again.

A second cop car rolled up. Then another. Then the watch commander. Christopher and I told our tales again and again. Each time Christopher had to describe how he slurred, "I like your boobs, Lucy," over the phone last night, he looked a little more suicidal.

A King County Sheriff's deputy arrived. Then the Seattle Police Department K-9 unit. Then a Washington State Trooper, for some reason. I'd never understood the division of labor among the police forces.

Then the media showed up. How ironic—the tables had been turned and the reporter became the reported! It was karmic punishment for my habit of mentally mocking my interviewees when they stammered and gave nonsensical quotes peppered with, "Uh, um, like, y'know."

I stammered into the cameras and microphones. I said, "Uh, um, like, y'know." I gave the worst interview ever.

Served me right.

Brigadoon

Saturday, March 31, 10:55 p.m.

When I was a child, a neighbor once told me about the land of Brigadoon. She was a one-time professional ballerina turned full-time anorexic. She had a flair for the dramatic. She told me that Brigadoon was a magical place that you could only stumble upon by chance. In Brigadoon, every day was a thrilling adventure. But if you left, you would never, ever find it again. Even if you searched for the rest of your life. I thought then, and I still thought to this day, that this was the greatest tragedy imaginable.

I called Jack nine more times before I gave up and went to bed.

Easter Sunday

Sunday, April 1, 10:04 p.m.

I didn't hear from Jack all day. I called him twenty-two times.

You have not reached Laptop Land

Monday, April 2, 8:56 a.m.

My cell phone rang just as I settled myself behind my desk at work. I glanced at the caller ID. It was prefixed by a 206 area code, meaning it was from Seattle proper. I didn't recognize the number. Normally I didn't answer unfamiliar calls—especially from the 206 area code. It was almost always someone mumbling, "Uh, yeah, I was wondering if you carry laptop cords?" Then, trying not to sound bitchy but always sounding bitchy, I was obliged to reply, "This is a private cell phone. Laptop Land is not at this number."

My cell phone was cursed with the discarded phone number of a small-scale computer repair business. The Yellow Pages called me once to check on the status of Laptop Land. I begged them to remove my number from their business listings. They said they would, and maybe they did, but the internet listing would never die.

In the last two days, I had been getting a lot of calls from phone numbers I didn't recognize—most of them prefixed by the 206 area code. Despite the threat of laptop inquiries, I had answered all of them.

Because it might have been Jack.

Because I was so worried about him.

Because I hadn't heard from him since Saturday.

The previous six times my phone rang that morning, prior to my arrival at work, it was:

1. The cops (Seattle Police Department)
2. The *Seattle Times*
3. Channel 5 News
4. The cops (King County Sheriff's Office)

5. Some Leo-like crime blogger

6. Laptop replacement battery request

I grabbed my ringing cell phone and said, "Hello?"

There was a long silence on the other end. Ordinarily, I would hang up when there was a long silence. In my experience, it indicated the unwelcome presence of a telemarketer. But then I heard a slow inhalation, cut off by a smoker's cough.

"Hey. It's me," a weak voice said.

"Jack?" I said.

"Yeah," he said, then coughed again. "You okay?"

"Oh, my God! Are *you* okay? I've called you about a hundred times. Where are you?"

"Harborview," he said. "Are you safe?"

"Me? I'm fine. Did you say Harborview? What are you doing at the hospital?"

There was another slow inhalation, then a belabored exhalation that was half-cough, half-sigh.

"Could you come?" he said. "Please? I have to talk to you."

The best place in the world
to have a heart attack

Monday, April 2, 9:37 a.m.

I sped the entire way to Harborview Hospital, situated just south of downtown Seattle. Sprawling, bloated with innumerable specialty clinics, and equipped with high-tech medical marvels with unpronounceable names, it was the place paramedics took you when something very bad had happened to you. It was not far from the headquarters of my second career, circa my mid-twenties. The war refugees to whom I played social worker used to bring their U.S.-born babies to Harborview's emergency room every time they had so much as a cold. They told me they'd seen too many babies (their own, sometimes several) die in the camps from simple diarrhea or a cough that turned deadly. When they went to Harborview seeking emergency care for a case of the sniffles or a tummy ache, none of their babies died. But it annoyed the triage nurses no end.

I asked after Jack O'Lies at the reception desk. I was directed to another desk on another floor. HIPAA privacy laws were invoked, then Jack's records were consulted via computer. For some reason, I was on his emergency contact list. I was directed to the intensive care unit down a long, greenish-gray hall lit by shuddery fluorescent lights.

Oh God…

I found Jack in a hospital bed. He was in a paper gown. He had an oxygen tube in his nose. His eyes were closed. He looked terrible. I crumbled inside.

"Oh God, Jack…" I murmured, stopping short a good six

feet from his bed. "What happened to you? Are you okay? No, obviously not. But…what happened?"

His eyes opened slowly. They drifted to me. They widened slightly…brightened slightly. This was the perfect time to breach the barrier at last. I could step up to his bed and place my palm on his chalk-white brow. Or take his blue hand and hold it tight in mine. And finally tell him the truth.

Instead, I awkwardly grasped a spindly chair stationed like an afterthought near his thrumming heart monitor. I scraped it loudly across the linoleum and sat next to his bed. Not too close. But sort of close. I was horrified and, to my shame, repulsed to see him reduced to this medical specimen. He resembled his Alzheimer's addled mother. When I looked at him, it made the marrow ache deep in my bones.

"Can you breathe okay?" I asked. "I had one of those things in my nose when I was in labor years ago. I hated it. Jack? Are you…can you answer me? Oh Jesus, what happened to you?"

Jack did not reach for my hand as he lay limp in his hospital bed. But his eyes reached for mine. He coughed the rheumy cough I knew so well back when I smoked.

"Katherine?" he said.

His voice was so ragged I could barely hear him.

"Yes," I said. "I'm here. Do you want to tell me what happened?"

Jack coughed again. He inhaled hard, his chest hitching under the paper gown.

"He tried to kill Lucy," he said. "But I saved her. She's okay. I…"

Jack coughed again. His eyes closed, then opened again, then slowly, slowly closed.

"Talk to me," I begged. "Please, Jack. I don't know what to say."

He opened his eyes, slowly, slowly.

"Don't leave," he said.

"I won't."

"Yes, you will," he said. "Can we talk? One last time?"

"Of course—yes, of course we can. And I won't leave, I

promise."

"You can't record this, Katherine," Jack said.

He paused to draw a breath. He was as pale as the moon.

"You can't take notes," he said. "Just listen."

He coughed for a solid sixty seconds, making his heart monitor pick up to a gallop. Then he laid very still, gasping shallowly as the monitor gradually slowed.

At last, he said, "I know."

I said, "You know what?"

He looked at me with the uncompromising gaze of one whose eyes have, at long last, been opened. He looked like the embodiment of revelation.

"I know the truth," he said.

My heart sank.

"From the moment we met, you made no sense to me," he said. "There was always something…false about you. Like you didn't belong here."

I didn't like where this was going.

"Now I know why you were so frustrating," he said. "You've been doing your best to live like a person in a book."

"We're paraphrasing Kurt Vonnegut now?" I said, with an uneasy half-laugh.

"I know, Katherine." Jack said. "I *know*."

I looked at him carefully; at his eyes, which had never been clearer or more wounded.

He did know.

"Damn," I muttered. "I should have killed him off when I had the chance."

I forgot to mention...

Saturday, March 31, 10:55 p.m.

On Saturday, the night before Easter, I called Jack nine more times before I gave up and went to bed. Just as I was tugging the quilt up over my head, I heard a far-off ringing.

My cell phone.

I jumped out of bed and rushed through the dark house, stumbling against furniture. I pawed through my purse blindly and fished my phone out. The glowing screen was blurry without my contacts or glasses. I couldn't make out the caller ID. I fumbled for the talk button.

"Jack? Is that you?" I said. "Hello?"

"Hey. It's me."

I slowly stood up straight. My heart began to pound so hard I felt dizzy.

"Spine," I said.

"Hi," Spine said. "Too late to call? Did I wake you?"

"What do you want? I told you never to call me."

"Don't get worked up. I've got something to tell you."

That sing-song voice, taunting and tempting.

"What?" I said.

"It's quite a story. You're gonna love it."

"What did you do this time?" I said.

"The best thing I've ever done," he laughed. "Better than you could possibly dream. Trust me, you are gonna *love* it!"

Slaughterhouse

Saturday, March 31, 10:58 p.m.

Spine told me such a tale.

Jack got a call on his cell phone two minutes after I left him sitting outside my house in his parked car. It was Leo. His voice sounded wrong. Like there was something around his throat. A hand, maybe.

"Slaughterhouse," Leo said.

That was all. The line went dead. It only took Jack a moment to realize what had happened.

"What? What happened?" I demanded. "I don't get it. Spine? What did you do?"

"I'm getting to that," Spine said, his voice infuriatingly unhurried. "I decided to take the bus today. I was heading up north to scoop up your boy Leo from that motel where you hid him."

The deep, silken timbre of Spine's voice made my skin crawl, even filtered through my cell phone's bass-poor speaker.

"Anyway," he continued, speaking so slowly he was nearly drawling. "Guess who I found riding alone in the back of the Ballard bus, all forlorn? Yes. *Her.* Did I mention I was wearing my green priest's cassock? I got it at a costume shop last Halloween."

Oh God. Poor Lucy. She never stood a chance. In my dark living room, I sank down onto the couch and cradled my cell phone gingerly against my ear. I desperately wanted to hang up so I wouldn't have to hear what he did to her.

"The kiddo was a mess," Spine said. "She told me everything. The back row of an empty bus makes a great confessional—have you noticed that?"

"I don't talk to people on the bus," I said.

"Not anymore, you don't," Spine said knowingly. "She does, though. She told me all the dirty details. That Christopher. What a sexual whack job."

"Well, he wants to be a priest," I said.

"And Lucy wants to be a nun," Spine laughed. "But now, she knows she can't. After she finished blubbering, I took her hand and told her, 'No, dear child of God, you are destined for greater things. You are destined to become a martyr.'"

"She went with you, didn't she?"

"Like a meek little lamb," he said. "She wanted to be a saint in the worst way. She's a hard-core zealot, that one."

"Tell me you let her go," I said. "You just scared her a little, then you let her go."

Spine chuckled.

"What fun would that be? I took her to my lair. You hide out in a cheap motel, I take over a slaughterhouse. That, my friend, is how I roll."

"I'm not your friend," I said. "Where are you right now? You're not standing outside my house, or hiding in my downstairs bathroom, or anything out of a horror novel, are you?"

"I am where I am. Don't worry about it," he replied.

"But—"

"Do you want to hear this story or not?"

I said nothing. Spine took my silence as consent. How like him.

"I told her I could give her full absolution of her sins at my private chapel. She bought it. She bought it right up until we got inside the slaughterhouse and she saw Leo hanging from a meat hook."

"You—"

"Oh, he wasn't dead," Spine hastened to amend. "I just trussed him up. I *really* wanted that dossier on you. You're so secretive!"

"Wait a minute," I said. "How did you get in there? Isn't the slaughterhouse still in operation?"

"No, those industrious Indians closed it down years ago. The casino business is booming."

"But why did you take her there? You're the Lake Washington Killer. The slaughterhouse is nowhere near Lake Washington."

"This is my story. Let me tell it my way," Spine said.

"This is not your story," I retorted.

"It is now," he said.

I bit my lip to keep from arguing. I didn't want to encourage him.

"What did you do to Lucy? And Leo?" I said.

"The thing is, you'll never figure me out. Never. That's why we've had such a hard time working together."

"Spine! Tell me what you did!"

"It's not what I did. It's what Jack did."

I had to hold the cell phone with both hands to keep from dropping it. My fingers were numb and my hands were shaking terribly.

"Did you kidnap him, too?"

Spine snorted.

"You call yourself a writer? You have no imagination," he said. "I did no such thing. No, good ol' Jack just showed up— a cavalry of one, gun drawn and ready for a fight."

"Gun?" I repeated. "Since when does he have a gun?"

"You tell me," Spine said. "It was very inconvenient. I had Lucy hog-tied. Leo was primed for a slow cutting. Worst possible moment to be interrupted. Terrible timing."

"Did you—"

"If you don't shut up, you'll miss the climax," he said. "So there I was, blade at the ready, and Jack kicks in the door. Leo starts screaming, Lucy's bawling, and Jack's pointing his gun all around, shouting, 'Let her go! Let her go!' Very dramatic. Very novelistic. I had my blade pressed right against Lucy's jugular. I knew what I was supposed to say—what you wanted me to say. Shall we say it together? 'You thought you could save the day this time, Jack? You can't. I'm going to rape and murder your daughter, just like your wife. But this time, you can watch.

It will destroy you.'"

"Oh, my God…" I whispered.

"But," Spine said. "But I didn't say it. I took a good, long look at Jack. He was standing in the middle of the rusted floor grating, wild-eyed, frantic. He was begging me to let his daughter go. Begging me not to destroy him. All of a sudden, I felt sorry for him. And, at the same time, I realized that I'm sick of following your plot. So I decided to ruin it."

"Wait," I said. "Spine. What the hell did you do?"

Spine paused luxuriantly.

"I told Jack the truth."

"The truth?"

"I told him that you made all of this up."

Even the combined grip of both of my hands on the phone was not enough. It slipped out of my fingers and bounced across the carpet. I was stunned. And so very angry I couldn't think. I stared at the blank, black TV screen, my mind blanker and blacker. Several feet away, Spine prattled on, voluble yet barely audible. It was several minutes before I could force myself to pick up my phone and bring it back to my ear.

"Hello? Katherine? Hello?" he was chanting in a tone of utter amusement.

"What the hell did you do that for?" I growled. "Damn you! You've ruined the book. You've ruined everything!"

"Exactly!" he said. "I told you this was my story."

"This—you—this is why I cut all your dialogue, all your scenes! You're so damned unpredictable! You never follow the plot."

"Have you considered that perhaps the plot was flawed from the start?" he inquired.

"Shut up," I snapped.

"You're the boss," he said, a sardonic lilt bedecking the last word.

"What am I supposed to do now?" I demanded. "Damn. I should have killed you off when I had the chance."

"But then you would've had no antagonist," Spine said.

"What about Leo?" I said.

Spine burst out laughing.

"You've got to be kidding!"

"Okay. What about me?"

"You? You've got too much sympathy for your protagonist. Stick to the omniscient narrator gig."

"I'm hardly omniscient," I muttered. "I didn't see this stunt of yours coming. Jack didn't believe you. Did he?"

"He's a writer. A better writer than you. All I had to do was point out the plot holes."

"What plot holes?"

"Good lord, where to start?" Spine mused. "Jack somehow knew the fat corpse from Lake Washington had 'Spine' written on the left heel. And he knew it was a name. How could he know?"

"Um."

"Jack knew you wanted him to write your obituary. He said it to your face: 'I left our obituaries with my editor because you wanted me to.' You had to put the brakes on that yourself, remember?"

"Uh."

"When Leo followed Jack to the Three Coins to, as he so eloquently put it, 'get some juicy pictures of him staggering out drunk,' why didn't he bring along his expensive camera? There was no reason for him to use his phone to snap blurry shots of Jack whaling on me in the alley."

"Well..."

"But the kicker, the thing that finally convinced Jack that I was telling the truth, was the photo of his wife."

"What photo?"

"The one he took right here, at the slaughterhouse, twelve years ago," Spine replied. I could hear his reptilian grin through the phone.

"What about it?"

"He took the photo of his wife feeding the ducks exactly one week before she died. Remember what he told you at that godawful bar? 'We went on a picnic. We did that every weekend. Except when I had to work.'"

"So?" I said.

"So," Spine said. "Every Sunday, Jack's wife went to the store to buy bread for the ducks, while Jack waited out in the car. And every Sunday, her killer watched her, waiting for his chance to strike. Right?"

"Right," I said. "So?"

"So," Spine replied. "I reminded Jack of a simple fact, then asked him a simple question. First, the fact: He told you himself that he'd been putting in fourteen-hour days for weeks. No time off, not even weekends. One week before his wife died, he didn't take his family on a picnic at this scenic slaughterhouse. He was at work."

I said nothing.

"Now, the question: How did he take a photo of his wife at the slaughterhouse if he wasn't there?"

I said nothing.

"Katherine? Hello?"

"Shit," I said. "I missed that."

"I didn't," Spine replied. "I spotted every plot hole. And so did Jack, once I started pointing them out. He's a much better writer than you. He wouldn't have made such mistakes."

"Shit," I repeated. "How did he take it?"

"His fevered brain grappled with the truth for a while. But then he…well. I think I'll let him tell you all about the next part himself. If he can," Spine added ominously.

He hung up on me. I sat in the dark for a long time, listening to the dial tone. Did he say, "if he can," because it wasn't my murder or Lucy's murder, but the truth that was destined to destroy Jack? Spine had known for a long time that he wasn't real. And he didn't care. But Jack was different.

I should never have written so many drafts of the chapters Spine dominated early on, before I gave up and relegated him to the role of "mysterious villain." All those rewrites acted on him like uncanny déjà vu, making him self-aware. Wasn't that exactly what déjà vu felt like—a passage you read long ago, the familiarity of the plot and characters and scenery and dialogue jumping into stark relief just for an instant?

I often experienced such moments. I wondered who was rewriting me.

The truth is worse than death

Monday, April 2, 9:52 a.m.

From his hospital bed, Jack said, "You are a murderer."

"Me? No!" I protested. "I've never killed anyone in my life!"

"You killed my wife," he said.

"The Westgate Serial Killer murdered her," I said.

"For the book?"

"Yeah."

"What kind of book is this, even? A memoir? A novel?"

"It was supposed to be a memoir. But my life is too boring. So I started changing things. Adding things."

Above the oxygen tube in his nose, Jack's blue eyes were steady.

"You killed her. You. You could have let me get to her in time. But you made her die just before I reached her."

"Yeah," I admitted.

"Why?"

"I needed you to be a widower," I said.

"For the book?" he said.

I nodded.

"That's so goddamned simplistic—don't you see?" he snarled.

"I...I don't know what you mean."

He struggled to sit up. His face was clotted with fury.

"If you'd let her live, do you realize how much less gimmicky and two-dimensional this story would have been?"

"No?" I said.

"Think about it!" he exclaimed.

His heart monitor trilled an alarm. He bit the inside of his cheek and waited until the noise subsided.

"You killed my wife. You gave me some vaguely sketched serial killer as an antagonist. And then...what? You showed up to watch me suffer?"

"What do you want from me, Jack?" I cried. "You want me to say this is all my fault? That I got it wrong—that I should have let your wife survive?"

"Yes!" he raged. "You did this to me. You made me a bad father and a failure and an alcoholic and a miserable, broken man, and it all started with her death. Change it!"

"How? Some kind of bullshit deus ex machina? Is that what you're asking for? A happy ending?"

"Let me get to her in time," he said. "That's what I'm asking for. Please."

He wasn't shouting anymore. His face was twisted, but not in anger. In agony. He reached for my hand. His fingers were dead white and shaking. I pulled my hand away before he could touch it. Because he couldn't touch it, because he wasn't real.

"Please, Katherine. You owe me—own me. You promised you'd help me. Just change it. Nothing else. Please?"

"Jack—"

"Please, Katherine. Please."

I sighed, long and hard and defeated. Spine was right. I had too much sympathy for my protagonist.

Rewrite

Thursday, March 22, 10:12 a.m.

The crime scene was located on the western shore of Lake Washington, where the coarse gray sand met rain-churned mud. I parked between a Washington State Patrol car and a Seattle Police Department cruiser. The King County Sheriff was on scene too, his car sandwiched between a pair of TV news vans. I'd never understood the division of labor among the various cop agencies. I wasn't that kind of journalist.

I didn't get out of my car. Outside, chaos reigned as cops and marauding ducks fought to defend their strongholds between the mucky bank, the gently lapping water, and the yellow tape emblazoned with the warning "Police Line Do Not Cross" that separated them. Through my windshield, I could see a major media convergence zone just outside the yellow tape. I covered a story here once before. I ought to have felt right at home.

When my press club buddy, John Whiteclay, and I set up our quasi-professional job shadowing scheme a few weeks ago, I did not expect I'd be tagging along with him to a murder scene. I figured I'd hang out with him in the hallowed halls of the *Washingtonian*, drinking a cappuccino from the lobby coffee cart and listening to the police scanners for a couple hours. Then I'd scoot back north where I belonged and add "on-the-job training in crime reporting" to my resume. Though he'd gamely gone along with the job shadow idea when I proposed it, I doubted John would ever avail himself of the opportunity to join me at my place of employment. I had described the dull rigors of my average workday too vividly.

I got out of the car. I pulled out my cell phone, scanning the journalistic crowd for John's unmistakable waist-length black braid and red Che Guevara T-shirt. I took a deep breath and begin to walk toward the other reporters. I dialed John's cell number, my eyes roving the crowd.

"Whiteclay," he answered in an irritable voice.

"Hey, it's Katherine. I'm here in the parking lot, knee-deep in cops. Where are you?"

"Huh," he grunted. "The Chief usurped when the AP wire started buzzing about it being a serial killer body dump instead of the usual hobo floater. God, I hate him!"

"So, where are you?" I said.

"Work. The jerk took the damned intern with him and left me manning the damned scanners for the damned Harbor Patrol. Yeah, that's right: the goddamned Harbor Patrol!"

Since the day we met, John had been complaining about his boss, an old-school editor who rose up the ranks from John's own position as lowly crime reporter. He habitually called his boss "The Chief." He only let his editor's real name slip once during a particularly baroque lament on his favorite topic, "Why I hate my job." Seated next to John at the Three Coins bar, where the press club met each month, I googled the unfamiliar name and cut him off mid-rant.

"Whoa!" I said. "Why is your editor hitting over and over with the words 'serial killer?'"

Annoyed at my interruption of his tirade, John had waved his hand dismissively.

"Yeah, his wife got involved or hurt or something when he was covering the Green River Killer or whatever about a hundred decades ago. Meanwhile, I'm on traffic court duty all day while the damned intern gets to photograph the erotic massage parlor raid on Highway 99. Prostitutes lined up for blocks, and I'm listening to, 'Eighty-dollar fine; pay the clerk and it won't go on your driving record,' repeated ad infinitum. God, I hate my job."

Ever since that night, I wanted to meet John's editor. I'd been hoping to run into him between the coffee cart and the police scanners today.

"Anyway, I'm stuck here," John was saying through the tinny speaker of my cell phone as I picked my way through the chaos of muddy shoreline, wandering cops, eager media, and belligerent ducks. "Want to come keep me company? I'm bored as hell."

"Oh, well, I'm already here and all. I think I'll check it out for a bit," I said, hanging up on him absentmindedly.

Where might John's editor be?

I was unsteady in the ooze that constituted the floor of the crime scene. I could barely navigate the slurry of sand mixed with mud. I stopped slogging and peered across the yellow police tape.

I had no idea what John's editor looked like.

I spied an idle newspaper reporter, identifiable by her jeans, sensible shoes, and decades-old but carefully pressed suit jacket. She was leaning against an ambulance, smoking and poking at her iPhone with a short-nailed thumb.

"Excuse me? You don't happen to know if Jack O'Lies from the *Washingtonian* is around here somewhere?" I said.

She pointed her cigarette at an open space beyond the yellow tape.

"Over there with the coroner. Can't believe Muhammad actually came to the mountain for once," she said.

The cigarette indicated a black guy in his fifties who was talking with a white guy. The white guy looked to be in his forties, with graying hair hacked into a super-short crew cut. He sported a couple days' worth of beard growth that would have looked sexy on a movie star in his twenties but didn't work for a professional man over the age of thirty. The black guy was wearing a dark blue windbreaker that loudly proclaimed "King County Coroner" in a sans-serif font across the chest.

I took a deep breath and contemplated the forbidding yellow tape that separated us. I glanced around. There was a gawky kid in a trench coat standing next to the white guy. His trench coat screamed "I'm a reporter!" more blatantly than mine. He was clearly an intern. I ducked under the tape and approached. Before I could reach the trio, the white guy smacked the coroner on the shoulder with his reporter's notebook (good-naturedly), jerked his head at the kid (brusquely), and began to walk toward me (blindly).

"Excuse me? Excuse me," I said, as he bore down on me. "Jack O'Lies? Jack?"

He halted. He turned to look at me. His pale blue eyes registered nothing at all.

"Hi," I said. "Sorry to bother you while you're working. I was wondering if you have a minute? I was hoping to talk to you about, um…"

How to say it? Your wife's kidnapping twelve years ago? What it's like to be married to a serial killer survivor? The worst thing you and your family ever went through?

"Uh…" I fumbled. "Could I set up a brief interview with you, possibly?"

"We aren't hiring," he replied curtly.

"No, no, I'm not—"

Before I could finish, he jerked his head at the trench coat clad kid a second time and resumed his march past me. I watched them go: Jack O'Lies striding purposefully through the squelching mud, his intern trotting dutifully behind him.

It felt wrong.

The Ballard of three lovers

Wednesday, March 28, 2:49 p.m.

I called Jack O'Lies to set up an interview (multiple times, all sent to voicemail) and I emailed him (multiple times, all unanswered). I never thought I'd eventually have to resort to the lowest of tactics, namely contacting his intern.

I'd had interns before. I understood their menial minds. It took me exactly two and a half minutes to gain the confidence of Leo Krakowski, a gung-ho whippersnapper majoring in journalism at the University of Washington, occasional contributor to the *UW Daily* student newspaper and various college lifestyle blogs, and valued intern at the *Washingtonian*. I promised to take a look at his writing samples and resume. He promised to set up an interview with Jack.

"Hey, even better! Why don't you come over to his place tonight?" Leo said eagerly. "You can tag along with me—I was planning to swing by after work."

"He told you to come to his house after work?" I said skeptically. That was a task I'd never asked my interns to undertake.

"No, but it's cool. I'm dating his daughter. She's real cute. He's totally cool with it."

Three hours later, I found myself seated uncomfortably on a grubby pink beanbag chair, clutching a glass of Hawaiian Punch liberally spiked with vodka.

"Dad'll be home at six," Lucy promised.

She was lying on her pink canopy bed, entwined in the arms of her gangly Boyfriend Number Two, while "cool with it" Leo flipped through old CDs stacked on top of her stereo.

"I wish you'd warned me before you gave me this," I said

for the second (or sixth?) time, as I set the half-empty glass unsteadily on the carpet. "Now I can't drive for at least an hour. Maybe two. I wish you'd warned me."

The bartender in this travesty of unintentional intoxication, Christopher, reached out and grabbed the glass before it could tip over. My God, his arms were eight miles long!

"Relax," he said, taking a drink from my glass. "Where've you got to be?"

"Home," I said. "It's a work night, you know. And a school night for you kids."

"Dad'll be home by seven-thirty at the latest," Lucy said.

Her voice was as flat as Kansas and her bare arms were gullied by old scars of varying depth. She looked a lot like Jack if he lost forty pounds. I had never seen a girl with so many bones poking at such odd angles through such lifeless, Kleenex-colored skin. Christopher stroked Lucy's hair and drank my Hawaiian Punch while she stared unnervingly at me from between eyelids demarcated by fat lines of cheap gray eyeliner.

"Or maybe nine. Who the hell knows with him?" she said. "What do you want to see him for?"

"It would bore you," I replied nonchalantly, trying to make up for the "school night for you kids" thing. When Lucy and Christopher started kissing, I rose unsteadily. Leo continued to flip through the CDs, their plastic cases ticking against each other steadily, like a clock. I'd had enough.

"Tell you what," I said. "How about I go wait for your dad downstairs?"

"Mom's downstairs," Lucy managed to mutter around Christopher's lips.

"Hey, cool! I love these guys! Let's dance," Leo enthused, brandishing a CD.

"Dance with her," Lucy snorted, tossing a look of scorn first at Leo, then at me.

"Yeah, no, I think not," I said, fumbling for words that didn't naturally slur. Now that I was vertical, the juvenile cocktail was making itself felt in a big way. "I'll just go chat with your mom."

Lucy sat up in alarm.

"She's sleeping," she said.

"It's fine, don't worry," I said, as I minced with exceeding care across the challenging terrain of Lucy's stained shag carpet.

"Don't wake her up," Lucy ordered.

"We'll chat briefly. Woman to woman."

"Leave her the hell alone!" Lucy shrilled.

Christopher gripped her shoulders, which were trembling as if she was in the throes of an epileptic fit. I glanced from Christopher to Leo. Leo shook his head at me. His face was stricken.

"Gotcha," I said.

I gave the teens a thumbs-up, wobbled away from their strange ménage à trois, and closed the door too hard behind me. I paused in the dim hall to regroup. Hard liquor was not my friend.

When I arrived at this dingy Ballard abode, there was a large lump lying on the living room couch, wrapped from head to toe in an orange and brown hand-crocheted afghan. I had passed it as I made my way through this house of lies—O'Lies, I mean. I remembered it was the size of a human body. Lucy had hustled me away from it with excessive alacrity.

I figured I'd go give it a poke and see what happened.

Jack's wife

Wednesday, March 28, 6:47 p.m.

The living room of the O'Lies house was deserted. The couch was vacant. There was no one in the kitchen or the bathroom. I didn't dare call out, for fear of teenaged Lucy's wrath. I didn't know what to do with myself. So I wandered out onto the porch to wait for Jack.

The evening air was chilly. I sat gingerly on a moldy 1970s-era sofa parked under the front window. I inhaled deeply. My head began to clear as the scents of salt water from Puget Sound and decaying fire-retardant fabric from the cushions mingled in my nostrils. The setting sun was throwing off bands of red and gold behind the neighboring roofs. This struck me as a great place to morosely smoke while contemplating the rusted Ford pickup truck on cinderblocks in the yard across the street, blue-collar philosopher style. I wondered if Jack ever did that.

I caught a flicker of motion in my peripheral vision. Someone was coming out the front door and was moving towards me. The sofa cushions jarred as someone sat beside me. I expected Lucy or Leo. Or maybe Jack, having arrived home unannounced through the back door.

I turned to see who it was.

It was Jack's wife.

When I saw her face, my heart stopped. My breath stopped. My blinking, my nervous toe-tapping, and my thoughts stopped. The entire world stopped.

It was the most gruesome face I had ever seen.

I dropped my gaze to the pitted cement of the porch. I swallowed hard.

I had to look at her.

I turned my eyes reluctantly back to Jack's wife. I focused on her scuffed white Keds, her mom jeans cut in an unflattering pegged style, her oversized University of Washington sweatshirt undoubtedly nabbed from her husband's closet, her mop of curly brown hair missing in odd patches along her scalp.

She darted a finger and thumb into a crumpled pack of cigarettes, a lighter clutched in the hollow of her palm. She turned her face away from mine as she hunched over the lighter, her hands cupping around the flame to protect it from the wind.

I felt I should say something. Simultaneously, I felt I should not. As she straightened up, I shot my gaze over to a broken-down swing set listing wearily against a stunted apple tree three houses down.

"Want one?"

Her voice was so normal. Her face was so horrifying. But I knew I had to look at it. Surely my avoidance was worse than the expression of barely contained shock in my eyes.

I couldn't look at her. Instead, I stared at the cigarette pack clutched in her hand. Ah, Marlboros! My brand of choice, back when I smoked.

"No," I said. "Thank you."

As I spoke, I realized that I had paused for so long my reply to her question sounded nonsensical.

"You're here for Jack?" she asked.

"Yes," I said.

"Mm," she said.

She was awfully quiet. Was she staring at me? Why would she do that? Well, if I happened to be napping on my living room couch and a strange woman showed up on my porch wanting to see my husband, what would I do?

It was imperative that I force myself to look at her. It was the least I could do.

I dragged my gaze to her face (her hideous, hideous face) and locked my eyes on hers. They were mud brown. One of them seemed larger and duller than the other. It didn't move. It was dead, like the plastic eye of a mannequin in a store window. Her eyelids were jagged, with frayed edges like torn newspaper. There were only a few eyelashes, and they were clustered at the corner of her left eye like the bristles on the back of a blowfly.

"I'm a journalist," I said. I thought I said it. My mouth moved in the shape of the words.

Gray smoke encircled her head like the dirty halo of a ruined saint. Her flayed lips parted in three sections rather than two, issuing more smoke. She had very, very few teeth.

"You're from the *Washingtonian*?"

"No," I said. "I'm from the *Journal*. It's a monthly."

"Yeah," she said. "We used to get it. Years and years ago. You don't work with Jack, then?"

"No," I said.

"Mm."

Her cigarette hovered in the void space where her nose should have been.

"I'm here to interview him," I said.

"Why?"

Could I look away yet? Had it been long enough? If I looked away too soon, I would seem shifty. Like I was lying. Or disgusted.

"Well," I said. "I'm actually interested in talking to you, too. For a book that I'm...um. I understand that you are...were...uh...."

Behold my bold interviewing technique! Further evidence that I was no heir to Barbara Walters, Diane Sawyer, or Rachel Maddow.

"Um," I concluded. "So, do you know when your husband will be home?"

"Ex-husband," she said.

"Oh, right," I said. "Wait. What?"

"Want a drink?" she asked, making to rise.

I noticed, for the first time, there was a metal cane resting against the couch next to her. I also noticed, as she gripped it, she was missing the tips of three fingers on her left hand. And I further noticed the remaining fingers didn't have nails.

"No, thanks," I said. "He's your ex-husband?"

"Jack will be home sometime," she said, fumbling with the cane as she got to her feet. "Seven, nine. Midnight. You never know with him. You should have a drink."

"I have to drive," I said. "He's really your ex-husband?"

"Yeah," she said.

"How did that happen? If you don't mind me asking."

She was grotesque, but Jack couldn't possibly be such a cold-hearted bastard. Could he?

"It's complicated," she said.

"I'm sure," I said.

"I'm gonna get a drink," she said. "Want one or not?"

To appease her, to get her peculiar plastic eye and the unmatched real one off me, I said, "Sure."

She limped into the house, her body nearly collapsing over the cane with each step. When she returned, she had a bottle of scotch and two glasses.

And five pictures.

Spared change

Wednesday, March 28, 7:39 p.m.

Jack arrived home as the sun was sinking with a weak blaze of color behind the neighboring houses. I was waiting for him on his front porch. His wife—his ex-wife—was sleeping in their bedroom, the door firmly closed.

He parked his run-down yellow Saab in the driveway. He shouldered the driver's side door closed, hefting a sizeable briefcase and a dented travel mug marked with a peeling *Washingtonian* logo.

He looked tired. I could tell he was stone sober. His eyes were sharper than I had ever seen them. They narrowed with recognition when they alighted on me. And with displeasure. I was taken aback. He had never looked at me with such loathing before. I wondered if he remembered me from the Lake Washington crime scene last week, when he curtly snapped, "We aren't hiring." Or maybe, just maybe, he remembered me from the previous story he rejected. Was there a glimmer of memory left from the time we sat on this very porch in a different draft of this day? I knew shouldn't hope so. But I did.

"Jack," I said, half-rising awkwardly, then sitting back down even more awkwardly. "Remember me?"

He didn't answer. He locked the car, pocketed the keys in his gray Members Only jacket, and mounted the porch. He stopped a good eight feet from the couch.

"Yeah," he said, staring down at me. "I remember you."

"Where do you remember me from?" I asked. "Does it feel like déjà vu? Or is it a real memory?"

He squinted slightly in confusion.

"What?"

Silence—the thick, uncomfortable kind—stretched between us.

"I—uh—met your wife," I stammered at last.

Jack jingled his keys impatiently in his jacket pocket.

"You woke her up," he accused.

"Yes," I said.

He exhaled hard. He jingled the keys harder.

"She's sick," he said. "It's dinnertime. You should leave. Is Leo still here? I'm writing him up for bringing you here. And don't bother to submit clips or a resume. Your name's going on the hiring blacklist."

He didn't remember me. After all we went through. I didn't think it would bother me so much.

"I felt sorry for you," I said. "I was supposed to stay objective and keep the plot on track, but you made me feel so sorry for you. I think I screwed everything up."

Jack should have looked at me like I was crazy. Instead, he walked to the couch and sat next to me. Not too close. But sort of close. He lit a cigarette, took a long drag, and sighed. He stared at the reddish-gold light that bejeweled his neighbor's roof as the sun slowly died behind it. It was pretty. I stared at it, too. What a picturesque white trash couple we must have made.

When he finally turned to me, I froze as the blue lasers of his eyes struck me. He had so rarely been sober with me, I didn't know how to handle it. His perceptive gaze penetrated me to the core. He must have been such a good editor.

"Let's cut to the chase," he said. "You're following me around because you want...what, exactly?"

"I don't want anything. Except a happy ending," I said. "For you."

He didn't say anything for a long time. He took a last drag off his cigarette, then pitched the butt into his sodden front yard. He dropped first his briefcase onto the porch, then his travel mug onto the couch cushions, and finally his forehead into his hand. He sat hunched on the couch, rubbing the worry lines above his eyebrows wearily.

"I do know who you are," he said. "I had Leo check you out after you left the first voicemail last week. I almost called you five times today. I don't know why. Why the hell would I want to talk to you?"

"Do you remember?"

"What?" he said.

His eyes swept me, then landed on the five pictures lying face down between us on the couch. He picked them up, glanced at them, then stuffed them into his briefcase.

"Oh God, Jack, I'm so sorry," I said. "She's so…"

"She's sick," he said. "While she was showing you these, did she tell you about the six times she's slit her wrists? She did it in front of our daughter the last time, explaining the best way to go about it while Lucy screamed at the 911 operator for help."

He stood.

"Look, I don't know what you're doing here, but you should leave."

I stood.

"Okay," I said. "Just tell me if this is better—if this works. Are you happy?"

"No, I'm not happy," he said. "Are you kidding me?"

"But your wife survived," I said.

"My wife—my ex-wife—do you know what she went through?"

"Not all of it," I said.

"She," he bit his lower lip hard, barely containing the rage I could see bubbling up through his pupils. "Did she tell you she has to have a catheter for the rest of her life because the bayonet tore through her uterus into her bladder? She lost all sensation down her left leg from nerve damage. She'll never walk without a cane again. She lost an eye. She's had nineteen reconstructive surgeries. There's brain damage from the strangulation. She has psychiatric diagnoses—plural. PTSD, alcoholism, compulsions I can't even count. She can't function—not as a mother, not as a wife."

"So you divorced her?" I said.

He let out a long breath and slumped against the outer wall of the house. Flecks of peeling paint dusted his shoulders like gray dandruff. He closed his eyes for a moment.

"I had to divorce her so we wouldn't lose the house when we couldn't pay the medical bills," he said. "It wasn't because she cheated with that guy in her therapy group. I understood that. It wasn't really sexual, what they did. He was just as mentally damaged as she is. It...you couldn't understand."

"Do you want me to try to change it again?" I asked. "I'm not sure I can. This was the best ending I could come up with."

Jack sank back down onto the couch. He covered his face with both hands. Between his fingers, he said something. I thought it was, "You owe me." But maybe the word was "own," and had been all along. His shoulders started to shake.

I'd never seen him cry before.

"Jack," I said. "This doesn't work. This is wrong, isn't it?"

He didn't answer. After a moment, he nodded.

"You can't have a happy ending."

I had to wait nearly ten minutes, but at last he shook his head.

Worse than death

Monday, April 2, 9:52 a.m.

I sat on a rickety folding chair not too close to Jack's hospital bed. I felt completely disoriented.

Jack was very still. His eyes were closed. There were tears on his lashes.

"Jack?" I said. "Are you okay?"

His heart monitor beeped. He was alive. But was he about to wink out of existence? Was I?

"Jack?" I said.

He opened his eyes. He looked up at me. I wasn't sure where I was. Which draft? Which story? Which version of the truth?

Jack opened his mouth to say something.

"You're still here?"

It was a flat female voice, toneless and without inflection. I turned and saw Lucy standing in the doorway. She was dressed all in black, which gave me no clues. Beneath her eyes were sooty smudges that could have been gray eyeliner or dark circles from a sleepless night.

Where was I? What kind of book was this? A memoir? A novel?

"You have to leave now," she said coldly. "You're gonna make him have another heart attack."

I stood.

I opened my mouth to say something. But I didn't know what to say. So I said nothing.

I left.

Brigadoon lost

Saturday, June 9, 3:32 p.m.

I went about my boring life. I didn't hear from Lucy or Leo or Christopher or The Chief or Coroner Dekins.

Or Spine.

I couldn't remember Jack's phone number, and it wasn't showing up in my cell phone's call record. All of my recordings of our talks were blank. All our texts were gone. I couldn't find any of his articles online, the *Washingtonian* building had disappeared, and Jack's Wikipedia page no longer existed.

I was in Ballard last month, working on an article. After wrapping up the interview, I tried to find Jack's house amid the tangle of post-WWII Scandinavian architecture, but I didn't have GPS in the press car that day and I had forgotten his address.

It was almost like none of it happened.

But I swear, it's all true.

THE END

ABOUT THE AUTHOR

Katherine Luck is a writer based in Seattle. She is the author of the novels *In Retrospect* and *The Cure for Summer Boredom*. Her articles and short stories have been featured in Reuters, *The Amistad*, *Seattle Woman Magazine*, *Oregon Literary Review*, and Crosscut.com. You can read more of her work, including the "Dead Writers and Candy" series, at KatherineLuck.com.